Adore

New York Times & USA Today Bestselling Author

NINA LANE

SNOW QUEEN
PUBLISHING

Cover photography: Jeanne M. Woodfin/JW Photography and Covers
Cover design: Najla Qamber Designs

Published by Snow Queen Publishing

ISBN: 978-1-7349747-8-2

And suddenly you know…it's time to start something new and trust the magic of beginnings.

—*Meister Eckhart*

Part I

CHAPTER 1

OLIVIA

*I*t's an epic meltdown. A part the seas, lightning bolts from the sky, plague of locusts, peanut-butter-smeared meltdown. His face is red as a beet, drenched with tears, his fists clenched. He's alternating between pounding the floor with his feet to flopping over like a beached whale and howling.

I've tried everything. Food. Changing. Toys. Reasoning. TV. Cajoling. Music. Going outside. Coming inside. Checking his temperature. Books. A vain attempt at a nap. I gave him the wooden spoon I'd been using to stir chocolate frosting because...*chocolate,* but even that didn't work.

Nothing is working. My nerves are shot. I'm exhausted, and the house looks like it's been hit by a tornado. I haven't showered all day. I look at the clock, calculating I have about three hours to calm Nicholas down and coax him to sleep, get my gourmet dinner prepped, and somehow wrestle the house into tip-top shape. And to make myself at least somewhat presentable.

"How about *Thomas?*" I suggest, quickly pulling up a video on my laptop.

Nicholas wails something incomprehensible and flounders around on the sunroom floor. A headache hammers at my skull. I turn the video toward him. He grabs the laptop from the coffee-table and sends it smashing to the floor.

"Tuck!" he yells.

"I know. I have given you five trucks." I point to the garbage truck, Mack truck, and three dump trucks amidst the clutter of cars on the floor.

"Tuck!"

"I don't think you have any more trucks," I say desperately.

"Fed!"

Fed. Fed what? Federal? Does he have an FBI truck? Does such a thing even exist? But if it did, what two-year-old knows that Fed refers to the FBI? Maybe he means something else, like red?

I rummage through the half-empty toy box and find a red bulldozer, which I hold up.

"This?" I ask.

"No!" Nicholas unleashes an ear-splitting scream.

"Are you thirsty?" I ask, deciding to change tactics even though I've asked him that question about a dozen times already. I grab his sippy cup of orange juice from the table and hand it to him. "Juice!"

For a second, his sobs decrease in volume. I almost hold my breath with hope as he grabs the cup from my hand. He throws it on the ground. Orange juice sprays all over the tile and splashes onto my sweatpants.

"No-spill" cup, my freaking ass.

I grit my teeth, clinging to what little patience I have left. My lack of sleep last night, thanks to Nicholas's penchant for flailing around when he sleeps in our bed, is yanking out the final threads of my frayed sanity.

Badly needing a break, I grab Nicholas and get him into the

playpen, where he can at least continue his meltdown without whacking his head against a hard surface.

I set the laptop back on the table, mop up the juice with a few napkins, then go into the kitchen and silently pray my darling, holy terror of a son will wear himself out and fall asleep. With his dark hair and thick-lashed eyes, he's adorable when he's asleep.

Now? Not so much.

I scribble "Buy orange juice" on a Post-it and stick it to the refrigerator along with all the other reminders of stuff I need to buy and do.

I grab a spatula and smear chocolate frosting over the lumpy, lopsided cake sitting on the central island. The stupid thing looks nothing like the elaborate, raspberry-chocolate layer cake on my Pinterest board, the one I thought would be "easy enough" to recreate.

I glance at the clock, wondering if I have time to run to the bakery. Then again, the last thing I need is to haul a screaming toddler into a bakery to buy a chocolate cake. We'd barely made it out of the grocery store without being disintegrated by the disapproving, death-ray stares of older women who apparently raised perfect, well-behaved angels.

Nicholas lets out a yell that sounds like he's being tortured. My heart plummets. I drop the spatula and run into the sunroom, where he is flailing against the mesh sides of the playpen.

"Nicholas, what?"

My headache intensifies, nails driving into my skull. I lean over to lift him out of the playpen. He swings a fist, catching my front teeth in a punch.

Pain radiates over my jaw. Tears spring to my eyes. I sink to the floor as he wiggles out of my grip and flops next to me with another screech of indignation.

"Ah, my beloved family."

Dean's deep voice washes over Nicholas's wailing. I jerk my head up in surprise to find him standing in the kitchen doorway, his briefcase in hand. Aside from looking travel-rumpled, he's as gorgeous as ever, his thick dark hair disheveled and his tall, muscular body clad in an open wool peacoat over his standard travel clothes of worn jeans and a forest-green rugby shirt.

He takes in the scene before him—the screaming child, the sunroom strewn with books and toys, the pile of dirty dishes and sippy cups in the sink, the disaster of a kitchen with cake ingredients and messy mixing bowls scattered over the counter.

Not to mention his wife collapsed on the floor in old sweatpants stained with spaghetti sauce and orange juice, her unwashed hair limp and tangled, and her torn T-shirt stinking of sour milk.

Dean smiles at me. "Hey, beauty."

I burst into tears.

He sets his briefcase down and comes toward us, one hand reaching for Nicholas and the other for me. Nicholas, oblivious to his father's homecoming, grabs a plastic hammer and pounds it on the rug.

I fall against the solid wall of Dean's body and give in to sobbing for a minute before pulling myself together for what feels like the hundredth time that day. I wipe my wet face and runny nose on his shirt and ease back to look at him.

"W-what are you doing home so early?" I hiccup. "You were supposed to be home at eight."

"There was room on an earlier flight, so I grabbed a seat," he says, pushing my hair away from my sweaty forehead. "Didn't you get my text?"

"Do I look like I got your text?" I retort, suddenly annoyed with both him and American Airlines for screwing up my plan to welcome my husband home after two weeks away.

"No," Dean admits reflectively, sliding his gaze over me. "You do not."

He pushes to his feet and reaches for Nicholas, who evades his grasp and toddles over to the basement door.

"Tuck!" Nicholas screams. "Fed!"

"Hold on." Dean hauls our son into his arms and sets him in the playpen, then goes down into the unfinished basement. He returns with a Lego Duplo-block fire truck and puts it in front of Nicholas.

And, like turning off a water faucet, Nicholas stops wailing.

My ears are still ringing, so for a moment the silence is deafening. Nicholas lets out a few lingering sobs and gulps. Dean grabs a napkin from the table and wipes Nicholas's face and nose, lifting him out of the playpen and onto the sunroom floor. Nicholas hugs the fire truck like it's a long-lost friend.

Which I suppose it is.

"Oh my god." I groan and bury my face in my hands. "Are you kidding me?"

"That's Fred," Dean says helpfully. "Didn't you know that?"

I take my hands away from my face to stare at him. "Do I *look* like I know that?"

"No," he admits.

"Why would I know our son has a fire truck named Fred? And moreover, why is Fred in the basement rather than the toy box where he belongs? I have spent all day dragging your son's toys out, trying to get him to stop wailing like a banshee, and now I find out there are more toys in the basement?"

Dean scratches his head. "Just a few. I put them there for safe-keeping when Nicholas was into throwing things down the stairs. He broke apart a fishing boat and had a tantrum, so I've been trying to keep the Lego Duplo sets intact."

"And you couldn't have told me?"

He shrugs. "I thought I did."

A wave of frustration almost makes me start crying again. With a grunt, I push to my feet and go into the kitchen. Nicholas rolls the truck on the floor and makes a high-pitched siren noise that sounds like the sweetest lullaby ever compared to his previous screaming.

I grab the spatula and slap frosting on the cake like I'm flogging it. Dean comes up behind me.

"I missed you," he remarks.

I growl in response.

"I love you," he adds.

Another growl rumbles in my throat. I turn and smack his chest with the spatula, leaving a smear of chocolate on his shirt.

"You were supposed to be home at eight," I repeat accusingly. "I had it all planned out. Nicholas was going to be sleeping peacefully, I'd be showered and all prettied up with *lingerie* on under my dress, waiting for you with a glass of scotch and a delicious gourmet dinner, followed by homemade chocolate cake. Afterward, I was planning to take you upstairs and actually *get sexy*. However, since you were inconsiderate enough to come home *three hours* early, you get nothing."

I wave the spatula in the air and turn back to the cake. "Nothing!"

"Oh, I've got something." Dean slides his hands around my waist and pushes his groin up against my bottom. "I've got the hottest, sexiest, most perfect wife in the universe."

"Hah. Good luck with that."

"Mmm." Dean pushes my hair away from my nape and kisses the back of my neck. "You smell like Spaghetti Os with meatballs. My favorite."

"Again…" I push my hips backward in a half-hearted attempt to shove him away, but the movement only presses my ass closer against him. "Good luck."

"I don't need any more luck." Dean presses his lips in a line over the ridge of my collarbone. "I've already got you."

Okay, so that wasn't bad. He continues pressing little kisses over my neck and shoulder, sending tingles raining down my spine. I lick a drop of frosting off my finger and make him work for a few more minutes before turning in his arms to face him.

The heat of his body flows into me, soothing the tight anger and frustration that have been gripping me all day long.

"I'm still mad," I warn him, holding up the spatula.

His eyes warm as he tracks his gaze over my face.

"You're so pretty," he says.

"Sure. You should have seen what I was *planning* to look like when you got home," I grumble. "It would have been a transformation like Cinderella at the ball, except *sexy*."

"You don't need a transformation to be sexy," Dean remarks. "But I'd be happy to provide you with a couple of balls."

That brings a chuckle out of me, despite my fatigue over the full-time care of our son. A few weeks ago, my good friend and part-time nanny Marianne moved out of town to be closer to her daughter and grandchildren. I hadn't realized how much I'd relied on her help with Nicholas until she was gone. And then with Dean's work taking him out of town more often than I'd like...

He licks frosting off the spatula I'm still holding before putting his hands on my hips and pulling me closer.

"Give me a kiss, beauty," he says.

"I haven't even brushed my teeth today."

"I don't care." He rubs his lips against mine. "I haven't kissed my wife in two weeks. No way am I waiting a second longer. Not to mention, you taste like chocolate."

With that, he tugs me against him and settles his mouth securely over mine. A muffled groan of pleasure escapes me involuntarily.

Oh, god, it's so good to have him home, despite the utter upheaval of my careful plans. I wind my arms around his waist and let myself fall into the familiar, compelling warmth of his kiss.

Arousal tingles through me like little bells, both surprising and welcoming. Over the past six months, Nicholas's launch into the terrible twos, complete with constant waking during the night, intense clinginess, and a mutinous refusal to learn potty-training, has sapped my energy right along with my sex drive.

Dean lifts his hands to the sides of my neck, tilting my head to just the right angle as he urges my lips apart. A rumble of pleasure echoes in his chest. Our bodies fit together seamlessly, the pressure of his hard muscles so good against my breasts. I slip my hands under his shirt and stroke the warm tautness of his lower back.

"Fed! Wee wee wee!"

Nicholas's siren noise breaks me and Dean apart. We both turn to see our son crawling into the kitchen, pushing Fred the Fire Truck.

"Daddy!" Nicholas yells, as if just realizing Dean is home again.

"Hey, buddy." Dean releases me to crouch and hold out his arms so Nicholas can barrel into them. They exchange a tight hug.

"So good to see you again." Dean pulls back and ruffles Nicholas's hair. "I swear you've grown in just two weeks."

"Haf Fed," Nicholas informs him, patting Dean's cheek.

"I see that." Dean glances at me with a wink. "I'll deal with him. Go take a break. Looks like you could use one."

"Don't you need to unpack your stuff?"

"I'll do it later. Go ahead."

I almost burst into tears again at the thought of locking myself in the bedroom *alone*. Figuring I can still salvage something of the evening, I hurry upstairs and strip off my clothes before getting into a scorching hot shower.

Oh, bliss. I stay under the water for at least ten minutes before soaping myself down from head to toe and shaving my embarrassingly prickly legs. Then I brush my teeth, dry my hair, and change into clean yoga pants and a pink fleece shirt—not the slinky silk dress I'd planned on to welcome my husband home, but I'm too tired and relieved to care.

Though I'm still exhausted, at least now I feel somewhat more human, and I certainly smell better. When I return downstairs, I find that Dean has cleaned up the clutter in the sunroom, put away the groceries, stacked the dirty dishes in the dishwasher, and washed all the mixing bowls I'd used for the cake. Now he and Nicholas are sitting on the sunroom floor, building a police car with Duplo blocks.

The sight of my two guys together never fails to make me all warm and mushy inside, especially when the younger guy isn't screeching like a howler monkey. Nicholas's features are a toddler version of Dean's, and though his hair is a lighter brown, it has the same wavy thickness. Put father and son side by side, and you have my entire heart.

Back together again. Since being awarded tenure at King's over two years ago, Dean has taken on more responsibilities and positions—not only with the Altopascio dig but with other historic sites. He holds a seat on the International Conservation Committee, which advises the World Heritage Center on the protection of sites and monuments, and he's regularly invited to European universities and museums to give lectures, join research projects, and organize conferences.

And yet, all those illustrious distinctions fall away when he walks back through the door of the Butterfly House and gently commands a kiss.

"Tell me about the site," I say, lowering myself onto the sofa. "How bad was the earthquake damage?"

"Bad." Dean's expression darkens. "Five point one. Fortunately, there were only a couple of minor injuries, but the medieval tower and church were damaged. The monastery took the worst hit. The whole north transept is destabilized, walls cracked, an entire section demolished. The IHR already says it can't afford to repair the damage, and the seismologists haven't even finished their assessment yet."

"Is there another way to save the monastery?"

"We need to get it on the World Heritage Center list of protected sites," Dean says, racing a toy car alongside Nicholas's. "That's the only way we can get funding from other sources to save it. The United Nations assembly meets this summer to vote on which sites should be added to the list. The deadline for proposals has already passed, but I'm hoping we can push ours through."

"What happens if you can't?"

"We could lose the site entirely." Dean lines up a few cars in front of what appears to be the starting line of a race. "And we think the monastery is only the start of a much bigger complex. There's no telling how much more we could excavate, but if we can't afford to stabilize the earthquake damage and continue the dig, we'll have to abandon the whole project."

A new worry gnaws me at the thought of Dean being forced to abandon a project that he and so many others have been working on with such dedication. I sit up to look at him.

"You won't let that happen," I say. "You'll find a way to save it. I know you will."

"I'm trying, but it means more work and negotiations I don't want to make."

Before I can question what that means, Dean reaches out to stroke his hand over my thigh.

"What about you?" he asks. "Toddler meltdown aside, everything's okay?"

"Mmm." I rest my head against the back of the sofa. "Busy, but fine. I have a gourmet dinner planned to welcome you home. Spice-rubbed Cornish game hens with a sherry *jus*. Lemon-mint braised artichoke hearts. Saffron rice pilaf. Raspberry-chocolate cake, if I can get it right. Mac and cheese, but that's for the boy."

"Sounds incredible."

"I've been shopping for groceries every day this week." I close my eyes, enjoying the sensation of his strong hand sliding up and down my thigh. "It's going to be delicious. I just need to rest for a second, and then I'll get the *mise en place* going."

"Bob!" Nicholas shouts.

Dean responds, but I don't pay attention to his words as much as the deep, soothing cadence of his voice. The house feels complete with him home again, his presence making the air warmer and richer.

As much as I love the Butterfly House, which Dean and I restored and renovated together, it's huge compared to the apartments we'd always lived in before. It's easy to feel a little lost, especially when Nicholas and I are rattling around alone. We stick together pretty closely when Dean is gone—Nicholas sleeps in the bed with me, and we spend the rest of our time in the kitchen or sunroom.

A sigh fills my chest, the anger and frustration of the day slipping into contentment with the knowledge that my husband is home and everything is as it should be, even if he did screw up my plans with his early arrival.

"George noodle," Nicholas remarks.

I have no idea what he's talking about, nor do I care at this point. I feel myself slipping into a doze and try to pull out of it, reminding myself that I need to clean the artichokes and stuff the game hens...

CHAPTER 2

OLIVIA

*D*ean's body is a wall of heat and muscle against my back. I wake with a start, disoriented for a second before realizing that I'm lying in bed, my head nestled on my cloud-soft pillow. Darkness slants through the curtains. I dimly realize Dean must have carried me upstairs. Would have been more romantic if I'd been awake.

Behind me, he mutters with annoyance at my shifting and settles his arm heavily around me, pulling me back against him. I'm still in my fleece shirt and yoga pants, but I can tell he's shirtless, wearing only his drawstring pajama pants.

He's also hard. His erection is pushing against my bottom. A spool of lust begins to unwind in my lower body as I absorb the sensation of his warm, muscled chest, his arm strong and tight around me, the pulsing stiffness of his cock. I wiggle a little experimentally, both surprised and delighted when my clit throbs in response.

Since giving birth to Nicholas, my libido hasn't been at all reliable, with more valleys than peaks. And as attracted as I am to Dean, after a long day working at the café, running errands, cleaning house, cooking, and taking care of a demanding toddler who often clings to me like a baby monkey…

By ten at night, all I want to do is fall into bed to *sleep*. These days, I need as much sleep as I can get, knowing Nicholas is likely to wake me up at least once or twice, needing water or to be soothed back to sleep, which often takes an hour.

But though things are always changing, especially with a toddler and our new work responsibilities, I am sharply aware I will always be Dean West's wife, and I never want to lose any part of our intense bond.

Which is exactly why I'd planned a romantic night to welcome him home. Maybe I can salvage part of the evening, at least.

Dean moves his hand around to cup my breast, his fingers toying with my nipple under my shirt. He nuzzles his face against my hair and rumbles a noise of pleasure.

There's certainly never been anything wrong with *his* sex drive.

I suddenly wonder what he's done about it, considering the number of times I've either outright turned him down, or made a breathy promise of *"later,"* only to end up asleep before we could get started.

A thought hits me. "The game hens!"

"That's not a hen." Dean pushes his erection harder against my rear. "That's a cock."

I laugh. "You don't say. I meant I forgot to put the hens back in the fridge."

"Already done."

"Oh, good. Thanks." I pause for a minute. "Hey, Dean?"

"Hey, Liv."

"You haven't been feeling…frustrated lately, have you?"

"About what?" He presses his lips against the nape of my neck.

"Sex."

"Does this feel frustrated?" He nudges his cock against me again, his body tensing slightly with growing lust. "Damn, I love your ass."

"I mean, over the past couple of years," I say as my skin starts to warm in response to him. "I know I haven't been on board much."

"I'm not frustrated," he assures me, snaking his other hand underneath me so he can fondle both of my breasts at the same time. "Though I do lust after you on an hourly basis."

"And what do you do when you're lusting and I'm sleeping?"

"I jerk off while thinking about you," he murmurs against my ear.

The admission fires me with an unexpected bolt of heat. I've always loved watching Dean masturbate—the easy, slow movement of his hand as he strokes himself to orgasm, the way his chest heaves with increasing breaths and his eyes glaze over with pleasure—but it occurs to me now I haven't actually seen him do it in ages.

I twist in his arms and turn to face him, my whole body folding against his. It's so good having him back in our bed, right where he belongs. I gaze at his chocolate-brown eyes framed with thick lashes, the strong masculine planes of his face, his rumpled dark hair. The woodsy, eucalyptus scent of his shaving soap drifts from his skin.

"You've stayed in practice," I remark.

"Had to. Traveling and being away from you doesn't leave me any other option."

Guilt simmers inside me. Once upon a time, he and I would engage in hot talk over the phone when he was away. Now I can't remember the last time I was up for that either.

But the thought of him pleasuring himself here at home…

"Do you do it in the shower?" I whisper, sliding my forefinger across his lower lip.

"Sometimes. Or up in my tower office. Or in bed."

"In bed?" I repeat. "When are you ever in bed without me?"

"I'm not."

I try to process that for a second. Dean raises an eyebrow, amusement flashing in his eyes. I gasp.

"Dean West! Are you implying you've been masturbating in our bed while I'm sleeping?"

"I'm not *implying* anything," he replies.

A riotous combination of shock and intrigue floods my chest. I push to one elbow and stare at him.

"Really?" I breathe. "You jerk off while I'm lying asleep next to you?"

"Uh huh." He slides one hand under my shirt, his fingers trailing against my skin. "That turn you on?"

"Um...I'm not sure." My heartbeat starts to increase in pace. "How come I've never woken up?"

"You sleep hard. And I'm quiet."

"You're not quiet when we have sex. Or when I watch you masturbate."

"What can I say? I'm versatile."

"So...How often do you do it?"

"Couple times a week, I guess." He moves his hand up to my bra. "Why are you so curious?"

"I don't know. It's just that my sex drive has been so weird since I had Nicholas, and you've obviously been deprived."

"I haven't been deprived."

"If you're jerking off beside your sleeping wife, you've been deprived." Now I sound annoyed. I can't even remember the last time I masturbated—not that I've ever had much reason to do so since I met Dean.

"I jerk off beside my sleeping wife because I fucking love

smelling her hair and feeling her body against mine when I come," Dean says.

A new flame of shocked heat rips through me.

"You smell my hair?"

"Uh huh."

"That sounds vaguely perverted."

"I'm okay with that," he remarks.

If my pulsing clit is anything to judge by, so am I.

I lean over him, drumming my fingers on his chest. "Why haven't I ever noticed it when I change the sheets?"

"First, because you don't change the sheets," he reminds me. "I do. And second, because I use a towel."

"Oh." Despite my shock at this revelation, hot images flash crystal-clear through my head of Dean stretched out on his back, his bare, sculpted chest patterned with shadows and moonlight, his big cock sticking straight up as he wraps his hand around the base and strokes up to the tight, shiny crown…

I shiver and press my thighs together. I'm starting to throb.

"So what…" I swallow to ease the dryness in my throat. "What do you fantasize about, then?"

"You."

"Oh, please." I roll my eyes and shift a little to rub my breasts against his chest. My nipples are straining against the constriction of my bra. I wish Dean had undressed me before carrying me up to bed. "You're a man."

"Yes, I am."

Yes, he is. I ease my hand down to brush against the stiff bulge in his pants.

"So men fantasize about all sorts of things," I remind him, cupping his erection in my palm. "What about when you're not in bed? When you're in the shower or up in your office? You can't smell my hair or grind up against me then. So what do you fantasize about?"

"Usually you in different scenarios."

"Like what?"

To my further intrigue, a slight flush crests his cheekbones.

"Dean?" I squeeze his cock lightly. "Come on. I've told you about my fantasies, right?"

"Mine aren't nearly as vivid as yours," he replies.

"Remember that dream you once had in which I was a librarian?" I ask, smiling when his cock stiffens even more. "That was pretty hot."

"That was a dream, not a fantasy."

"A dream is an unconscious fantasy," I remind him. "But I want to know what you fantasize about when you're awake. Am I a nurse? A farmer's daughter? A vestal virgin?"

He shakes his head.

I try to think. "Oh! Am I a dominatrix?"

"Beauty, as much as I love the idea of you in leather, I'd never be up for that." He slides his hand over my ass.

I can't really see it either—even in my imagination, sexual submission and Dean West are a total mismatch. *Control* is just one of the things that makes him who he is, and though it's also the characteristic that has caused the most problems between us, I've accepted that it will always be part of him.

"What do you fantasize about, then?" I ask.

"How about you tell me?" he suggests. "You have some pretty imaginative, elaborate fantasies. Elves and pirate captains and all that, right?"

Right. I *used* to have elaborate sexual fantasies. Now my most intense fantasies involve sleeping past five a.m., or eating an entire meal without getting up once, or having time to read a book whose plot doesn't revolve around Arthur or the Berenstain Bears.

Stay on track, Liv. No thinking of Brother and Sister Bear...

"So?" Dean prompts, winding a lock of my hair around his finger.

"Um, so I had this fantasy where you were...uh, a deliveryman," I say, "and I was…a bored, lonely housewife and you were delivering some sex toys…"

"Sounds more like a porn flick."

"Yeah." I sigh. "I guess I haven't fantasized much lately."

"So instead of talking, why don't we just get dirty?" he suggests, tugging at the hem of my shirt. "Take this off."

Though I'm not entirely ready to be done with this conversation, I'm getting hot, and my breasts are aching. I lift myself up to take off my shirt and unhook my bra, tossing both to the floor. Cooler air caresses my skin, and Dean's breath hisses out in pleasure at the sight of my bare breasts.

I shiver, desire rolling through me at the darkening heat in his eyes, the visible strain of his muscles.

Yes.

Oh, it feels good to be aroused, even if we haven't done much of anything yet. *Especially* because we haven't done much of anything yet.

"C'mere," he mutters roughly, grabbing my waist and hauling me toward him. He fastens his lips around my nipple and tugs, the light pull sending a current of heat right to my sex.

I move over him to straddle his waist, bending forward so he has full access to my breasts. His body tenses as he palms and squeezes my breasts until waves of heat wash through me.

"God, Dean." I squirm on top of him, rubbing against his torso. "I'm getting really hot."

He pushes his hips upward, nudging his cock against my ass. He grips the waistband of my pants, and I shift so he can tug them down my hips and slip his hand between my legs. He groans.

"Ah, fuck, you're wet already." He yanks at my pants. "Get these off. Now."

I maneuver around to pull my pants off and ease down Dean's body, pressing kisses to his gorgeous chest, down the line bisecting his abdomen, following the trail of hair leading right to the tantalizing hardness of his erection.

I grasp his hips and press my mouth onto his cock, right over the cotton of his pants. Dean groans, fisting a hand into my hair. His heat burns through the thin material, his thigh muscles tightening like corded wire. I pull his pants down just enough to release his erection, the beautiful, thick length almost gleaming in the dim light.

I glance up at him through the veil of hair that has fallen over my face. He's watching me, his dark eyes smoldering. He reaches down to squeeze my breast, pinching the nipple between his thumb and forefinger.

"Use these," he says huskily.

A shiver rains through me. I get to my knees and cup my breasts. He grasps the base of his shaft. I position myself over him and press my breasts together to create a deep cleavage before sliding his cock between them.

"Oh, god." I inhale a sharp breath, my skin tingling at the sensation of him against my damp skin. "Is that good?"

"Hell, yeah." He grits his teeth and pushes his hips upward. "Fuck me with them."

I squeeze my breasts together tighter and slide them up and down his stiff cock, the pathway eased by the slickness of our skin. My head fills with his scent. I'd almost forgotten how uninhibited and sexy I can be with him, how good pure, undiluted lust can feel.

Mesmerized, I watch his thick erection push in and out of my cleavage. Heat pours through me. I pause, circling my tongue over the tip of his cock before easing him past my lips. Slowly I move my head up and down, fucking him with my mouth.

A groan shakes his chest. I let my eyes drift closed and breathe, focusing on the sensation of my husband's body, the quickening breaths signaling his increasing drive toward release.

His fingers tighten briefly on my nape before he slides his hand down to rub my back in an almost soothing motion.

"Come here," he orders gruffly.

I release him, crawling back up the length of his body, my thighs hugging his hips and my breasts crushed against his chest. Our lips meet in a hot, full kiss as he strokes his hands down to my rear end. In one movement, he turns me over onto my back.

"Open," he whispers against my lips.

My breath catches. I spread my legs, letting him move between them. I rake my gaze over him, the planes of his chest and thighs, the ridge of his erection, the burning gleam in his eyes. He slides his fingers into my cleft. The first touch is a delicious shock, his thumb circling my clit as he pushes two fingers into me.

"Oh, god, Dean…" I clench my fists into the sheets, feeling as if I'm aroused for the first time ever.

I'm vibrating with sensation—streams of blue and gold coursing through my veins, the press of Dean's fingers stimulating my nerves, the heat-drenched air pressing against my skin. All thought slides away into a warm, heady pool of sensation.

"Fuck me," I murmur, hooking my legs around his thighs. "I want to come with you inside me."

He needs no further invitation, pushing into me with one slow, easy surge. I grip the sheets tighter as he starts to thrust, his deep movements blazing heat over my nerves. I arch upward to meet his repeated plunges, our bodies pushing and pulling in a rhythm as powerful and natural as tides.

Tension winds through my lower body. I crave the intense explosion of pleasure I haven't felt in weeks. Sometimes I can hardly remember not having to work to get into the moment, to push away all the worries, plans, and schedules cramming my head.

There's always something to think about, whether it's the café staff schedule, profit and loss, what to make for dinner, Nicholas's daycare payments, or...

Oh, shit, I forgot to give the monthly payment to Christine last week, which means I need to double-check that there's enough to cover—

"Ah, good." Dean, still thrusting into me like a well-oiled piston, braces his hands on either side of my head and lowers his mouth to mine. "Put your legs up...yeah, like that..."

I writhe under him, trying to get my head back in the game, but my rhythm is off, and we both pull back at the same time. He slides out of me and stops, his breathing hard. His expression darkens.

"Where did you go?" he asks.

"Nowhere. Just, um..." I dig my fingers into his back and wiggle again. I strain for the resurgence of arousal, but it's like trying to grasp a fistful of water.

Dean slips his hand between my legs. I sink back against the pillows, playing with my breasts and waiting for delicious arousal to coil through me again.

Did I tell Christine about the change in my work schedule? I can't remember. I need her to take care of Nicholas on Thursdays instead of Tuesdays, and I need to shift the pickup time to...

I shake the thought off and reach down to palm Dean's erection and guide him back inside me. I arch upward. His body grows taut with familiar urgency as he pushes into me again.

I squirm, disliking the edge of unfulfilled lust, but knowing he won't succumb to his own release until he knows I'm satisfied. For the first time ever, I wish he weren't such a gentleman.

"Oh, Dean..." I breathe his name and wrap my legs around his hips. "You feel so good, so big...fuck me harder, please...yes, yes!"

I dig my fingers into his shoulders, simultaneously straining for both arousal and something to say in order to keep him, at least, in the zone.

"Do me, baby, good and hard. I'm coming...Oh my god, I'm coming. Yes...oh, yes!"

I shriek and writhe my hips, pushing up against him the second I realize he's stopped moving. I open my eyes. He's looking at me, his arms still braced on either side of my head and his chest heaving.

"Really?" he asks dryly.

A hot flush crawls up my face. Dean gives a half laugh, half groan and thrusts a couple more times. Though he comes, I can tell it's hardly as powerful an orgasm as it usually is for him.

He rolls off me, throwing his arm across his face.

"You're the love of my life, Olivia," he mutters. "But you're a terrible actress."

My embarrassment intensifies. I should have known better than to think he wouldn't notice. But after two weeks away from each other, I was sure I'd have no trouble reaching the finish line.

I turn toward him and put my hand on his damp torso. Lines of frustration etch his forehead, and his chest rises and falls with heavy breaths. Guilt stabs me.

"I'm sorry." I prop myself up on my elbow to look at him. "It's really not you. It's me. I don't know where my sex drive goes sometimes."

He opens his eyes to meet my gaze.

"So what happened?" he asks. "You were into it before."

"I started thinking about something I have to do tomorrow," I admit.

"I'm guessing it wasn't *ride Dean's cock*," he mutters.

I can't help giggling. "No, but I'll put that on my To Do list."

I ease closer to rest my cheek against his shoulder. I slide my hand down his abdomen, tracing the ridges of his abs with my fingertips. Not only does my husband have an incredibly gorgeous body, he knows exactly how and when to both make love and fuck hard. *He's* certainly not the reason I have trouble keeping my head in the game.

"Don't do that again," Dean says, his tone so implacably stern that I glance up.

He frowns down at me, his eyes narrowing with a sense of menace I've never before seen directed at me. For some reason, a shiver of excitement runs down my spine.

"I won't," I promise.

"You'd better not," Dean murmurs, his deep voice rolling over me like a hot breeze. "You're not allowed to fake an orgasm. *Ever.*"

"Oh." I dart my tongue out to lick my lips, wondering why his unyielding command is making me all quivery inside. "Okay."

"If you do that again, I'll have to punish you," Dean warns, leaning back against the pillows and closing his eyes. "We wouldn't want that now, would we?"

Given the little tingles racing through me, I'm not sure what the right answer to that question is.

CHAPTER 3

*W*ell, shit.

After two weeks away from my wife, I was unapologetically expecting explosive sex within a few hours of my return. But after last night fizzled out like a wet firecracker, and with Liv's sex drive here one minute and gone the next, I don't know when *explosive sex* will be on the agenda again.

Not that I'm deprived. Just a little tired of my right hand.

I take a deep breath and finish shaving. Despite the fact that last night hardly went as planned, I'm glad to be home. Thirteen days away from my family was thirteen days too long.

I'd hoped Liv could come with me to Italy—I've been working on the Altopascio dig for almost three years now, and she has yet to see the site—but the timing didn't work out. It never has. We've made plans a few times for her and Nicholas to join me, but work and schedules always get in the way.

When I go downstairs, the high-pitched voice of Elmo comes

from the TV, and the smell of coffee drifts in the air. The picture windows in the sunroom reveal a sky the color of metal and a springtime growth of weeds and plants sprouting from the mushy ground.

"Morning." Liv is standing at the central island, putting out coffee mugs. She's bundled into her padded robe, her hair all loose and tangled around her shoulders. Exactly how I like it.

"Morning, wife." I slide a hand around the back of her neck and pull her in for a kiss. A surge of unfulfilled lust hits me at the feeling of her lips against mine.

After a minute, Liv pulls away from me and rests her hand on my chest. Guilt flashes in her pretty brown eyes.

"Sorry about last night," she says.

So am I. I've never not been able to make her come, especially after two weeks apart. *Never.*

"It had just been such a bad day," Liv continues. "And I wanted to make you happy."

"I am happy." I twist a lock of her hair around my finger. "But knowing you're faking it makes me very *not* happy. You ever do that before?"

"No."

I narrow my gaze. "You sure?"

"Of course I'm sure." She slides her hand up to my neck. "And clearly you figured it out last night. Don't you think you'd be able to tell if I'd done it before?"

Yeah, I *think* I'd be able to tell, but doesn't every guy?

"You're the one who said I'm a terrible actress," Liv reminds me. "Really, Dean, I promise I've never faked it before. I was just exhausted. Nicholas had been pitching a level ten fit *all day,* my cake turned into a disaster, and my plans to welcome you home were a wreck. Honestly, I consider it a win that we got as far as we did."

Can't say I agree with that.

"Stop frowning." Liv reaches up to smooth her thumb against

the crease between my eyebrows. "You've always rocked my world hard, professor, and you know it."

"Not *always*," I mutter darkly. Not as recently as last night.

"I'm sorry," she says again. "I swear upon everything holy that before last night, I have never faked an orgasm or anything else with you, but honestly, sometimes I can't get into it. I mean, we're so busy raising a toddler and working... Sometimes just snuggling up together in bed is better than the hot sex we used to have."

Again, not agreeing.

Liv slides herself into my arms and hugs me around the waist. The feel of her against me eases my frustration. I guess I'll consider it a *win* too, for her sake only, but I hate that she can switch gears right in the middle of sex—and then actually lose interest in what we're doing.

It used to be that fucking was overwhelming enough to block everything else out. Now it takes work for her to even stay focused.

"I promise, things will heat up again," she murmurs, pressing her lips against my neck.

I bite back a retort of *"When?"* because neither of us knows the answer to that, and being irritated about our sex life when everything else is so good...well, I'm not such an ass that I'll complain about it.

Much.

"Hey." Liv rubs her hand over my cheek. "I know you're getting all hot and bothered. I really think once Nicholas starts sleeping through the night, and I start getting more sleep as a result, we'll get back on track again."

And if we don't?

Again I don't bother asking that question aloud.

"In the meantime, take your wounded male pride into the family room and watch *Sesame Street* with our son," Liv says. "As an apology, I'll make you a very manly breakfast of eggs, black coffee, and thick-cut bacon."

"Will you serve it to me naked?" I pull her closer.

She smiles. "Hold that thought for a morning when our son is actually sleeping in."

At the rate we're going, that'll probably be when Nicholas is a teenager.

"Go," Liv commands, gesturing to the family room.

I feel her up a little—squeeze her breasts, rub her ass—just to make sure she knows who's still calling the shots. Then I obey her order and go to join Nicholas on the sofa.

He's transfixed by the TV, but he edges over to lean against my chest when I sit down beside him. He smells like sleep and Cheerios, his hair rumpled and his sturdy little body clad in train-patterned pajamas.

My tension eases as my brain makes the shift to Big Bird and Oscar the Grouch.

"*Sesame*," Nicholas tells me, pointing to the TV.

"Excellent choice." I rumple his hair, feeling a familiar and yet still overwhelming rush of love fill my chest.

It's a different kind of love than the one I have for Liv. My love for my wife is powerfully intense and secure, bone-deep, the essential part of me. It's the solid ground under my feet, a feeling as inevitable as a sunrise.

With Nicholas, my love is almost scary in its fierceness and layered with so many other emotions I can't even define them all. Awe. Wonder. Fear. Amazement. Hope. Every day, every time I see him, the love surges anew, like a tidal wave submerging my heart.

"I make puzzle." Nicholas shoves off the sofa, apparently having lost interest in the cartoon, and waddles over to the puzzle of wooden pieces scattered on the rug.

I sit on the floor with him as he fits the dinosaur picture together, his face set with concentration. Tantrums aside, he's a good kid—smart, curious, funny, creative. Half the time I can't imagine he was ever a tiny newborn, and the other half I can't imagine him ever being older than two.

"Hey, come talk to me," Liv calls. "I want to hear about your trip."

"Come on, Nicholas." I grab another puzzle and push to my feet. "Let's go hang out with Mommy."

He follows me into the sunroom, where the kitchen table sits beside the windows. After settling Nicholas on the rug with the new puzzle, I pour a cup of coffee and join Liv at the table.

As we eat breakfast, I tell her more about my trip to Altopascio—the process of damage assessment after the earthquake, the cataloging of archeological finds, the details of my proposal to get the site on the World Heritage list of protected monuments.

"Brought you some things too," I say, going to the travel bag still sitting beside the door. "I found Nicholas a set of Italian blocks and a pop-up book, which I'm sure he'll destroy in about five seconds."

I bring the packages back to the table, handing two to Nicholas and the rest to Liv. I'd gotten her Italian chocolate and coffee, a culinary travelogue, and a print of a Tuscan village.

"This will look perfect on that wall." Liv gestures to the opposite wall and leans in to press her lips against mine. "Thank you."

"Here's one more." I push a wrapped package across the table to her.

She opens it and takes out a leather journal with hand-cut pages. I'd had it specially made at a printer's in Tuscany and embossed with Liv's name on the cover. For a few years, she's kept what she calls her "manifesto" of thoughts and ideas, and I've noticed her journal is getting a little ragged.

"Dean, it's beautiful." She runs her hand admiringly over the cover. "Thank you so much. Did you get one for yourself?"

She eyes me pointedly, as always unimpressed with my own habit of scrawling things on the pages of a loose-leaf notebook.

I'm saved from having to answer by the buzz of my cell phone. I smile at Liv and get up to answer the call.

"Dean West."

"Dean, it's Hans Klasen," an accented male voice announces over some crackly static. "Did you arrive home safely?"

"Last night, yes. Thanks."

"Good. I'll be in Mirror Lake next week," Hans continues. "I was hoping you'd have a chance to meet, perhaps for lunch? We need to talk about the Altopascio proposal and your role with the World Heritage Center."

"Sure." I pick up my notebook, which I'd left on the desk. "Where are you staying?"

Hans gives me his hotel info. "Have you thought more about interviewing for the job?" he asks.

Shit. Not a conversation I want to have right when I just got home.

"No," I reply carefully. "You know my priorities are the site and my work at King's."

"I understand," Hans says. "But we continue to believe you'd be an excellent candidate for the position. Look over the documents I sent you, and we can discuss it more when we meet. I'd also like your opinion about the Novgorodian dig and the manuscripts."

"Happy to provide it," I tell him. "Do you need a ride from the airport?"

"No, I'm driving. I'll let you know when I arrive."

We exchange goodbyes. I toss my cell back on the counter and pick up my empty breakfast plate.

"Who was that?" Liv asks, coming into the kitchen.

"Hans Klasen, director of the World Heritage Center." I load my plate with scrambled eggs. "He's planning a visit to King's next week. We've known each other for years, but haven't had a chance to work together until recently. He stepped in to help with the aftermath of the quake, and I'm hoping he can push the proposal through to the UN Assembly."

"Is that what he was calling about?"

"Partly. He's also working on an archeological dig in Novgorod and wants my opinion on some things."

"Please don't tell me you're going to Russia now." Liv slips her arms around my waist from behind.

"Nyet, lyubimaya moya."

She chuckles. "What does he want your opinion on?"

"Birch bark scrolls preserved by the unique chemical qualities of the Novgorodian mud."

"Mmm. Sexy." Liv reaches up to kiss the back of my neck.

I put my plate down and turn to face her. Liv's perspective has always made me see things from a different angle. She was the one who told me I had to go work on the Altopascio dig almost three years ago—and though I'd refused at first, the work has turned out to be one of the most rewarding projects of my career. And because it's expanded my professional reputation into areas beyond academia, it's also bringing up new challenges I haven't yet figured out how to handle.

"Hey." Liv puts her hand on my chest, her forehead creasing. "What's going on?"

"Nothing." I slide my hands down to her hips. "Just office politics. What time are you working today?"

"Morning shift. Do you need to go to campus?"

"No. I'll spend the morning with Nicholas and go back to campus on Monday." I kiss her nose, then pick up my plate and join our son at the table. "Are Archer and Kelsey back from California? I need to drop off Archer's financial portfolio this afternoon."

"They got back a few days ago, but I haven't seen either one of them yet." Liv puts the milk back in the refrigerator. "Kelsey emailed me that they're getting the Spiral Project ready, so they're both busy. I can take Nicholas for the afternoon, if you two want to stop by the café."

"Sure. Call me if you need me."

"I always need you," she replies with a smile.

She heads upstairs to get ready for work. I leaf through some mail that accumulated in my absence, picking up a worn postcard with a photo of the Bronze Horseman statue in St. Petersburg. In scrawled handwriting on the back is the message:

Liv,

Candy-colored onion domes, painted nesting dolls, sour cream so thick you can stand a spoon in it. Serpentine canals, wedding-cake palaces, the Bronze Horseman caught in a moment of impossible glory. History both grim and beautiful embedded everywhere.

My adventure continues.
North

Northern Star Richmond—Liv's old friend from the California commune where she once stayed with her mother and later found refuge when she had nowhere else to go.

I look up at the sound of her entering the kitchen. She spots the postcard and smiles.

"Once upon a time, I thought North would never leave Twelve Oaks," she says. "Last month, he was in China, now Russia. No telling where he'll end up next. Hey, I need to get going. You okay with the tornado over there?"

"Sure."

She reaches up to kiss me, the air around her fragrant with

the sweet smell of cherries, before she gathers her things and leaves. I turn my attention to Nicholas. He and I spend the morning racing cars, watching a wildlife program, constructing tall buildings with blocks and pretending we're monsters knocking them down.

We break for apples and peanut butter, then head to the park for an hour to practice on the monkey bars before stopping at the Wonderland Café to see Liv as her shift ends.

"Hey, cute stuff." Allie Lyons, Liv's partner and close friend, emerges through the swinging doors of the kitchen.

"You've never called me cute before," I tell her. "I like it."

She laughs and holds out her arms for Nicholas. "*Cute* is not a word I'd use to describe you, Dean, and I mean that in the nicest possible way. You guys here for lunch?"

"Scarecrow Straws," Nicholas says.

"Your wish is my command, captain." Allie ruffles Nicholas's hair.

"Liv around?" I ask.

"Yeah, she's in the office working on the plans for the festival."

"What festival?"

"The Mirror Lake Bicentennial Festival."

"Mirror Lake is having a bicentennial festival?"

Allie nods. "Liv is in charge of it. Didn't she tell you?"

"No."

"She took over the planning committee to celebrate Mirror Lake's two-hundredth year," Allie explains, shifting Nicholas to her other arm. "I'm helping organize the entertainment. It's going to be held in Wizard's Park. There'll be concerts, an art fair, a children's stage, tons of food, and a fireworks show at night. Liv is also planning a charity auction to benefit the Historical Society."

I take in that barrage of information. "When did she start all this?"

"A few weeks ago." Allie shrugs. "Maybe she told you, and you forgot."

I'm pretty sure I wouldn't have forgotten hearing that my already overworked wife is now planning a town festival and charity auction.

"I need to talk to her," I say, gesturing toward the kitchen. "Can you deal with Nicholas for a few minutes?"

"Sure. I'll get him set up in a booster seat." Allie sets Nicholas on the floor and leads him over to an empty table by the window.

I go through the bustling kitchen to the offices in the back. Liv is sitting at the cluttered desk, working at a computer whose edges are decorated with scrawled Post-it notes.

"Oh, hi." She looks up at me, her face blooming with a smile, and for a second my resolve falters.

I manage to frown at her. "Hi."

"Why are you scowling?"

"Because apparently you're planning a festival to celebrate the town's bicentennial, which I didn't even know was taking place," I say. "And some sort of charity auction, which I also did not know was taking place."

"Well, it's to benefit the Historical Society's restoration of the train depot near Wizard's Park," Liv says. "So you shouldn't be scowling."

"When were you going to tell me this?"

"I thought I did." She looks at the computer. "I mean, I wrote down all the...Oh."

She plucks a Post-it off the computer and hands it to me. Written in her loopy handwriting is: *Tell Dean about festival and auction.*

She gives me a sheepish grin. I crumple the note in my fist.

"Is there a reason you wanted to take this job?" I toss the note into the trash.

"They asked me to."

"Who asked you to?"

"The city council. The original festival director got a job in Indiana, so she had to move away. And the city council knows how involved the Wonderland Café has been with local events, so they asked if I'd be interested in taking over the festival."

"And you said yes?"

"Well, obviously. And I wanted to do the charity auction because the Wonderland Café has always been involved in Historical Society projects. Why are you so annoyed?"

I'm *annoyed* because my wife seems to have plenty of energy and ambition for everything except our sex life...to the point where she had to fake an orgasm.

Irritation grips my neck. Apparently her little act was more of an insult than I'd initially thought. Since when does she think of *something else* when we're fucking?

"I appreciate you wanting to help," I say evenly. "But I don't get why you'd take on the task of planning a festival when you're already overbooked."

She narrows her eyes. "You don't think I can handle it?"

Oh, fuck.

"That's not the issue, and you know it." I step closer to her, still frowning. "You have shifts almost every day, you've been talking about expanding the café, you're busy every weekend with birthday parties, you've got Nicholas registered for toddler sports and swimming classes...and while you know I'll help however I can, I'm not happy about you taking on more work right now."

"Dean, most of the festival work is already done," she says, spreading her arms out. "Linda, the former director, already had so much in place. I just need to schedule the events, make sure we have all the permits, confirm the details, and set up the charity auction."

"That's it, huh?"

"I promise, it's not that big a deal." She puts her hand on my chest in an obvious ploy to weaken me. "Just phone calls and emails, a meeting or two. It's going to be a wonderful event for the whole town. And I'm doing it partly to create more visibility for the café and secure our reputation as an important institution. That's all part of our success."

I look into her brown eyes and feel an old, familiar twist in my chest. Liv has tried so hard to find her place in Mirror Lake, and I know this is one more way of ensuring that her roots here run strong and deep. It's one more way of making herself an integral part of the town that has become her home.

But as strongly as I understand that, I still don't have to like it.

"Do you have an assistant?" I ask. "Have you asked other people for help?"

"There's a whole planning committee, and I'm delegating duties to everyone," Liv says, faint irritation flashing in her eyes. "Look, I haven't complained about you being so busy lately or gone so often. Haven't you been overextending yourself for the past two years? You know, it's not always easy taking care of Nicholas by myself."

My jaw grinds. "I have told you countless times since Marianne moved away that I want us to hire another nanny."

"I don't want another nanny. I want *you*."

I take a breath and try to smother a surge of guilt. Liv sighs and strokes her hands over my chest.

"Dean, not once have I resented the work you're doing," she says. "I don't *like* it when you're gone, but I know how important the excavation is, and I would never ask you to change anything. I have always supported you, so don't make it sound as if I don't know my own limitations, okay? Please."

I drag a hand down my face. Frustration pushes at my chest. My work isn't going to slow down anytime soon.

For weeks I've been dealing with the fallout of the earthquake, assessing damage to a site that had previously stood for a thousand years, battling governmental officials and institutions who want to kill the whole project. Not to mention making decisions

I don't like. Then sex with my wife last night was hardly a hero's welcome—not that being angry about that will help anything either.

At this point, however, I'm not sure what will help.

"I don't want you to scale back your work, especially now," Liv says. "I know you need to save the site, and I'm proud of your dedication and commitment. But I want to do things too, and being asked to plan the festival is an honor I can't turn down. Okay?"

I don't respond, but I nod.

"I promise, I'm recruiting more people every day," she continues. "In fact, I'm going to recruit you to help out during the festival, maybe with one of the stages or setting up for the auction. You know how much I love watching your muscles flex when you do heavy lifting."

She strokes her hands down my arms and looks at me from underneath her long lashes. Some of my tension eases. Though I'm well aware Liv is playing me, I decide to let her. Because anything that gets my hot, sweet wife thinking in a sexy direction —and then *staying* there—is a win.

"What will I get in return?" I slide my hands around to squeeze her gorgeous ass.

"Whatever you want."

"Then I happily volunteer."

"I knew you would." She reaches up to kiss me. "I'll let you know what I need you to sign up for, okay?"

"Sure."

As if I could ever tell her *no.*

CHAPTER 4

DEAN

*A*fter leaving Nicholas with Liv, I drive to the east side of the lake where clusters of rental cabins, outdoor shops, and restaurants cater to the tourist crowd. Next to a sandwich shop is the place my brother Archer bought with his inheritance money. It's a rundown garage attached to an office, which he's in the process of turning into a motorcycle repair and sales shop.

I go through the main office to the back room where Archer does all the paperwork. I stop and knock on the closed door. After a moment, his voice tells me to come in.

I push open the door. The air feels thick, laced with tension. Archer is sitting behind the desk in grease-stained overalls, his expression set. Kelsey March, Archer's girl and one of my best friends, is standing on the other side of the room.

"Hey, man." Archer rises and extends a hand. "Welcome back."

"Thanks." I shake his hand and go to kiss Kelsey on the cheek. "Thought you'd be on campus today."

"I'm heading over to Edison Power to finalize the details of funding for the Spiral Project," she replies, brushing a hand through her blue-streaked blond hair. "How was your trip?"

"Good. Got a lot done." I step away from her. "How was California?"

She and Archer exchange glances before Kelsey shrugs.

"Okay," she says. "We had to meet with the Explorer Channel producers about the upcoming season. Contract details and stuff. Did you bring me my panettone?"

"Yeah, it's at home." I glance from her to Archer, aware of the lingering tension. "Guess I'm interrupting something."

"No." Kelsey rolls her shoulders back and fidgets with her cuffs. "You're not. I was just leaving."

Archer's gaze follows her as she heads out the door. Something is off, but I'm not about to try and figure out what it is.

I lower myself into a chair without comment. While I know well that dealing with Kelsey can be a challenge, I've learned to stay the hell out of her and Archer's relationship.

The air crackles with faint awkwardness. My relationship with my brother is no longer overtly hostile, but we haven't entirely figured out how to get past years of estrangement and anger.

I give Archer full credit, though—after meeting Kelsey, he settled in Mirror Lake and completely turned his life around. He opened the garage two months ago, after a year of searching for a place and working out a business plan. For years, it seemed as if Archer would never even hold a job, let alone own his own business, and he proved all our doubts wrong.

"So what's going on?" Archer asks.

I hand him the folder I'm carrying. "That's the details of your investments. I made some recommendations you can look over. Good rates on some newer gold-star funds."

"Thanks." He glances through the papers.

"Looks like you're starting to pull in some customers," I say, nodding toward the window.

"I put out a few ads and got some word-of-mouth." Archer puts the investment papers into the filing cabinet. "Hey, I haven't seen Nicholas since I got back. He's in daycare today?"

"No, he's at home with Liv for the afternoon."

"Maybe I'll text her, see if I can stop by." He reaches for his phone. "I might have a lead on a truck for her."

"A truck?"

"Yeah, for the party thing she and Allie want to do."

"What party thing?"

"The *thing*." Archer works the apps on his phone. "You know."

"I don't know."

Archer sets the phone aside. "Liv and Allie are trying to get a loan to buy a used truck for the café. I guess they want to be able to go to kids' houses for birthday parties or whatever. I said I'd help them find something that'd work. She didn't tell you?"

I shake my head. "First I've heard of it."

Apparently there's a lot going on in Liv's life that I don't know about. Or at least, that I'm the last to know. I don't like the idea that I'm out of the loop when it comes to my wife.

As I leave Archer's office, I suppress the urge to call Liv and tell her I'll donate a truck to the café. She still doesn't like it when I offer to give her something that she wants to work for—and while I love her drive and know where it comes from, it's still frustrating when she doesn't want my help. Or when she wants it only on her terms.

I leave the garage and cross the street. Kelsey's car is parked at the curb, partly hidden behind a row of trees. She's in the driver's seat, her forehead resting against the steering wheel.

Concerned, I walk to the car and knock on the driver's side window. Kelsey looks up and rolls down the window. Her eyes are glistening with a faint sheen of tears.

I pull a clean handkerchief out of my pocket and hand it to her.

"Thanks." She blows her nose and gives a humorless laugh. "Don't tell anyone you caught me being girly."

"It's in the vault." I pause, knowing she won't want me to probe too much. "What's going on?"

"Your brother is a goddamned stubborn ass."

"You say that like it's a bad thing."

"He wants to get married."

"To you?"

Kelsey glowers at me. "Of course to *me*."

"The bastard. You want me to beat him up?"

"Maybe." Kelsey groans and rests her forehead on the steering wheel again. "I don't get it, Dean. Everything has been perfect, you know? We live together, we have an amazing time storm-chasing, we fuck like rabbits whenever and wherever we want—"

"I get the point."

"I'm just saying, it's all good. Why does he want to screw it up by getting married?"

"Kels, I'm guessing he wants to get married *because* it's all good."

"Well, I told him I don't need to get married," she replies. "When we were in LA, he wanted to go to Vegas and do it, then he got pissed when I refused. He doesn't know how to take *no* for an answer."

"Why aren't you saying *yes*?" I ask.

"Dean, I'm thirty-eight," Kelsey says curtly. "I've never been married, and I see no reason to *get* married. It's not like Archer and I are going to settle down and have kids. Why can't things just stay the same?"

"If things stayed the same, you might never have met Archer."

She shoots me a glare, like that's exactly what she didn't want to hear.

"Hey, you want to go for a run tonight?" I ask to change the subject. "Or racquetball?"

Kelsey studies me. "How often do you hang out with your guy friends?"

"Huh?"

"I mean, you play football and stuff with them, right?"

"Yeah, sure."

"Who are they?"

"What?"

"Your guy friends," she says impatiently. "Who are they?"

"Other professors," I say. "Archeologists, historians. A few grad students. Max Lyons and I shot some hoops the other day. Why?"

"And none of them wonder why you hang out with a chick?" Kelsey asks.

"Since when are you a *chick*?"

"You know what I mean."

"I doubt they notice or care," I say. "What's this about? You don't want to hang out anymore?"

"Of course I want to hang out," she replies, glancing past my shoulder to the garage. "But have you ever asked Archer to join your football games or whatever?"

"Uh, no. But he's been busy with the garage." I shake my head with faint disbelief. "Are you trying to find buddies for your boyfriend?"

"I'm trying to figure out what the hell is going on between my *boyfriend* and his brother," Kelsey replies. "Archer has been living in Mirror Lake for over a year. And you and he never do anything together."

"We went to dinner and that concert last month."

"With me and Liv," Kelsey reminds me. "And, as usual, you both let us do all the talking."

"Actually it was more that we couldn't get a word in edgewise."

A faint smile tugs at her mouth before it's replaced with another frown.

"Look, as far as I can tell, you guys talk business, but that's it," she continues. "You know how crazy Archer is about Nicholas. And it kind of sucks that you and he still can't get over your shit. Maybe if you did, you could set him straight about this marriage thing."

"Whoa. Don't get me involved in your issues. I learned my lesson, remember?"

She gives me a pointed look and starts the car. "Not about how to fix your relationship with your brother, you haven't."

She rolls up the window and pulls away from the curb. I stand there for a minute, knowing—and hating—that she's right. My relationship with Archer, though better now, has always been the one thing in my life I haven't known how to fix. He's great with Nicholas, and he and Liv have become good friends, but he and I are still like two animals wary of each other.

Years ago, we used to be comrades-in-arms, fighting zombies, dragons, and monsters from our tree house, which we'd built in an old oak tree in the backyard of our California house. Known as The Castle, the tree house had served as a fortress, a UFO, a Wild West saloon, a robber's hideout, and a dozen other head-quarters.

I start back toward the office. Maybe I'll ask Archer if he wants to grab a beer tonight. He's standing outside next to a rundown motorcycle, talking to a customer.

I stop. Even if he did want to hang out with me—which I doubt—I don't know what we'd even talk about. Neither one of us is into rehashing the past or filling in details of all the years we were estranged.

Archer walks back into the garage, a clipboard in one hand. I watch him go, suddenly feeling a rush of sympathy. I can't imagine what I'd have done if Liv hadn't wanted to marry me. Don't want to imagine it. *Won't.*

I turn and walk back to my car. I've had to learn a lot over the past few years. How to stay out of Liv's business and not jump in to rescue her. How to give up control of certain aspects of my work. How to let my family fix their own problems. How to leave Archer and Kelsey's relationship alone.

I've had to learn how to back off, stand down, retreat, when everything in me wants to fight. I've had to stop trying to fix everything, even when I've wanted to do nothing more. Even when I still want to.

CHAPTER 5

OLIVIA

I hit the publish button on my latest blog entry, "What the Truck?," which is an unvarnished recounting of Nicholas's meltdown and my ruined attempt at a welcome home dinner for Dean.

I'd started my *Liv in Wonderland* blog as an extension of the café website, using it to describe our birthday parties, community outreach, and to post pictures of our dishes and desserts. But after Nicholas was born, my blog posts started becoming more personal and focused on the struggles of motherhood and work.

And while I keep certain things private—I'd never get into my lackluster sex drive, for one thing—the blog has become popular among other working mothers, who leave comments sympathizing with me, thanking me, and offering advice.

While I have plenty of real-life friends who are also mothers, some of whom also read the blog, it's fun to have a little community of online "fans," and I've even started earning a bit of extra money from advertising revenue.

I shut down my laptop and take out the Italian notebook Dean brought back for me. I open to the first page and write:

Get my groove back.

Though the book is so beautiful I feel like I should be using it to write a masterpiece rather than a To Do list, frankly that list is a mile long. And it has to start with my husband. Guilt nudges at me.

Even though Dean has been the model of patient understanding for two years, the discovery of his rather frequent self-pleasuring, not to mention the disaster of my badly faked orgasm, has made me realize I need to do something about this.

It's definitely time. Maybe I need to stop making excuses about being tired and overworked. I've lost all—okay, *most*—of my pregnancy weight, I feel pretty good about myself, I *think* about sex practically every time I look at my hot husband, and I miss the intimacy we once had. Plus I finally found a birth control pill that doesn't give me any side-effects, which means we can be entirely spontaneous.

Sex has always been an intensely powerful part of our relationship, but it also encompasses so much more than just physical pleasure. It's intrinsic to what we are to each other, a strong, glittering thread throughout our history, the singular, brilliant place where nothing exists except us.

Now with both of us so busy, and especially before we start resenting each other's work, we need to find that place again. And I'm the one with the map. Not to mention, I'm still curious about Professor West's hot masturbatory fantasies.

I add to the page:

Learn Dean's fantasies.
Act them out.

Surely that will get us back on track, though I'd better have some other plans too. I do some Internet searching for how to revive one's sex life. Maybe I should even start a Pinterest board of sexy images and ideas. My boards are all about home decorating, elaborate cakes and baked goods, craft projects, and a million "good mothering" tips and ideas. I've clearly forgotten one of my main priorities.

I log in to my Pinterest site, create a new board, and pin a few erotic pictures up. Before I can peruse a *31 Days of Hot Sex* website, I hear Nicholas calling from the living room that his cartoon is over.

I switch my brain to Mommy Mode and bring Nicholas upstairs to get ready. I don't have a full work shift today, but I stop at the café to get some paperwork done.

I love the café—it's a bright, airy fun place with murals covering the walls, diamond-patterned upholstery, and a potted topiary pathway leading up the "yellow brick road" staircase to the Wizard of Oz rooms.

Over the years, our clientele has mostly been mothers with children and families on weekends. Teenagers drop in often, their coolness belied by their half-smiles of pleasure as they're served edible teacups and peppermint twist cupcakes, and elderly ladies come in regularly for our Mad Hatter high tea.

I'm so proud of what Allie and I have created together, despite some bumps in the road. Not only is the café successful as a family-favorite place of fun, whimsical warmth and good food, we've also become actively involved in the community through our charity work, participation in the local theater festival, collaborations with the Historical Society, and most recently our work for the Mirror Lake Bicentennial Festival.

After settling Nicholas in the playpen I keep in our office, I sit at the desk to pay bills and figure out the work schedule.

"Hey, Liv, guess what?" Allie stops in the doorway of the office, her curly red hair caught up in a high ponytail. "A guy from Edison Power stopped by earlier, wanting to talk to us about catering their company picnic in August. It would be incredible for publicity, and it might bring in enough money that we could afford a deposit for the birthday party truck."

"Edison Power? I just sent them the sponsorship package for the festival." I pull open my festival file. "What was his name?"

"Mike Harrison, head of marketing. He also said his wife wants to have their daughter's fifth birthday party here, but I don't think we can pull it off. Mrs. Harrison wants her daughter's entire class invited, plus her other friends. We can't handle that many kids and our regular customers at the same time, and we already have reservations for that day so we can't close for a private party."

"Maybe we can double our staff for a few hours." I open the birthday party calendar and staff schedule. "If we can host a great birthday party for Mike Harrison's daughter, Edison might be even more inclined to sponsor the festival."

"And let us cater their picnic," Allie adds. "But we don't have the capacity for thirty-one kids in the party room. Plus a lot of the parents might stay."

"We'll use the Kansas Farm room too," I say. "And the outdoor terrace. This is great, Allie. We'll show them how good we are and establish a relationship. Do we have his wife's contact info?"

Allie digs in her apron pocket for the party request form and hands it to me. "I already emailed her this morning and told her we couldn't host that many kids."

"I think we can do it." I unfold the paper. "When did she schedule the party?"

"Three weeks from Saturday. She wants the full *Wizard of Oz* package."

"I'll call her." I reach for the phone. "If we plan for enough staff, we'll be fine."

A hint of irritation radiates from Allie. I try to ignore it as I leave a message on Monica Harrison's voicemail.

"It's not just about the café, Allie," I say apologetically, putting the phone back onto the receiver. "I didn't realize I'd be responsible for finding sponsors for the festival. But I asked Edison Power to be our highest level sponsor, and if they agree, we'll be able to have a children's stage at the festival and hire Slice of Pie to play."

"But the festival has nothing to do with the café," Allie says with a frown.

"Look, I'll handle it all," I promise her. "And I won't schedule anything without your okay."

She shrugs, not looking entirely convinced or happy. Regret twists my insides as I watch her turn and leave the office. Since becoming partners, Allie and I have disagreed on things over the past couple of years, but we've always managed to reach a compromise and never stayed irritated with each other for very long.

I start to go after her with the intention of making amends when the phone rings.

"Wonderland Café," I say into the receiver. "This is Liv."

"Liv, it's Monica Harrison. You left a message about my daughter Becky's birthday party?"

"Yes, thanks for calling me back. I wanted to tell you we'd be happy to host it for you, and after talking to my partner, we found a way to accommodate your entire guest list."

"Oh, that's wonderful. Thank you so much. Becky will be thrilled."

I write down the details of her request and email them to Allie before gathering my things to leave. I get Nicholas into his car seat and text Dean, asking if he can join us for lunch. When he doesn't respond right away, I drive to King's University.

The campus is milling with people walking to and from class, boots sloshing in the melting spring slush. The grass of the quad is starting to turn green, the bare trees budding with leaves.

The door to Dean's office in the history department is half-open. His baritone voice drifts into the corridor, along with another man's accented tone. They're talking about the Altopascio monastery and the damage from the earthquake.

I stop outside the office, taking Nicholas out of the stroller before he starts fussing. A young woman with brown, curly hair caught back in a bun comes down the hall toward me, her stride purposeful and a stack of folders in her arm.

After a second, I realize it's Jessica Burke, Dean's whip-smart, former grad student who earned her PhD a few years ago and has since been doing postdoc work in England.

"Jessica?" I stop and wave at her. "I didn't know you were back in town."

"Oh, hey, Liv." She approaches to give me a quick hug. "I just got in a few days ago. My father passed away last week."

"Oh, no. I'm sorry."

"Thanks." Sadness flashes behind her attempt at a smile. "He was sick for awhile, so it wasn't unexpected but still..."

She shakes her head and turns her attention to Nicholas. "Wow, look at how big Nicholas is getting. I've been keeping up with him by reading your *Liv in Wonderland* blog. He's adorable."

"Thanks. If there's anything you need or anything I can do to help, please let me know."

"Actually, I might be on the lookout for a part-time job," Jessica says, letting Nicholas wrap his fist around her thumb. "My postdoc at the University of Leeds is over, so I'm looking for a professorship somewhere. I'm also hoping to be able to stay with my mom for awhile since she's pretty broken up about my dad. I'd like to help her out as much as I can."

"Of course. Are you looking for a professorship around here?"

"If I can find one, but my chances are slim just because all the positions are already taken," she replies. "Dean is keeping an eye out for me, and he's going to spread the word to other state universities."

Before I can respond, the door of Dean's office opens wider.

"You'd be an excellent fit for the WHC, Dean." The other man's lightly accented voice carries into the corridor. "I don't have to tell you that opportunities like this don't come around very often."

"I appreciate that, Hans," Dean says. "And I'm honored that you'd think of me."

Something in his voice indicates he really is honored. I wonder what opportunity they're talking about.

The two men step into the corridor. Hans is a slender, blond man wearing a well-cut gray suit and small, round glasses. He looks vaguely familiar, though I can't immediately place him.

"Hey, Liv." Dean catches sight of me and lifts his hand in greeting. "What are you doing here?"

"We thought we'd see if you were free for lunch." I walk toward him as Nicholas starts to squirm, reaching out for his father.

"Hans, Jessica, and I are heading to a meeting over at SciTech," Dean explains, hefting Nicholas into his arms. "They're helping us with analyzing the seismic reports from the quake. Hans, this is my wife Olivia. Liv, Hans Klasen. You met at the Medieval Studies conference a few years ago. Hans is the director of UNESCO's World Heritage Center."

"Of course." The pieces click, and I hold out my hand in greeting. "Pleasure to see you again, Dr. Klasen."

"Hans, please. You as well." He indicates Nicholas with a smile. "You hadn't had your son last time we met. He is two years now?"

"He turned two in January, yes."

"Beautiful child." Hans touches Nicholas's brown hair. "Strong resemblance to his mother."

"Lucky kid, huh?" Dean asks, winking at me.

"Indeed," Hans agrees.

"Charmers," I remark, flattered nonetheless. "Hans, how long are you staying? Maybe both you and Jessica can come for dinner one night."

"I'm afraid I leave tomorrow for Washington, DC," Hans explains. "I stopped for a lecture in Chicago and the SciTech meeting. Also to convince your husband to come for the interviews."

I swing my gaze to Dean. "Interviews for what?"

He shakes his head. Jessica glances from me to Dean and touches Hans on the arm.

"I think Professor Hunter was looking for you," she tells him. "We still have a few minutes before we need to leave."

They both walk toward the main office. Dean hands Nicholas back to me.

"Interviews for what?" I repeat.

"Hans thinks I'd be a good fit for an open position at the World Heritage Center," Dean says.

I blink in surprise. I know Dean's professional reputation is immense, extending beyond the scope of academia, but strangely enough, not once have I considered the possibility that another institution might want to lure him away from King's University.

"What's the job?" I ask.

"Assistant director."

Assistant director of the World Heritage Center, a division of the United Nations?

Before I can process that astonishing idea, Nicholas whines and reaches for the sippy cup in his stroller. I turn, getting him settled and giving myself a second to regain my composure.

I love Dr. Dean West, *summa cum laude* from Harvard, the brilliant professor, the distinguished scholar and archeologist, but I don't often think of him that way. To me, he's far more often my warm, sexy husband, the doting father of our son, my best friend who brings home my favorite ice cream just because he thought I'd like some. The man who puts his hand on my lower back to guide me with such ease, as if I'm an extension of his body.

So it's something of a shock to remember just how internationally renowned he is and to realize other people want him.

"So you're...you applied for the job?" I ask.

"No." His expression pensive, Dean brushes his hand over Nicholas's hair. "But the WHC knows my credentials. Last week when I was in Italy, Hans mentioned the board was eyeing me for the assistant director position."

"And he asked you to take it?"

"He asked me to interview for it." Dean pushes back his cuff to glance at his watch as Hans and Jessica round the corner from the office.

I step away from him, taking hold of the handle of Nicholas's stroller.

"I'm sorry, we've got to get going." Dean leans in to brush a kiss across my cheek. ""I'll tell you more about it later, okay?"

I nod, but something inside me rustles with unease.

CHAPTER 6

OLIVIA

*A*fter Nicholas is asleep that evening, I take the baby monitor up to the Butterfly House's tower room, which is now Dean's home office. It's one of our favorite rooms—a circular space lined with windows that show off a view of the lake and downtown, all nestled within the embrace of the mountains.

Last year during the final phase of renovations, Dean put in oak shelves, which are now packed with hundreds of books, and I created a little sitting area with a comfy sofa and chairs near the wood-burning stove that radiates a cozy warmth in winter. The wall space is lined with framed family photos and various prints of medieval manuscripts. Dean is seated at his big desk, which is cluttered with books and papers.

I gesture to the clock. "Half past later."

He turns to face me as I sink into an oversized chair beside the window and put the baby monitor on the side-table.

"So what did you tell Hans when he said they were considering you for the job?" I ask.

"I was going to say no," Dean says, "but since we're trying to get the World Heritage Center to put the monastery on the list of protected sites, I knew it wouldn't be a good move politically to turn them down right away."

"What does the position entail?"

"Analysis and evaluation of historic sites in different countries," he explains. "The assistant director determines which sites should be listed by the WHC, how to protect sites in war zones, assesses landscapes, natural properties, conservation. Whoever takes the job has to get involved with cultural areas far beyond medieval sites. They'd chair the annual convention, deal with lobbying, fundraising, United Nations meetings."

"You'd be an international diplomat." I feel like I just said, *"You'd be president of the United States."*

"I went to college to be a historian, not a diplomat."

"You went to college to learn how to study and preserve history," I remind him. "And this sounds like you could do that on an international level. Actively, too…working with the physical part of history like you've been doing at Altopascio. I know how much you love that."

"I also love living in Mirror Lake and teaching at King's," Dean says. "It would be more of a change than we can make."

"Why?"

"We'd have to move to Paris."

My breath catches in my throat.

Paris. Sweet, hot memories fill my heart and mind.

Despite my nomadic childhood with my mother, I had never been out of the United States before Dean whisked me off to France almost seven years ago for our wedding and honeymoon. We'd gotten married at the family villa of a friend of Dean's before spending a soft-edged, intense month together in Paris. I'd felt like I was floating the entire time, as the world unfolded all the dreams I'd kept secret in my heart.

Even now the word *Paris* sparks thoughts of the museums and art galleries where paintings glow like jewels, the cafés with round tables and wicker chairs, the sandcastle façade of Notre Dame cathedral guarded by looming gargoyles, the lamp-lit bridges arching over the Seine. Buttery madeleines, fresh fruit at the outdoor markets, rich wine from Provençal vineyards...

Dean, carrying a fragrant bag laden with fluffy croissants, closing the door of the apartment that had once been an artist's atelier. Flowers blooming from window boxes, framing views of rooftops and chimney stacks, tall oak doors embellished with gold molding, scuffed wooden floors.

My new husband. My *husband.*

I stare at him now—the thick hair falling over his forehead, the stubbled planes of his jaw and dark-lashed eyes. He's wearing worn jeans and an old King's T-shirt, his feet planted on the hardwood floor in a solid stance that looks as if he's holding the earth in place. As if he's holding *our life here* in place.

"*Move* to Paris?" I repeat weakly.

"If I were even offered the job, I'd have to work from the World Heritage Center headquarters," he says. "But it wouldn't only mean a move to France. It's a position that requires global mobility, moving wherever the WHC sends me. Sometimes only for a few weeks or months. We'd have to completely uproot our lives."

"Do you think you'd ever consider it?" I ask.

"No. It would be a full career move, not something I could do part-time from King's, like I'm doing with the Altopascio dig. I'd have to resign from King's and start all over again."

Resign.

The word sticks me like a pin. He resigned from King's three years ago—for no other reason than to protect me from the hideous fallout of a false sexual harassment allegation. And while the university asked him to rescind the request and keep his job —later rewarding him with full tenure—the very idea of Dean leaving the department he created elicits a wave of apprehension.

I can't imagine him resigning from King's again, not even for a good reason rather than a disgraceful one. In the few years since he started the Medieval Studies program, it's developed a widespread reputation for being one of the best and fastest growing history programs in the country.

Move. Resign. Start over.

"Um...wow." I can't think of anything else to say. Because...*wow.*

Dean shrugs, like it's no big deal. "I appreciate the interest, but we could never make it work."

Of course we couldn't. But I wonder how he's figured that out in the week since Hans told him about it.

Though I'm aware of a faint relief that Dean doesn't seem interested, it's not like him to do something without considering all the angles first. I mean, this is the man who looked up the university *rules* before he even asked me out, just to make sure there would be no repercussions if a professor dated a student.

"Do you think you'd want the job?" I ask.

"It doesn't matter if I want it or not," he replies. "We have Nicholas, I have tenure at King's, you're busy running the café and all your other activities...Why would we even consider moving anywhere?"

"So what's this business about the interviews?"

"That's what Hans and I were talking about," he explains. "Once a year, the World Heritage representatives meet at a United Nations Assembly to vote on which sites to add to the protected list. With the Altopascio proposal still under consideration and the assembly meeting in July, it wouldn't look good if I turned down the job right away. If the representatives think I'm still a strong candidate, that will help our case. And with the earthquake damage, the site needs all the help it can get."

I know Dean wouldn't hesitate to pick his family over any professional opportunity. I also know he's not the kind of man to sit complacently in one place—he's a natural leader who likes to move, to do things, to effect change. And what greater influence could he have than to actively help save historic sites throughout the world?

I gaze out the window at the glassy darkness. Condensation clings to the edges, framing my image. Sometimes when I see my reflection, I see Liv the confident woman, the capable mother, and other times I still see a ten-year-old, uncertain girl.

Those glimpses make me realize that girl will always be a part of me. I wonder if that's true for everyone—do we all still sometimes feel like the children we no longer are?

I look away from the window at my tall, strong husband. It's in him too—the twelve-year-old child who fought with his brother and divulged the secret that tore them apart. The son whose father pushed him excessively to be the best. The young man who believed in chivalrous knights and bold, momentous quests.

The boy who dreamed of traveling to far-flung, exotic places, seeking adventure, leading the troops to victory.

Discomfort hits me. It's also not like Dean to pretend to be interested in something he's not.

"So what's going to happen when the WHC committee discovers you're not really considering the job anyway?" I ask.

"Nothing's going to happen." A crease appears between his eyebrows. "I don't like not being able to say no right away, but I also don't like the idea of doing something that could thwart all the progress we've made."

"But they'll think you're interested in the job," I point out. "That sounds a bit…"

Unethical. I don't like that either. Nothing about Dean has ever been *unethical.* Just the opposite.

"I'm trying to save an important site that's been badly

damaged by an earthquake and is now in danger of being destroyed," Dean says in a measured tone, faint tension lacing through his body. "And I'm not hiding my position. Everyone knows I'm advocating for the site."

And that's just one of the reasons they want him. The World Heritage committee can easily see how Professor Dean West's undeterred advocacy and persistence on behalf of a medieval monastery could extend to sites around the world.

I walk to the other side of the tower and look out the window that affords a view of downtown.

It's silly, I know, this feeling of something perilously close to fear. It also reminds me that no matter what else we do in life, some things run so deep they're engraved in our bones. I don't like instability, restlessness, unpredictability. I crave safety and permanence.

That's just one of the reasons I love the lake—the water moves and shifts, but stays in one place, encircled by trees whose roots run deep into the earth, by rocks and boulders that have been there for centuries, by a town that was founded two hundred years ago by people who were looking for a *home.*

The lights of Avalon Street shine in the darkness like the stars of the Milky Way. Our little apartment is down there somewhere, the place where I'd be reading in a cushy chair by the French doors when Dean would come in from his bedroom office, rumpled and scruffy, kiss the top of my head, and tell me he was going to the corner bakery to pick up some doughnuts.

"Liv, there are dozens of other candidates being considered for the job," he says from behind me. "A request to interview isn't a job offer."

"What if it turns into one?"

"I'd say no. Hans already knows I'm not going to uproot our lives."

Because we both have everything we always wanted right here. Right now.

Neither of us has to say those words aloud.

We've worked so hard. We have so much. I'd been so over-the-moon happy when Dean was offered tenure at King's almost three years ago, solidifying his position there and ensuring we could stay in Mirror Lake as long as we wanted.

Never did I imagine that either of us might one day *not* want to stay.

But if I block out everything else, I can see this for Dean, like a single, crystal-clear star. It's in his nature, the very core of him. Everything he is centers around his fierce, basic urge *to protect*.

Since becoming a mother, I've understood Dean's protectiveness on levels I never had before, solidifying the bone-deep knowledge that I would do anything to keep my child safe.

Now, as I think of Professor Dean West merging his intense, protective instinct with his love of history, it's painfully obvious that no one on earth is more perfectly suited to advocate for the global protection of historic sites.

I swallow hard. "I wouldn't want you to miss an incredible opportunity."

"I'm not missing anything," he says. "We have a life here I don't want to change."

And yet he didn't say he doesn't want the job.

I let out my breath in a long rush. I have never understood the meaning of the word *wanderlust*. I was not the college girl who had dreams of backpacking through Europe or South America. I will never understand Kelsey's love of packing her truck and hitting the road for weeks on end, chasing storms and sleeping in roadside motels.

My travel journey has been an inward one, mapping out all the rivers and valleys of my soul, finding my way, charting new territory toward a place that I could call *home*.

I've done that now. I know who I am. I have bloomed right where I was planted.

And while change has always been a nerve-wracking concept

for me—as a child, change never led to anything good, and it's the thing that has caused the most rifts between me and my husband —I'm not as afraid of it as I used to be.

But for me, *change* is having a toddler who is learning something new every minute, restoring and moving to the Butterfly House, figuring out ways for the café to reach into the community, visiting Altopascio one day, enrolling Nicholas in preschool, trusting my ability to plan a town festival.

It's not giving up what we've built here and moving overseas.

"If we were living back on Avalon Street," I say. "In our little apartment, just you and me, no child yet...would you want the job?"

"Not if you didn't want to consider moving."

"That's not an answer."

He pushes to his feet and goes to the window, looking out at the expansive view of the lights. His profile is like that of an ideal king or emperor—strong and beautiful with a straight nose and angular jaw. His hair is getting longer, in need of a cut, the thick strands brushing the back of his collar.

"You spent enough time supporting me when we were first married," he says. "I wouldn't ask you to uproot your life again, especially on this scale."

The unease inside me intensifies, like a wave building slowly beneath the surface of the ocean.

"That's still not an answer."

He drags a hand through his hair with a sigh. "I don't know. If it were just the two of us living in the apartment, then I'd be a lot more inclined to want it."

"Regardless of what we have here?"

"Liv, for almost ten years, I've never done a damn thing *regardless* of what we have." A note of irritation edges his voice. "I've done everything with you—with *us*—in mind. Everything. So you're asking a pointless question because it's not just you and me anymore, and we don't live in the apartment, and we do have a child to think about."

"I'm trying to get at whether or not you'd even want the job," I tell him.

"And I told you it doesn't matter."

I hold up my hands in a placating gesture. "Okay. I just don't want you to make a decision you'll later regret."

"I'm beginning to regret having told you about this," he mutters.

I blink. "Wow."

He sighs, turning to cross the room to me. He brings his hands up to the sides of my neck.

"I just don't see the point of this conversation," he says. "Why are you even asking these questions? I need to do some political maneuvering, but do you want me to seriously consider pursuing the job?"

I stare at the warm, vulnerable hollow of his throat that is one of my favorite places to kiss. Of course I don't want him to consider the job. I want him to stay happy right where he is. I don't want him to notice another door on the other side of the room, away from us, and wonder what would happen if he walked through it.

"No," I finally say. "I don't want you to take a new job. Certainly not one in Europe. But I also don't want to be the reason you turn down an amazing opportunity."

"Liv, you're the reason I do things, not the reason I don't." He brushes his thumb across my lower lip. "Why are you so upset?"

"I'm not upset. I'm proud of you." The instant I say the words, I realize just how true they are. I put my hand against his jaw. "The United Nations, for heaven's sake. I mean, I knew you were good, but I didn't know you were *that* good."

"Yes, you did."

I smile. "Yes, I did."

He pulls me against him, his strong arms encircling me in a

warm, protective embrace. A rush of selfishness fills me so fast my throat aches. I can't stand the thought of sharing my husband with anyone.

Since the day we met, this man has never looked beyond me, beyond us, beyond the fortress of our marriage that we've fought so hard to build and defend.

But what would happen if he did? What if my white knight decides to lower the drawbridge and let the rest of the world in?

CHAPTER 7

OLIVIA

I didn't have a key. I was eleven. I couldn't get into the apartment. I had no idea where my mother was.

I can't remember where we were, what city it was. Indianapolis, maybe, or Milwaukee. It was a cold, glittery night. We'd been there for two days, having driven from Florida where my mother earned some cash selling woven bracelets on the beach. She'd used the money to put down a deposit on a first-floor, downtown apartment that smelled like mold.

She'd sent me out to get milk and bread from a store a few blocks away. When I got back, the apartment door was locked. I didn't have a key. I rang the bell. No answer. Knocked. No answer. Tried to peek in the window. Dark inside.

Dark inside.

My heart thumped low and heavy against my ribs. I clutched the plastic bag. My hands were sweaty. I waited for a long time, huddled up against the door. Every now and then, I'd ring the bell or knock, as if she'd suddenly open the door and tell me she'd been in the shower all this time.

The night air grew colder. When my fingers started getting numb, I pushed to my feet and walked back to the grocery store. Even if I had no one to call, at least it would be warm there. Lights shone from the windows, neon beer signs flashing.

I walked with my shoulders hunched. I didn't notice the group of men loitering outside the store until I straightened. They were big, maybe five of them, dressed in ratty jeans and jackets. Cigarette smoke, bottles of hard liquor, raspy laughter.

"Hey, honey, why you all alone?" one of them called.

I stopped. I'd been forced to deflect plenty of leering, wrong looks from men. I'd been looked at, touched, and spoken to in ways no young girl should be. My mother had never protected me, so I'd had to learn how to protect myself. Even if it was by being invisible.

A guy with a beard stood between me and the entrance to the store. He narrowed his gaze on me.

"You know how to answer a question, girl?" he asked.

My stomach knotted. Their stares burned into me. I'd have to pass them all, walk through the gauntlet they'd created, to get inside the store.

"You're a pretty little thing," another guy remarked, tilting his head back to drink out of a bottle. "You shouldn't be out alone this time of night."

"You got a boyfriend?" the bearded guy asked with a leer.

The others laughed, the sound cracking through the air like a whip.

I dropped the bag and ran. Better than trying to be invisible was not being there at all.

Their laughter followed me as I ran, my tennis shoes pounding on the cracked sidewalk. Instinctively, I ran back toward the apartment, but fear propelled me faster and faster. By the time I stopped, gasping for breath, I realized I didn't know where I was.

I stopped on a street corner, looking around. An empty lot, car repair shop, boarded-up house. Yellowish pools of light cast by streetlamps. Panic flickered in my gut. I didn't know what to do except keep walking. There was no one else around, not that I'd have trusted anyone enough to ask for help.

I walked through the maze of streets until my feet ached, passing closed stores and noisy dive bars I was too scared to enter. Everything scared me—passing cars, shadowed alleys, underpasses thick with weeds. I didn't even dare try and find a police officer for fear they'd involve Child Protective Services after taking me in.

When I was too exhausted to keep walking, I found a sheltered stoop where I could hide in the shadows. I nodded off into an uneasy sleep, waking when the sky began to lighten.

I pushed to my feet, hugging my arms around myself as I started walking again. A grocer was just unlocking the door of his shop as I approached. Desperate and longing to be back at "home," I hurried up to him.

"Sir, can you help me?" My voice was hoarse, cracking. "I'm lost."

He eyed me warily, trying to figure out if I was a runaway kid, beggar, or both.

"P-please," I begged. "I know the street where I live, but I can't find it. Could you just l-look it up for me? Tell me how to get there. I'll walk home."

He finally relented and gestured for me to enter the store. He told me how to get to Sycamore Street, and it turned out I'd walked ten miles away from the apartment. Then he gave me an apple and told his wife to drive me back.

A light was on in the apartment. I knocked. I didn't know

whether to be enraged or relieved when my mother answered the door. She looked like an angel, the light glowing on her honey-blond hair, her features as fine as those of a princess. She looked at me with her thick-lashed blue eyes and blinked.

"Where were you?" she asked.

"You told me to go to the store for milk and bread last night," I said, my throat tight with the urge to fling myself into her arms, to feel her embrace. "When I got back, you weren't here. I didn't have a key. I've been walking all night. I got lost."

She blinked again, like she didn't remember. At times like that, I almost wished I could blame drugs or alcohol for her lack of concern. Using the excuse "She was drunk" or "She was strung out" seemed far easier than admitting the truth, which was "She just doesn't give a shit."

My mother opened the door wider to let me in. A man's jacket was flung over the sofa, his shoes next to the coffee-table. A heavy thickness hung in the air, one I'd learned to recognize as a male threat, menacing and lewd.

I glanced toward the bedroom. The door was closed.

"Well," my mother said. "Where's the milk and bread?"

"Paris?" Allie's eyes widen behind her purple-framed glasses as she sets a roast-beef sandwich in front of Florence Wickham at the counter. "That is so awesome. I wanted to do a year abroad in Paris when I was in art school, but I ended up going to Madrid with a friend. We traveled all over Europe, though. Had a completely amazing time. I love Paris."

"Moi aussi," Florence says, pursing her lips around the straw of her cherry soda. "The city of lights and love. How can you not be happy there?"

"How many times have you been?" I ask.

"Oh, countless." She waves her hand in the air. "But no matter how many times my husband and I visited Paris, we always found something new to see and do. And the food is incomparable."

"Liv and Dean went to Paris on their honeymoon," Allie tells Florence. "Isn't that romantic? They were married at a villa in the south of France."

"Oh, how lovely," Florence says warmly. "Have you been back, Olivia?"

"Dean has. I haven't."

"Why not?"

I shrug, not wanting to admit I haven't had a reason to return to Paris. "Well, Dean has gone for work reasons and I've just stayed here."

"I'd never pass up the chance to go to Paris," Allie remarks. "I'll never forget this chocolate profiterole I had at a café on Boulevard Montparnasse."

"My niece and her husband went on a food tour of France a couple of years ago," Florence says. "They took cooking classes, went wine tasting, even shopped at the market with a chef so they could pick fresh produce. They had such a fantastic time they're planning to do it again next year, either in Paris again or Rome."

"You could totally do that, Liv," Allie says, her voice tinged with excited envy. "Take French cooking classes or pastry classes in Paris. And you could write about all your experiences on your blog. *Liv in a Parisian Wonderland*."

I hadn't expected such an enthusiastic response from her. "Well, we might visit Paris again, but we're not going to move there. Dean hasn't even been offered the job. It's just an opening."

"Well, I imagine Dean is rather exceptional at fitting into openings," Florence remarks, dipping a French fry into a pool of ketchup.

Though of course that's true, I shoot her a mildly disapproving look.

"Not this opening," I say. "Besides, even if he were offered the job, there's no way we could move overseas with a child. And it's not just Paris either. We'd have to move to different countries for weeks or months at a time. Wherever the World Heritage people send us."

"Well, that sounds incredible," Florence remarks. "What an opportunity."

"We can't go globe-trotting with a two-year-old," I say.

"People move all over the world with children all the time," Allie remarks. "Don't you ever watch *House Hunters International*?"

"We're not on *House Hunters International*," I remind her.

"Oh, you should totally apply."

"Allie, I'm not moving overseas! I can't believe you'd want me to leave the café."

She blinks. "I don't want you to leave the café. But I wouldn't want you to think the café is the only reason you'd have to stay. I always believe you're more likely to regret the chances you *didn't* take than the ones you did."

Florence nods in sage agreement. I scrub down the counter with unnecessary force. I'd secretly hoped that by mentioning the possible job to Allie, she would laugh and agree it would be ridiculous for Dean to ever consider such a move, thereby validating my own response. I hadn't expected her to wax rhapsodic about pastries, cooking classes, and *House Hunters International*.

Over the next few days, I wonder if I'm the only woman in the world who can't imagine moving to Paris. Admittedly, in some tiny part of my brain—fueled by travelogues set in Provence, Isabelle Adjani movies, and buttery croissants from the French bakery where I used to work—I can see the romanticism of the opportunity. I can imagine Dean reaching the apex of his career, he and I raising our son to be a citizen of the world, me learning French, visiting museums, making new friends for myself and Nicholas.

But I know the difference between an idealized image of something or someone (*Hi, Mom*) and reality. And I know that a move to Europe, even Paris, would not be like a soft-edged romantic movie where I wander down the Rue de Rivoli in a chic scarf, buying fresh flowers and *macarons* for my dinner party comprised of international diplomats.

Global mobility means Dean could be sent anywhere. I looked at the list of World Heritage sites, which includes monuments in China, India, Chile, Malaysia, Peru, Turkey…

There's no telling where he would have to go first and for how long. It's painfully reminiscent of my constant moving with my mother, except on a far bigger and more frightening scale.

Even if I could get past my deep-seated hatred of moving to unknown places, the price of the WHC position is not one I would want to pay—leaving Mirror Lake, selling my half of the café, selling the Butterfly House, saying goodbye to the friends who have become my family, trying to adjust to raising our son in foreign countries. Through hard work and struggle, my dreams of life in Mirror Lake have all come true, and I could never leave them behind for dreams I don't even have.

But I'm distinctly aware I'm not the only one with dreams. And I don't know what my husband's dreams are anymore. I know he wants to protect his family, to do whatever he can to ensure we're safe and happy, to forge new paths in academic research, expand the Medieval Studies department, and guide his students to achieve their best. But all those dreams focus outward or on other people.

Does Dean have any dreams for himself?

I try not to let the disquiet of that question affect me too much. I don't want to even consider the idea that Dean might ever give up any dreams for my sake. But the question of the interview fades after Hans Klasen leaves town, and Dean and I settle back into our steadfastly familiar routine.

Though Dean isn't teaching this semester, he goes to campus to work and meet with grad students. One Thursday afternoon,

Nicholas and I head to Wizard's Park to join a weekly playgroup of other children and their mothers.

The park is a grassy expanse of land dotted with sculptures and topiaries of wild animals—a tiger, elephant, a flock of penguins, a giraffe. A large playground sits in the middle of the park, and the landscape slopes down toward the lake.

The moms—or The Moms, as I've come to think of them, like an army guarding their children—are wandering around with takeout cups of coffee, talking and keeping an eye on the kids, who swing on monkey bars, cross the rickety bridges, and go down the slides.

Today Nicholas and I are in charge of bringing snacks, and I set up containers of grapes, apple slices, cookies, and milk on a picnic table before going to supervise Nicholas on the jungle gym.

When he starts shoveling sand into a plastic bucket expressly made for the purpose of filling and dumping, I sit on a nearby bench and take out my phone to text Dean.

LIV: Tell me a fantasy.

DEAN: I have office hours.

LIV: Ooo. A sexy office fantasy. Am I a naïve little secretary, and are you the big, domineering boss?

DEAN: I'm on campus and I have student office hours right now.

LIV: Is there a student in your office?

DEAN: No. Where are you?

LIV: With other moms and kids at the park.

DEAN: And you're texting me about sex fantasies during a playgroup?

LIV: I know, it's so wrong. So…naughty.

DEAN: Yes, it is.

LIV: Am I a bad girl in your fantasies? A slutty French maid?

DEAN: No, but now I want to buy you a French maid costume.

LIV: I would wear it for you, you know.

DEAN: Yeah, you would.

LIV: Do you really fantasize about that?

DEAN: No, but I will now.

LIV: Come on, give it up, then. What do you fantasize about?

DEAN: It's in the vault, baby.

LIV: I'm not a nurse, am I? A cheerleader?

DEAN: No.

LIV: A stripper? Catwoman?

DEAN: Uh, no, but that sounds promising.

LIV: Dean, there can't be that many fantasies left.

DEAN: You'd be surprised.

LIV: Tell me!

DEAN: Gotta go. Student just walked in.

LIV: I will break you, Professor West.

DEAN: You already do every time you smile at me, beauty.

Well, crap.

A smile tugs at my mouth as I tuck my phone back into my pocket and reemerge into the world. Even though Dean and I don't have nearly as much time alone together as we used to, these little stolen moments still have the power to sweep me off into the space that belongs to us alone.

"Snack!" Nicholas calls, dumping the bucket of sand out.

"Come on." I hold out my hand, feeling that warm glow when he closes his chubby fingers around mine.

We return to the picnic table, and I hand him an individual container of milk, a cookie, and a few grapes.

"Do you have soy milk?" Susan, a young mother of twins whom I met at the last playdate, pauses beside the table. "Bailey is lactose intolerant."

"No, sorry." Because I have become well-versed on the hot topics of The Moms these days, I add, "But the grapes are organic, and the double-chocolate cookies are gluten-free and nut-free."

She appears somewhat mollified as she takes a juice box out of her bag and hands it to the pigtailed blond girl at her side.

"So I heard you've taken over the planning for the bicentennial," Susan says. "Between that and the café, you must be swamped. Is Nicholas in daycare?"

"A few times a week," I say, hating the stab of guilt and the sense that I'm being judged—even though the question was innocent enough.

"And how is the festival planning going?" Susan asks. "I don't know how you do it all."

I don't, I think ruefully. At least, I'm not doing my husband.

"It's going well," I tell Susan brightly. "Just looking for a main sponsor."

"I heard you were going to have a children's stage." Joan, a mother of two teenagers and an unexpected three-year-old, reaches for a cookie. "What kind of entertainment do you have planned?"

"Hopefully a magician and an acrobatic group," I say. "But if I can bring in a high-level sponsor, Slice of Pie will be the headliner."

"Slice of Pie?" Susan and Joan exchanged impressed looks at my mention of the red-hot children's band, which is fronted by a charismatic and curly-headed young guitarist and singer known as the Pieman. "Wow."

"I hope they don't play 'Rumble in My Tumble.'" Another

mother, Wendy, approaches, pushing her sunglasses on top of her head. "If I have to hear that song one more time, I'm drowning myself in chardonnay."

"Oh, please." Joan rolls her eyes. "As if you need an excuse to drown yourself in chardonnay."

We all laugh, and Wendy acknowledges the truth of the remark with a good-natured grin.

"So will we need tickets, Liv?" Joan asks.

"There will be a few VIP seats, but since the stage will be in the park, it's all part of the festivities."

"What about backstage passes?" Susan asks. "Can we meet the Pieman? He's so adorable."

"Noah wants to be the Pieman when he grows up," Wendy says. "He'd lose his mind if he got to meet him in person."

"Well, nothing is confirmed yet," I reply. "I'm waiting to see if Edison will sponsor the festival so we can afford more entertainment."

I glance at Wendy, wanting to change the subject. "So didn't Noah start pre-K this year? How is that going?"

"Oh, it's wonderful. I really should have had him tested for early enrollment."

"Liv, Louise said you have Nicholas on the waitlist for Preschool of the Arts," Susan says. "Have you heard from them yet?"

"No, but he won't be three until next January. They won't take him before then."

"Oh, they will if your child is advanced," Susan assures me, patting Bailey's head. "I've had Bailey on the list since she was one. I expect she'll be enrolled this fall."

"Dylan just started at P of A." Carol, the mother of a three-year-old son and newborn daughter, approaches the table. "It's been incredible. They emphasize arts and music as well as academics, so the children go into kindergarten really well prepared.

Some of them are even reading at advanced levels by the time they start."

My heart sinks a little. I dropped a ball I didn't even realize I was holding. I make a mental note to call the preschool as soon as I get home, once again feeling like I'm falling behind in some sort of race, even though I don't even know where the finish line is.

"…the Bahamas," Susan is saying, the conversation apparently having shifted to another topic. "We usually stay on Paradise Island, but this year we're going to Nassau. We've never been there before."

"Are you taking the kids?" Wendy asks.

"No, they're staying with my mother." Susan gives a sigh of relief. "I can't wait. I've already booked two spa days and a snorkeling trip."

"Bob and I are going to Colorado in August," Joan says. "At least it's a getaway. The kids are going to visit his sister for about a week."

The other women chime in with their upcoming summer vacation plans. I stay silent. I can't remember the last time Dean and I went on a trip alone together. We've taken Nicholas to California to visit Dean's father, and to Chicago a couple of times, but other than occasional talk about going to Italy *someday*, we haven't gone anywhere else.

I'm beginning to think with our focus on Nicholas and our work, Dean and I have lost sight of each other in ways that have nothing to do with sex. I can't even remember the last time we managed to go on a date—mostly because by the time evening rolls around, I'm too exhausted to want to do anything but sit on the sofa and watch TV, though even then I'm usually falling asleep before a program is half over.

"Hey, there's my main man." A deep voice booms over the park chatter as Archer strides toward us from the parking lot.

"Unca Archer!" Nicholas launches himself at Archer like a little rocket and hugs his legs.

Archer rubs Nicholas's head and extends a fist. Nicholas obliges with a return fist bump, and then they simultaneously flare their fingers out into "fireworks."

"How's it going, man?" Archer grabs Nicholas's legs and swings him upside-down to carry him back to the playground. Nicholas shrieks with laughter.

There's a palpable shift in the air as the other mothers watch Archer approach—big and muscular with black hair and the hard edges of a biker, Archer West draws a great deal of feminine interest and fascination.

"Hey, Liv." Archer hauls Nicholas upright and upside-down again, causing him to burst into a fit of giggles. "You get my text?"

"Yes, thanks. Can you drop us off at home after we pick up the chairs?"

"Sure." Archer flips Nicholas around a few times before setting him back down.

"Swing," Nicholas shouts, tugging on Archer's hand.

Archer obligingly follows Nicholas to the swings.

"He is so hot," Carol mutters to me under her breath. "What's he doing here?"

"I asked him to help me transport some used chairs from a furniture warehouse," I say. "They're for the festival auction."

"You're auctioning old chairs?" Carol asks.

"I'm collecting old chairs," I correct. "The auction is going to be called the Chair Fair. We're going to give a chair to anyone who wants one, and they can paint it with whatever design they want and return it to me. Then we're going to auction the chairs along with the travel and dinner packages that local businesses have donated."

There's a murmur of impressed appreciation among The Moms, which makes me feel good. With the exception of Susan, who claims she can't "draw a straight line," all the other women agree to participate in the auction by painting a chair.

"I'm going to keep all the chairs in the shed at the Butterfly

House, so you can come by any time to pick one up," I tell them. "I'm going to do a garden-themed chair, and I'm hoping I can get Archer to paint a comic-book chair to go along with a gift certificate from a game store."

"He could *be* a comic book hero," Carol remarks, eyeing Archer as he catches Nicholas coming down a slide. "Is he married?"

"*You* are," Susan reminds her.

"Yeah, but Frank doesn't look like that," Carol replies. "Archer could put the rumble back in my tumble, if you know what I mean."

Susan chuckles. "Every mother of young children knows what you mean. That's why we need these vacations alone."

Good heavens. Is that true? Do we all have this dearth in our libidos and sex lives? Are The Moms so caught up in running households and raising children that sex has fallen by the wayside?

"Honestly, I'd rather have a spa day than a romantic night with Frank these days," Carol says. "The idea of being alone and pampered is way more exciting than having to do any actual work. Maybe if I were more relaxed, I'd feel sexy again."

"Yeah, well, Paula had a full-time nanny and plenty of time to pamper herself…you know what a babe she is…and her husband still ended up having an affair," Wendy points out. "Less than a year after their son was born!"

The other ladies shake their heads and cluck their tongues. I eat a cookie and sigh inwardly.

I really do need to do something—not because I think Dean would start eyeing other women, but because I know how lucky I am to have him. In the chaos of the past two years, he's always been right there, steady as an oak tree—walking with a colicky Nicholas at night so I could sleep, going to work every day after making breakfast and coffee, asking one of his grad students to babysit so he can take me out, always ensuring Nicholas and I have everything we need and want.

He and I have struggled with dry spells before, but not for longer than a few months. This one seems to have been going on for two years.

And my husband *does* look like Archer. Heck, my husband is a zillion times hotter and sexier. And still, even when he's thrusting inside me and murmuring dirty things in my ear...I start thinking of daycare payments.

Really, Liv?

I need to do something more than just get my groove back.

I turn to pack up the snack containers. Archer runs around with Nicholas and a few of the other kids, much to both their and their mothers' pleasure.

If these other women can manage to take vacations alone with their husbands, why can't I? Schedules are certainly adjustable. But though I love the idea of Dean and I going on a trip alone together, I can't prevent a nagging worry. If we're alone in a hotel room, there's some serious pressure to get uninhibited and raw.

Which would obviously be the point and, under the right circumstances, I'd be all in. But now I can just picture myself gorging on an expensive, room-service meal that I didn't have to cook and then falling facedown on a huge, feather-soft bed to sleep for eight hours straight.

Leaving my husband to his own devices. Again.

But what if I don't tell him about it at all? That would give me even more motivation—I could plan a hot, romantic trip just for the two of us and surprise him with it. How incredible would that be?

Ideas start sparking in my mind. I'll buy new lingerie, get a mani/pedi, maybe a new haircut. I'll study the *31 Days of Hot Sex* website for new ideas, read some smutty novels. Heck, I might even check out a couple of dirty movies.

If I follow the Dean West belief that *a plan* is the bedrock of

every action, then I should be raring to go by the time we close
the hotel room door.

That's it! That's the answer. It has to be.

As Archer returns with a giggling Nicholas slung over his
shoulder, I think I should have found—or at least looked for—the
answer sooner.

Maybe if I had, Dean wouldn't have turned his attention to
work so much over the past few years. And maybe he wouldn't be
facing the lure of a fancy, international job that feels like it might
suddenly be my new competition.

CHAPTER 8

OLIVIA

*A*fter we get Nicholas buckled into the car seat in Archer's truck, I direct him to the furniture warehouse where we load a bunch of old wooden dining chairs, a rocking chair, and an Adirondack chair into the back of the truck. Then we head over to an industrial area of town, one populated by junkyards and manufacturing buildings. He parks near a warehouse whose parking lot is lined with trucks and vans.

The side door opens, and Kelsey strides out. In contrast to her usual professional attire of a tailored suit and silk shirt, she's wearing jeans and a tank top smudged with dirt.

She smiles as she greets us, but a faint awkwardness crackles between her and Archer. Archer unbuckles Nicholas from his car seat and hefts him into his arms.

"What's up with the chairs?" Kelsey asks, nodding to the truck bed.

I explain about the auction as we walk around to the back of the warehouse.

"I'm recruiting both of you to paint chairs," I tell her and Archer. "Kelsey, you could do a weather-themed chair or maybe one based on Russian egg painting designs. And, Archer, what about a superhero theme or a Blue chair?"

Tension winds through the air at my mention of Blue, the superheroine Archer created after he and Kelsey met. Based on Kelsey, Blue is a fierce, powerful character who derives her power from the forces of weather and uses tornadoes to defeat her enemies.

"He can't paint a Blue chair," Kelsey mutters. "Blue is private."

"Blue is fearless," Archer says, shooting her a pointed look.

Kelsey's mouth tightens. Their gazes clash, like sword blades striking. I suddenly wonder what I've started with my innocent remark about chairs.

"Yeah, I'll paint a chair, Liv," Archer tells me.

"He's not painting Blue," Kelsey says, her gaze still on Archer. "Blue is mine."

"Blue is mine, storm girl." Archer shakes his head and strides ahead of us. "You know it. Now you just have to admit it."

Good heavens. With their strong personalities, Kelsey and Archer still often clash, but I have no idea why a comic-book character is a source of tension. I wait until Archer is a distance away before I lean closer to Kelsey.

"What was that all about?" I whisper.

"Him being a stubborn ass."

"Dean mentioned something was going on with you two, but he didn't elaborate."

Kelsey sighs. "Did Dean push you to get married?"

I blink. "He didn't have to push me. I wanted to marry him."

I don't think I'd wanted anything more in my life than to marry Dean West. Not even the love and attention of my mother.

"Does Archer want to marry you?" I ask Kelsey.

"You don't have to sound surprised."

"I'm not. I mean, I'm surprised he didn't want to before now. You've been together for two years, right? You're living together, you work together, you love each other. What's left to do but get married?"

"Why does that have to be the goal?" Kelsey replies curtly, running a hand through her blue-streaked hair. "It's so good the way it is, you know? Why change it now?"

Exactly.

The word pops unexpectedly into my head. Kelsey has always been such a no-bullshit friend—a risk-taker, the woman who went up against the male-dominated meteorology department in order to get her Spiral Project funded. And she succeeded. She drives right into storms and tornados. So it doesn't make much sense that marriage would be the one thing Kelsey March doesn't want to face.

On the other hand, I can certainly relate to her desire to keep things *as they are.* Because when it's so good, why risk change?

"Hey, Liv, this is Roger Jameson." Archer approaches with a thin, balding man who extends his hand to me.

"Liv West." I shake his hand before looking past him to the food truck that has a faded burger logo and milkshake painted on the side. "Is that it?"

"Needs work, but it's got a burner stove and prep space." Roger pulls open the door, and I go inside. "Plenty of storage space."

The scent of grease hangs in the air. I look at the rusted fixtures, the old propane tank, and try to envision Allie and I working here. If we fixed the truck up, we could run a mobile unit of the Wonderland Café, serving a limited selection of our menu.

But that's not all we want to do. Last year, we talked about the idea of a birthday party truck where we could bring themed parties to children's homes—including the decorations, costumes for kids, character actors, all the party supplies and food. A turnkey party, delivered right to your front door.

I shake my head. "I'm sorry, but this isn't quite right. We want to be able to serve food, but we need more than a kitchen in a truck."

As we step outside, I notice an old, silver trailer parked in a corner of the lot overgrown with grass and weeds. The shell is dented and rusty, the metal tarnished, the windows cracked.

"Whose is that?" I asked.

"The silver Twinkie?" Roger glances toward the trailer and laughs. "That's an old '72 Airstream. Used to belong to my father-in-law. Hasn't been used in years."

"Can I see it?" I ask. "Is it for sale?"

Roger shrugs. "I never really thought about it, to be honest. Didn't imagine anyone would want to put the time and money into it."

We walk toward the Airstream—and even though it looks like a huge, old piece of metal pipe, I have a flash of what it could be. A sleek, shiny vehicle emblazoned with the Wonderland Café logo.

We go inside. The interior is a mess of scarred furnishings and torn carpet, but I can see it as a delightful miniature version of the café, with a checkerboard floor, striped curtains, whimsical clocks, and mismatched, cushy furniture.

We'd have Alice in Wonderland murals on the walls and ceilings, teacup-shaped tables, and teapot lamps. We could set up a red-and-white striped awning outside, with table and chairs for the party-goers. If we had a trailer like this, we could even host birthday parties at parks and gardens.

"The shell is good," Roger remarks. "You'd probably have to gut the interior. Exterior work too, of course. I can look into a price, if you're interested."

"I might be."

I feel Archer looking at me as we walk back outside.

"You'd need another truck to pull it," he warns me. "And the restoration would cost more than the sale."

Though I know he's right, I take a few pictures of the Airstream with my phone and send them to Allie. The whole project will likely be more than we can afford, but the vision is in my head now, crystal-clear. Once upon a time, my decorating ideas were limited to a two-bedroom apartment, but since Allie and I revived and opened the café, and Dean and I restored the Butterfly House, projects like this are exciting rather than intimidating.

After Roger tells me he'll also ask around about a used pickup, he and Archer start talking about motorcycles. Kelsey and I return to the truck with Nicholas.

"Will you be around on Memorial Day weekend?" I ask her, as I get Nicholas situated in his car seat again.

"Yeah, why?"

"I'm planning a surprise getaway for Dean," I explain. "With him being gone so much, and all our work, we haven't gone away together in ages. I figure it's about time, so I want to surprise him with a weekend trip. Can you and Archer take care of Nicholas?"

"Of course. Archer has been wanting to take him over to that miniature train show in Forest Grove, so we'll do that when you guys are gone."

I smile and thank her. Though I experience the usual Mom Guilt about leaving our son in the care of other people, even Archer and Kelsey, I console myself with the reminder that not once in over two years have Dean and I been away from Nicholas at the same time.

In fact, I've never been away from him at all—Dean has gone on trips and to conferences, but I've always stayed home. Surely I don't need to feel guilty for planning to spend a few nights away from Nicholas for the first time in two years.

And I try not to think about the stark reality that something could potentially happen to him while we're gone. Of course, it *won't,* and he'll be *fine,* but...

But nothing. He'll be *fine.*

Archer drives me and Nicholas back to the Butterfly House. I sort through the day's mail while Nicholas plays with his fire trucks. At the bottom of the stack, there's a postcard addressed to me, the postmark and stamp from Sri Lanka. Scrawled, slanted handwriting covers the card:

Liv,

Mangroves, lagoons, tea plantations, Temple of the Sacred Tooth, gilded rooftops, stilt fishing, elephant sanctuaries, sunsets like crayons exploded in the sky.

My adventure continues.
North

I read the card over a few times, the simple words evoking bright, vivid pictures. For two years, my friend North has been traveling around the world with nothing but a walking stick, his backpack, and his uncanny sense of understanding.

"Going on walkabout," he'd told me when we'd spoken on the phone shortly after Nicholas was born. "See what I can see. Do what I can do."

I'd been surprised and baffled—even when I'd first met North, I'd thought he would never leave Twelve Oaks. He was such a part of the place, like a tree whose roots twined deep and secure into the California earth.

But he'd uprooted himself, shaken off the dirt, and left Twelve Oaks after twenty years to tour the world. Over the past two years, I'd received postcards from Japan, India, Poland, Brazil, China, Tanzania, South Africa, Australia. Always a list of places, people, sites, and food that made the country come to life.

I put the postcard in the kitchen drawer where I keep all of North's postcards. I don't know if he plans to return to Twelve Oaks, but one day, somehow he and Dean will finally meet—the two men who proved to me, who still prove, there is such intense good in the world.

They've always been linked by an everlasting, invisible thread —the man who put me on a path that led to my husband. And one day North will meet Nicholas, the boy who changed every cell in my body. All loves of my life in such profoundly unique ways.

After getting dinner prepped, I sit at the kitchen table with my laptop. I make reservations at a hotel in Madison and the lodge in Door County where Dean and I used to stay often. I make a list of Things to Do, though I expect we'll follow it loosely since the whole point of this trip is to relax and have *fun*. Lots of hot, spicy fun.

The more I plan, the more excited I get. I picture Dean and me walking hand-in-hand down State Street, stopping to explore the shops and used bookstores before going to a café for a leisurely coffee. I see us strolling through the botanical gardens, eating dinners in intimate restaurants, candlelight and shadows, and then returning to our hotel room for bubble baths, massages, and plenty of sex that's both raw and romantic.

Exactly what we'd had during our first year together, when we'd lived in a lovely, intense world that belonged to us alone. I can't wait to give that world back to my husband and to remind him how perfect we can be together.

CHAPTER 9

Dean

*P*aris. *United Nations. Cultural heritage. Conservation. Assistant director. Chartres Cathedral. Durham Castle. Fontainebleau. Speyer Cathedral. Rhodes. The monuments of Ravenna.*

I did my master's degree work in the city of Ravenna. That was when I knew I wanted to be a historian—despite my father's decree that I should go to law school and follow in his footsteps.

Instead I've spent my career following the footsteps of countless people into the past. I've studied the minutiae of their lives—coins, paintings, tools, manuscripts—to discover their secrets. I've measured their cathedrals and translated their poems. I've unearthed their pottery and mapped the layout of their castles.

And while I've always worked hard to be the best at whatever I've done—a drive instilled in me when I was a kid—I never considered the possibility that being a great medieval historian could lead me to a diplomatic position with a worldwide organization.

Spring rain sleets outside the window of my campus office, rivulets of water spilling over the glass. I work a loop of string between my fingers, creating a geometric pattern of triangles and squares.

I *could* end up working for an international organization, I remind myself. But I won't. Despite the many fascinating aspects of the job, not to mention the intellectual and professional challenges and the fact that it would secure my career on an entirely new level, I can't pursue it. Even if part of me wants to.

I unwind the string from my fingers and drop it onto the desk, turning to my computer. After pushing thoughts of UNESCO and the World Heritage Center out of my mind, I spend the next hour working on a paper about medieval guildhalls.

My phone buzzes. An image of a busty, sexy French maid shows up on the screen, with Liv's face pasted over the model's.

I pull up her number.

"Yes?" Her voice is sultry and low.

"Nice picture," I tell her. "But your body is far superior."

"Well, I haven't yet found a French maid costume that would fit well." She heaves a sigh. "I think I need to buy all new lingerie."

"You don't need lingerie to turn me on."

"I'm trying to give life to your fantasies, professor," Liv says.

"You're already my fantasy come to life."

"Oh, for Lord's sake." She groans. "Would you work with me here? Do you understand that I am willing to *act out your hottest fantasy*? I'll be a cheerleader, a stripper, a policewoman…hell, I'll be a hooker, if that's what it takes. The deal is you have to tell me what your fantasy is first."

I know she's expecting some elaborate scenario. When Liv fantasizes, she dreams up entire worlds involving pirate captains and their prisoners, or battles between fairies and elves. I, on the other hand, just picture her spread open in front of me, gasping and moaning as I pound my cock into her sweet, warm pussy.

"Dean?" she prompts. "Tell me."

Though this is not my strong suit, it's a measure of how much I love my wife—and how badly I want our explosive sex life back—that I give it a shot. At this point, I'm willing to try anything.

"What if it's not so much who you are," I say, lowering my voice an octave, "as *where* you are?"

"Oh." Her breath catches with a little gasping noise that makes my blood burn. "You mean like a spaceship or something? Am I your alien princess sex slave?"

Where does she come up with these?

"No," I admit. "But I like the princess idea."

Not to mention the sex slave.

"You've seriously never thought of that before?" Liv asks.

I must have the imagination of a doormat, because the answer is no.

"Not once in your entire sexual history have you ever acted out your fantasies with a girlfriend?" Liv asks.

"I didn't say that."

"Then what have you done?"

"I can't remember."

"You lie like a rug."

I glance at the door, which is closed but not locked. Because I'm not stupid, I go to lock it before returning to my desk.

"Where are you?" I ask Liv.

"Home and on the sofa," she replies. "Nicholas is napping, and of course he could wake any second so we shouldn't stall."

Okay, I can do this. Ignoring the fact that what goes on in my head are really just stripped-down fantasies about fucking my wife dirty. I don't have the time—or, apparently, the imagination—to visualize even a tenth of the elaborate scenarios Liv dreams up. I'll admit to a few ideas, but I'm still not willing to share them.

"I imagine making love to you on a deserted island," I remark.

"Go on."

"With you in a little bikini that barely covers your breasts and ass."

"What color is it?"

"Uh, blue. With white polka dots."

"How did I find a bikini on a deserted island…oh!" Liv's voice warms with enthusiasm. "Unless we're the sole survivors of a shipwreck?"

"Yeah, that's it."

"And we have to live off the land, right? And of course you can't keep your hands off me."

"Of course."

"Do we just wander around naked? No, wait, you said I'm wearing a bikini. What are you wearing?"

"A…uh, a loincloth?"

"How did you get ahold of a *loincloth*?"

"It was a dishtowel from the ship."

She laughs. "No way would a dishtowel cover *you* up."

"Maybe I made the loincloth out of palm leaves, then."

"So we're on a tropical island."

"Well, it's not an island in Antarctica," I mutter.

"Okay, okay, sorry. It's your fantasy. I'm just going to get comfortable and listen."

An expectant silence follows. Any lust I might have had disappears as my brain works to think up a creative scenario.

"So it's a hot, tropical island with white-sand beaches and a cool ocean breeze," I say.

"Mmm."

"And you're…in this blue bikini with white polka dots…"

"You mentioned that."

"And I'm…okay, let's just say I'm naked."

"I like it so far," Liv remarks.

I'm trying hard to picture her spread out on the sofa, maybe even with her skirt hitched up and her hand between her legs, but the pressure of this fantasy is seriously killing my desire. I much prefer just telling her all the hot things I want to do to her. Or will do to her. Soon.

"Are you turned on?" I finally ask.

"You mean right now?"

"No, I mean yesterday," I say dryly.

"What?"

"Yeah, I mean *now*."

"Well, I was getting there a little when you started talking about the loincloth," Liv admits. "But we're off to a rather slow start."

"Considering I was just thinking about medieval guildhalls, I'd say we're not doing too badly here."

"Are you hard?"

"No."

"Then let's get back to the fantasy. Are there coconuts?"

"Where?"

"On the tropical island, of course."

"Probably."

"What do you do with them?"

"What?"

"The coconuts."

I try to think of what the hell I'm supposed to say.

"Eat them?" I suggest.

"I mean, do you break the coconuts open with your big, strong muscles and then pour the coconut milk over my naked, glistening body…oh, crap."

"What?" I ask. "That was starting to get good."

"Yeah, well, your son is awake and screeching," Liv says in resignation. "The Fantasies of Professor West will have to wait."

"Too bad," I remark, while sending up thanks to whatever god is in charge of overly imaginative wives for getting me out of this.

"Call me later," Liv suggests.

"I have two lectures and a seminar later," I say, trying to sound regretful.

"Okay." Her voice lowers into a husky tone. "But I'll see you tonight."

"Yes, you will."

I put my phone back on my desk. I love Liv even more for trying. But it used to be that we didn't have to try. Other things have been rough over the years, but sex has always been so damned easy. So damned good. At least, until recently.

I drag my hands over my face. Even taking sex out of the equation, we don't spend much time alone together. I've tried making the romantic part easy again. We've had date nights and nice dinners out, though more often than not Liv has ended up falling asleep on the way home. I write her love notes, cook dinner regularly, help take care of Nicholas, do everything I should be doing. And still it feels like we're not getting it right.

But if we were in Paris...

We could live in an apartment like the one we had on Avalon Street. Take Nicholas to parks and gardens, boat rides, carousels. Liv and I could visit all the museums again, sit at corner tables in cafés, take the train to visit London, Venice, Berlin. In the summer, we could get a little farmhouse in the south of France and...

I shake the ridiculous thoughts out of my head. Even if I were offered the job, we'd never be able to create a life like that. I'd be required to travel more than I do now, and to remote places where it would be difficult for Liv and Nicholas to come along. And no way could I stand leaving them for weeks on end. The travel I already do now is too much as it is.

My phone rings. I refocus on the fact that I'm in my office and should be working. I reach for the phone.

"Dean West."

"Dean, it's Simon Fletcher," announces the booming voice of

my friend and director of the Altopascio dig. "Did you hear the news yet?"

"What news?"

"The UN Assembly agreed to vote on the Altopascio site, if we get the proposal to them by the fifteenth."

"Really?" A combination of surprise and disbelief fills me. "But the deadline was three weeks ago."

"I'm guessing Hans Klasen had something to do with the extension," Simon remarks. "We need you back over here to finish work on the proposal."

I flip through the calendar on my desk, trying to ignore the sinking of my heart at the thought of leaving my family again so soon. "I'll try to catch a flight early next week."

"I know you just got home, man. How's Liv and your boy?"

"Both great, thanks."

"Bring them with you," Simon suggests. "I haven't seen Liv in ages, and you guys could go to Rome or Paris for a few days when we're done. Take a vacation."

I've lost track of how many times I've suggested exactly that to Liv. I haven't yet been able to convince her to come to Italy with me—despite promises of leisurely strolls through medieval towns and lunches on terraces overlooking vineyard-covered hills.

"I'll ask her," I tell Simon. "Figure ten days or so?"

"At least. Mateo Rinaldi is getting the Italian team on board, but you're the guy who has to put it all together."

"Okay." I turn to my computer and pull up an airline website. "I'll be there as soon as I can."

After making the arrangements, I walk down the corridor to Frances Hunter's office. A formidable, gray-haired woman, Frances has been one of my staunchest supporters and friends since she hired me to start the Medieval Studies program at King's.

She's sitting at the desk in her office. I stop at the open door.

"You want me to bring you back some grappa?" I ask.

Frances stops typing and turns to peer at me over her glasses.

"It's a good thing you're not teaching this semester," she remarks dryly.

I move to sit in the chair in front of her desk. "The UN agreed to vote on the Altopascio proposal. That has to mean they understand how urgent it is."

Frances sits back in her chair and studies me. "I have a question for you, Dean."

"Sure."

She takes off her glasses. "I don't think I've ever told you this, but I was surprised when you accepted the job offer from King's."

"You were?"

"Yes. I knew you'd have multiple offers from universities with much bigger names. So why did you accept our offer?"

I lean my elbows on my knees, linking my hands together. I remember the day Frances had called offering me the job. Liv and I had been living in a two-bedroom apartment in Los Angeles, and my postdoc fellowship with the Getty Institute was almost completed. I'd had professorship offers from Cambridge, Princeton, UCLA, Cornell, and the University of Toronto, as well as two other postdoc offers in Germany and Italy.

Through months of interviews and travel, Liv had only said she wanted me to take whatever job would make me the happiest. *"Whatever job you really want, Dean. It doesn't matter to me where we live."*

She'd come with me to Mirror Lake for my interview at King's. We stayed a few nights at the Wildwood Inn, walked along Avalon Street, and went hiking on one of the mountain trails.

When we stopped on a rocky outcropping surrounded by trees, Liv looked out at the glistening expanse of the lake and said in an offhand way, "I've always dreamed of living in a place like this."

So taking the job at King's University, and making my wife's dream come true, was what made me the happiest.

"I accepted the offer at King's because I liked the idea of creating a Medieval Studies program from the ground up," I tell Frances, which is also the truth. "Starting something new."

"It's been phenomenal, as you well know," Frances remarks. "But as the program has become more and more successful, I've suspected it was only a matter of time before other institutions came knocking at your door."

A strange sense of foreboding fills my chest. "Are you firing me, Frances?"

"Heavens, no." She laughs. "I'd actually give anything to keep you here. But I heard the World Heritage Center is eyeing you for the assistant director position."

Discomfort stabs at me. "I haven't been offered the job. The only reason I didn't turn it down right away was—"

She holds up a hand to stop me. "I'm not upset you didn't tell me. In fact, it made me think you might be under-utilized in your current position."

I don't know what to say to that, though her implication that I'd like to do other things besides teach is partly true—and the reason I've enjoyed getting back into archeology and travel.

"I talked to Hans Klasen yesterday," Frances continues, picking up a glossy blue folder embellished with the gold UNESCO logo. "I told him he'd be a fool not to offer you the job."

"What?" I sit back and stare at her. "Why?"

"Because I've been around scholars for most of my life," she replies. "And it's rare that I have the privilege of working with one of your caliber. I believe you should use your God-given talent on a global scale, to actively work with sites and monuments the way you've been doing with Altopascio."

For a minute, I can only look at her, again smothering the persistently ambitious thought of taking my career and reputation to a whole new level. I shake my head.

"I appreciate that, Frances. But there's no way I could ever leave King's or Mirror Lake. And it doesn't matter anyway because I haven't been offered the job."

"Yet." She pushes the folder across the desk to me. "Your devotion to your work is the reason the World Heritage Center is interested in you. It's hardly a wonder you didn't even have to formally apply. Your integrity and single-mindedness are your application."

A weighty silence falls between us.

"I can't believe you want me to consider another job," I finally admit.

"I know. I'm amazed that I'm being so generous." Frances gives me a little, self-deprecating smile. "If it were any other job, I wouldn't be. But frankly, you taking the job would also be great for King's University, especially if you did joint programming between us and the WHC."

She turns back to her computer. "Really, Dean, I don't believe you've reached the limits of what you can do or the difference you can make. And honestly, I suspect that unless you look beyond this university, you never will."

She puts on her glasses and begins typing. I glance at the thick, blue United Nations folder on her desk, not sure if it seems more like a time bomb or an announcement that I just won a coveted prize.

Without picking the folder up, I turn and leave the office.

CHAPTER 10

DEAN

Though tourist season hasn't started yet, Mirror Lake is getting ready. Flowers bloom from wooden planters lining the sidewalks, and several storefronts have freshly painted façades.

Last summer, Liv and Allie had an outdoor terrace added to the Wonderland Café, and it overlooks a grassy expanse of land leading to Wizard's Park. In a short time, the café has become more than just a restaurant and birthday party place—it's become a new Mirror Lake institution, thanks to word of mouth from local mothers, as well as Liv and Allie's outreach efforts in the community.

As I enter the café to the sound of happy chatter, a stab of guilt hits me at the thought that I'd ever—even in the most closed-off place of my mind—resent the café for taking so much of my wife's time.

Never. I'd never think that. I can't.

The conviction solidifies when I see Liv maneuvering around the tables in the Tea Party Room, her hair swinging in a high ponytail, her skin flushed and her eyes bright as she stops to deliver a tray of checkerboard sandwiches and bread-and-butterflies.

She smiles at a little girl seated at a table and bends to say something. The girl smiles back and nods, touching the barrette in her hair Liv must have commented on.

My heart tightens. Sometimes I still feel guilty over not wanting to have kids for so long. I'd known from the start Liv would be an incredible mother, though I was never sure about my own abilities as a father. But watching her with Nicholas and other kids, it's painfully obvious this is what she was meant to do and be.

If I go into that dark place, I know exactly why I'd resisted having children. And my reasons had less to do with worries about fatherhood and more to do with not wanting to share Liv with anyone. Because that would mean she was no longer completely mine.

It was a stupid, selfish thought—one I still don't want to admit to—but it was there. And I do have to share her now. She belongs to the café, to her volunteer work, to the people who count on her for employment, advice, help, support, friendship. And she belongs to our son, a fact I wouldn't change for anything. There is no better gift Nicholas could have been given than to have Liv for his mother.

The thought of our son disintegrates all those old fears. If Liv hadn't convinced me to battle them back a few years ago, we might not have had the boy who fills my heart with color and light.

Liv walks to the front counter, her face breaking into a smile when she sees me.

"Hi." She stands on tiptoe to kiss me. "What are you doing here? Still thinking about coconuts?"

"Uh, no. I thought I'd see if you could take a break."

"I'm sorry, but I can't. We're swamped." She squeezes my arm. "I have an hour left in my shift, then I'm meeting with the planning committee for the Bicentennial Festival."

I deflect a stab of disappointment, figuring it would be better to tell her at home that I'm leaving again.

"Okay." I reach out to gently tug her ponytail. "You need me to pick up Nicholas?"

"No, I'll get him on the way home."

"Call me if you need me."

She flashes me a smile. "I always need you."

I return her smile and start toward the door just as Kelsey comes up the steps of the front porch. She enters the café and whips off her sunglasses.

"Hey." She blinks at me. "What're you doing here?"

"Just came to talk to Liv. You?"

"Looking for Archer." She glances past my shoulder. "He's not answering his phone. Is he here?"

"I don't think so."

"I wanted to tell him the Spiral Project just got approval to do a chase in Australia this fall."

"Really?" A rush of pride in her fills me. "Congratulations."

"Thanks." She smiles. "It'll just be for a few weeks, but the university already approved my leave."

I'm about to ask if Archer will go with her when an elderly female voice rises above the chatter of other patrons.

"Dean!"

I turn to find Florence Wickham, trustee of the Mirror Lake Historical Society, approaching from the dining room. In a pink suit with her white hair and bright blue eyes, she looks like an inquisitive bird.

"How nice to see you," she says warmly.

"Hello, Florence." I take her hand in greeting, leaning in to brush my lips across her powdered cheek. "Nice to see you too."

"Don't you look handsome, as always." Florence picks a piece of lint off my lapel and touches my silk tie.

Kelsey, looking amused at Florence's fussing, exchanges greetings with the other woman. I ask Florence if she's heading over to the Historical Society offices.

"Yes, we have a meeting this afternoon." Florence pats my chest. "I'm so glad I ran into you. I'm sure Liv has told you the Historical Society is planning to renovate the old railroad depot near Wizard's Park."

"She told me she was doing an auction to benefit the restoration, yes."

"She is just a powerhouse, I tell you," Florence says. "We're going to turn the depot into a transportation museum, with the shed next door used to display restored train cars and engines."

Though I'm impressed by the idea, my heart is already starting to sink.

"That's great," I reply carefully.

Florence beams. "It is, isn't it? I told the board I would recruit you and your formidable historical expertise to help with the restoration process. We need a project director, and you're the perfect man for the job."

She blinks at me expectantly.

"Much as I'd love to help out…" I begin.

"Oh, lovely!" Florence claps her hands. "I'll send you all the info to get started."

"…I can't," I finish weakly.

Kelsey snorts with suppressed laughter.

"It won't take much time," Florence assures me, patting my chest again like she's stroking a cat. "Archival research and writing up a few reports, maybe doing some work on the engines. You did such a beautiful job with the Butterfly House the Historical Society just can't tackle this new project without you."

"I'm really not—"

"You are such an extraordinary help to us." Florence turns to

Kelsey. "A pleasure seeing you, dear. I'll be in touch, Dean. You are a gem, did I ever tell you that?"

She squeezes my biceps, gives us a little wave, and heads out the door. I sink into a nearby chair with a groan. Kelsey is outright grinning now.

"Professor Marvel, browbeaten by a little old lady," she teases.

"Little old lady, my ass," I mutter darkly. "She's Xena the Warrior Princess in disguise."

"Hey, engine restoration sounds more like Archer's line of work," Kelsey says. "You should call him, ask if he can help you out."

"Good idea." I take out my phone to text Archer. "Maybe Florence will pat his chest and squeeze his biceps for a change."

"Hah." Kelsey rolls her eyes. "Knowing him, he might like it."

I send the text to my brother. Though I'm aware Kelsey's suggestion is a ploy to get me and Archer to spend time together —in her belief that we need to—I also know Archer would be a great addition to the project.

I slide my phone back into my pocket as Kelsey and I head out to our cars.

"You have time for coffee?" I ask, thinking she could give me a good perspective on this whole job situation.

"No, sorry." Kelsey stops by her car, digging into her purse for her keys. "I'm heading over to the warehouse to check on some equipment. Gym tomorrow around four?"

"Sure."

She gives me a wave and gets into her car. I watch her drive away, then start toward my car. After a block, I turn and go in the opposite direction.

Our former apartment, the place where Liv and I first lived when we moved to Mirror Lake, sits above a row of shops on the corner of Avalon and Poppy Streets.

There's a wrought-iron balcony that used to be filled with Liv's potted plants. In the summer, she'd leave the French doors open and the blue-and-white striped curtains would flutter in the breeze from the lake.

I'd always liked coming home—walking toward the building and seeing those curtains like they were waving hello. Knowing my wife was in the rooms behind them.

Now the balcony is empty, the French doors shut. The landlord rented out the place shortly after Liv and I moved to the Butterfly House. No idea who's been living there since.

I walk back to my car and head toward campus. Strange how when your life gets richer and bigger, you still sometimes miss the days when it was smaller.

I work late at the university, finalizing my travel arrangements and reviewing the criteria needed for a site to be inscribed on the World Heritage protection list.

By the time I head home, the sky is charcoal-gray, streaked with a few reddish clouds. The porch lights are on, and I go into the foyer—expecting the usual noises, Liv cooking dinner, either kid's music or the TV on, Nicholas coming to greet me.

Instead it's oddly quiet inside.

"Liv?" I drop my briefcase on a table and go into the kitchen. There's a wrapped package on the central island with my name on it.

I wonder if I've missed an important date—birthday, anniversary of our first date—but no. I unwrap the package and pull out a ream of typing paper.

Huh. There's a note typed on the first page:

> *While I wandered soft and lonely as a cloud*
> *that floats on high over vales and hills,*
> *You saw me and snatched me down*
> *to love among the utility bills.*

Interesting. It sounds like a clue. Since we keep our bills in the first drawer of the kitchen desk, I walk over to open it.

A bunch of bills are wrapped around a box with a rubber band. I unfasten the band and open the box, which is full of cotton balls. Each cotton ball has a paper letter affixed to it. I dump them all onto the desk, arranging and rearranging the letters until they spell out:

S-H-A-R-P D-R-E-S-S-E-D M-A-N

I think for a minute, then go upstairs to the bedroom. I open the closet, revealing one of my suits hung neatly on a hanger. A leather belt is buckled through the pant loops, with a note attached to the buckle.

I take it off and read another clue that leads me to a box in Nicholas's room, which reveals an apple. A fourth box near the living room fireplace contains a block of wood, and a fifth has a bag filled with candy and a note that says:

> *Professor West to the dark tower came,*
> *saying fum, fie and fee*
> *I smell peaches and cream—is it she?*

Amused and intrigued, I climb the spiral staircase to the tower. A box is sitting on the landing, and I open it to reveal a spool of copper wire and a skein of wool. I knock once on the door and push it open.

All the breath stops in my lungs. Tiny white lights glitter around the windows, casting a soft glow on my wife, who is standing in the middle of the room.

I can only stare at her—stunning in a white dress that hugs all her gorgeous curves, her hair adorned with little white flowers. She's smiling that smile that makes my heart fill to breaking every single time.

"Hi," she says.

"Hi." I let the doorknob slide from my grasp and put the box down. "You look incredible. Isn't that your wedding dress?"

Her smile widens. "It's a bit tighter now, but yes. Thanks for remembering."

"I remember everything about that day." I walk toward her, lifting my hand to touch her thick, shiny hair. "Every stone in the terrace. The hills covered with grapevines. The way Jean's mother stopped you halfway toward me to straighten the hem of your dress. The flowers you were holding, the golden retriever lying in the sun. The officiant saying, *'Magnifique'* when you came closer. Everything. But mostly you."

"I'd tell you it was the best day of my life, but that wouldn't be true," Liv says. "I've had so many *best days* with you. More than I can count."

"I haven't had any best days with you."

A crease appears between her eyebrows. "Why not?"

"Because you *are* my best day."

"Aw." She smiles. "Good one."

I slide my hand under her chin, lifting her face to mine for a kiss, but she puts her hand on my chest to stop me.

"Did you understand the clues?" she asks.

"Paper...you're going to write me a really hot love letter."

"No."

"Cotton...uh, we're going to have a naked pillow fight?"

"No."

"I'm going to tie you up with a leather belt."

"No." Intrigue sparks in her pretty eyes. "But hold that thought for later."

"The wood...well, one look at you and I get a hard-on, so that's self-evident."

She grins. "Wrong again."

"Then I didn't understand any of them."

"Paper is the traditional gift for a first anniversary," Liv says.

"Cotton is for the second, leather for the third, fruit for the fourth, wood for the fifth, and sugar for the sixth."

"Ah. Let me guess. Seventh is copper and wool."

"I always knew you were brilliant."

"Our seventh is coming up this year," I remark, sliding my hands around her waist to pull her closer. "July twelfth."

"You remember."

"Of course." I frown at her. "Haven't I brought you flowers and gifts on July twelfth for six years running?"

"Yes, you have." She smooths her hands over my suit jacket. "But for this year, I was thinking we should do something extra-special. Seven is considered to be a very lucky number."

She gestures to another larger box on the coffee-table, this one tied with a red ribbon. Since she's already covered traditional anniversary gifts, this has to be something different. I let go of her and walk over to sit on the sofa.

I open the box and take out the items one by one. A white rose. A University of Wisconsin baseball cap. A postcard printed with one of the distinctive Union Terrace chairs. A Madison, WI keychain, a Bucky Badger stuffed animal, a picture of the Wisconsin State Capitol building.

"Do you get it?" Liv asks.

"If I had to guess, I'd say this has something to do with Madison, Wisconsin," I remark.

"Excellent guess."

"Our first year together." I look at the gifts on the table. "One of the best years of my life."

"Mine too." Liv sits beside me, reaching out to put her hand on my knee. "With our seventh anniversary coming up, and us not having been away together in so long, I've planned a trip for us back to Madison."

"Yeah?" Warmth fills my chest. "Just the two of us?"

"Just the two of us. Kelsey and Archer are going to take care of

Nicholas." She picks up her notebook and opens it to a page filled with notes.

"We're staying in a lakeside suite at the Edgewater," she says, showing me the page. "I have dinner reservations at the White Rose and tickets to a show at the Overture Center. We can go to the zoo, the botanical gardens, the farmer's market, and I booked our favorite cabin in Door County for the last night. We'll do all the things we did during our first year together."

For a second, I can't even speak. The idea of having my wife all to myself for several days, reliving those months when I was falling for her so hard, so fast…

Liv smiles. "Okay?"

"Yeah." I clear my throat. "More than okay."

"Since the festival is in the summer, I planned it for Memorial Day weekend," Liv says. "Sheryl said she would cover my Friday shift, so we can leave early in the morning and be in Madison by noon, which means we'll have all afternoon and evening."

My heart begins a slow, heavy descent to the pit of my stomach.

"Memorial Day weekend?" I repeat.

"Yes, since we'll both have Monday off, that gives us a whole extra day."

Now I can't speak for a different reason. Liv looks up, faint confusion furrowing her brow.

"What's wrong?" she asks.

"I…uh, Liv, I have to leave town the Thursday before Memorial Day. I just found out this morning. The United Nations Assembly agreed to vote on our proposal, if we can get it to them by the end of the month. I have to go back to Tuscany, and then Paris. I'll be gone for about ten days."

She blinks. "Oh."

Shit. Shit. Shit.

"Simon called this morning," I say in a rush. "I was going to tell you at the café. If the Assembly votes to put the Altopascio site on their protected list, we'll be able to raise more money for the repairs, increase the size of the team, even get enough funding for the third phase of the project. There's a few dozen people who are counting on this, not to mention the whole town. I'm so sorry."

Liv shakes her head. A petal falls from her hair onto the floor. She starts putting all the Wisconsin gifts back into the box.

"It's okay. I shouldn't have made all the plans without checking your schedule first."

"No, it's not...I mean, it's...there's nothing I want more than to be alone with you."

Curses blister my brain. I can't fucking stand the look on her face. The disappointment she can't hide.

"Liv..."

"Dean." She puts her hand on my wrist, giving it a gentle squeeze. "Really, it's okay. I know how hard you've been working for this, especially after the earthquake. It's great that the Assembly has agreed to vote on it."

"It's just...we thought we'd missed the deadline, but they gave us an extension."

"I know. It's *okay*."

But it's not okay. It's not fucking okay that my wife planned an anniversary trip that we have to cancel because my work is taking me out of the country again. It's not okay that we haven't been alone together in weeks. It's not okay that having *everything* means we're losing sight of each other.

And it's a goddamned disaster that I can't figure out how to fix it.

"Forget it." I grab Liv's arms, pulling her toward me so she tumbles onto my lap in a rush of sweet, flower scents and warmth. "I'll tell Simon I can't make it. We're going on our trip."

"Dean—"

"It doesn't matter. They can do the work without me."

"No, they can't. You've been working on the site for years

now, and there's no way you can insult the WHC by not showing up. What if you need them in the future?"

"I'll figure it out."

"Dean, love of my life." Liv puts her hands on my cheeks and turns my face to look at her. Her brown eyes are warm with love and understanding. "You're going to do this. You're going to give your proposal to the UN because it's what you've been working toward. Because there is no way you can risk losing the site completely. We'll just postpone our trip until we can figure out a time that works for both of us. Maybe even *on* our actual anniversary."

My chest is tight. I hate the unease simmering in my blood, the disquiet that started the second I heard I had to leave again. I take a breath and reach up to pluck a flower from Liv's hair, crushing the fragrant petals between my fingers.

Not only do I remember every last detail of our wedding day, our honeymoon is imprinted on my mind like a painting. Liv sitting on the balcony of our rented apartment, her body clad in a flowered sundress that flowed over her bare legs, her head bent over a Paris travel guide.

My wife…my *wife*…laughing at a comedian street performer, gazing at Vermeer's *The Lacemaker,* stopping to look at the old books in one of the stalls along the Seine. Her long hair falling across the side of her face, the movement of her arm as she reached up to push it back.

That was poetry. Right there. Poetry.

Determination fills me in a hard rush. No way am I letting my wife's plans be postponed.

"Come with me," I tell her.

She blinks. "What?"

"Come with me to Europe," I say. "Instead of reliving our first year, we'll relive our honeymoon in Paris. We'll go to the same restaurants, visit the museums and that little café where you couldn't get enough of their macaroons. I'll bore you to tears telling you all the architectural details of Notre Dame. We'll go to—"

"Dean." Liv touches my hand to stop my barrage of words. "I can't go with you. We can't do all that."

"Why not?"

"I can't leave the café for more than a couple of days," Liv says. "We're too busy right now. And the week after Memorial Day, I'm swamped with meetings about the festival. Besides, you'll be so focused on work we wouldn't have time to do all those things together anyway."

Frustration fills my throat. Liv presses a kiss against my lips and eases away from me.

"We'll figure it out, I promise," she says. "It'll take some adjusting, but we've been doing that for awhile now."

I don't want to adjust. I want to grab things and force them to work the way I want them to. The way they *should.*

"I'll go make us a quick dinner." Liv glances at the clock. "Archer is dropping Nicholas off at seven, so I'll call and see if he wants to eat with us too."

I watch her go, my gaze sliding over the straight line of her back, her legs and round hips, the thick, dark hair falling like a curtain over her shoulders.

My beauty. It feels like a weight is pressing on my chest. I can't figure out why I'm so knotted up, but then it hits me.

My wife gave me the chance to make her completely mine again. Just for a few days. And I have to say no.

CHAPTER 11

OLIVIA

I'd launch Plan B, except I only had Plan A. I look at our wall calendar in the kitchen, which is filled with color-coded details about our daily activities and schedules. With Dean leaving again and the festival scheduled for the second week in July, there's no way we can have a romantic weekend getaway anytime soon.

Maybe we could go somewhere after the festival. Except then we're getting into the end of July and August, and summer is always a busy time for the café, especially if we end up catering the Edison company picnic. But I might be able to get away for a few days.

Unless Dean suddenly discovers he has to go to Siberia to excavate a wooly mammoth.

Now, Liv, stop it.

I give myself a mental kick and get a sippy cup of milk for Nicholas, who is occupied with a toy toolkit on the sunroom floor. I open my laptop and pull up my *Liv in Wonderland* blog. I'm half-tempted to write a blog post about the trials and tribulations of a busy married couple trying to get away together, but that isn't something I want others to know about.

Instead I write about the multiple preschool and kindergarten options available for children today and title the post "Finger-painting en route to MIT."

After I publish the essay, I turn to my Pinterest boards. Started as a source of inspiration, the boards have now become the bane of my existence.

My Sexy Ideas board mocks me with pictures of lithe, gorgeous couples locked in passionate embraces that will never be interrupted by waking toddlers or mommy guilt. My Recipes board is filled with photos of polenta fries, beef Wellington, and "toddler-friendly" snacks of roasted chickpeas and vegetable risotto balls that I have yet to actually make.

And my Parenting Ideas board taunts me with images of crafts that I planned for rainy Sundays after Nicholas and I make whole-wheat pancakes while listening to Mozart. Melted crayon art, homemade play dough, an airport made out of a pizza box *with landing lights that work.*

While many rainy Sundays have passed since I created the board, my son and I have spent them lounging around in our pajamas, watching cartoons and eating microwaved popcorn rather than being creative and healthy.

Maybe if I hadn't been working so much lately, I'd have had time to make tissue-paper suncatchers with Nicholas before preparing a healthy, gourmet dinner and then rocking my husband's world in the bedroom.

I close the Pinterest boards and give myself a mental shake. *Don't be so hard on yourself.* The Moms tell each other that all the time, since we all seem prone to self-doubt and criticism.

I shut off all my internal mutterings, tell myself I'm doing great, and go to get Nicholas ready for the day. After leaving him at daycare, I head to the café for the morning shift.

"Hey, Liv." Allie pushes through the kitchen doors. "If you still want to deal with the birthday party for the Edison Power guy's daughter, you need to call her mother."

I straighten from refilling the tray of éclairs in the cold case. "Why?"

"She heard that Slice of Pie is headlining at the children's stage during the Bicentennial Festival." Allie waves a piece of paper at me. "Apparently they're little Becky's favorite band, and now her mother wants them to play all their hit songs at her party."

"Seriously?" I take the paper from her, my heart sinking. "Slice of Pie isn't even confirmed for the festival yet. I need Edison's sponsorship before we can afford to pay them. And I don't know if they do birthday parties."

"According to their website, they do, but they're expensive."

"Well, I'll tell Monica she'll have to pay for it, if they're even available."

"Liv, we don't have the capacity for a band!" Allie says. "Especially one that big."

"We'll put them out in the garden." I wave to the window. "The kids can use the terrace as a dance floor."

"I thought we were using the terrace for lunch and cake," she says. "Besides, don't we need some sort of permit for that kind of entertainment?"

"I'll call the city and find out," I promise, reaching for the phone. "Or maybe the band can just send the Pieman and his guitar."

"Good luck telling Monica Harrison to scale back her kid's party," Allie mutters. "She already put in an order for a three-tiered Wizard of Oz cake. Can you imagine what she'll do when her daughter gets married? Mother of Bridezilla."

I suppress the urge to remind Allie that *her* parents went all out for birthday parties when she was a girl, including the big Alice in Wonderland tenth birthday party that eventually sparked the idea for our café.

Maybe Monica Harrison is going over the top, but I can appreciate a mother who is trying to give her daughter everything she wants. Frankly I'd have loved this kind of birthday party when I turned five. I don't think my mother even remembered my fifth birthday. I barely remember it myself.

"I'll handle it, Allie," I say. "Remember, if this works out, we get to cater Edison's company picnic, which will help us buy the birthday party truck."

"The Airstream *would* be awesome." Allie looks somewhat mollified. "But you have to make sure we have enough staff and organization."

"I will, I promise."

After Allie leaves, I look at the lists spread out on my desk. Despite my encouraging words, I'm in more of a time crunch than I'd anticipated. I haven't even thought about what would happen if I *don't* come up with a festival sponsor. I can't think about that.

Which is why I'm going to make it work, if it kills me. I study the spreadsheet of festival details, trying to ignore the simmering worry about whether or not I can pull it off. The city council approached me because they knew I would do a good job—and if I fail, I'll not only hurt my personal reputation, but also my reputation as a business owner. And that would be bad for the café, our marketing efforts, even Allie…

I shake off the growing fear. I'll work things out with Edison, get all the events scheduled, host the birthday party, run the auction, and ensure the Mirror Lake Bicentennial Festival is a success. It's sort of like Dean's and my sex life—when things are on track, it will be perfect.

It has to be.

CHAPTER 12

OLIVIA

"*H*ey, Liv, have you seen my extra shaving soap?" Dean calls from upstairs.

I set the pot I'd been washing into the dish drainer and push a damp tendril of hair away from my forehead.

"It should be in the bathroom cabinet," I call back.

"It's not. I checked."

Check again, I think somewhat peevishly, when an expectant silence indicates he's waiting for me to come upstairs. I look in on Nicholas, who is banging on a xylophone in the sunroom. I trudge upstairs to the bedroom, where Dean has his suitcase open and half-packed. Suit jackets, ties, and pants are strewn over the bed.

He's standing in the bathroom doorway, holding a package of Nicholas's pull-ups.

"I keep my shaving supplies in the bottom cabinet, but this was there instead," he says.

"Oh, since Nicholas has been sleeping in our bed so much, I put those in our bathroom in case he needs changing in the middle of the night," I explain. "I had to rearrange a few things."

"So what did you do with my shaving soap?"

Since I can't remember, I go into the bathroom and search the cabinets. I finally find Dean's shaving soap pushed to the back behind a box of tampons.

"Sorry." I hold a wrapped disk out to him. "I'll rearrange everything again so you can have a cabinet just for your stuff."

"Please don't rearrange again," he replies, pressing a kiss against my temple. "I'll just hereby designate the bottom shelf of the left-hand cabinet as the exclusive zone for *Dean West's Stuff.*"

"I dunno." I shoot a dubious look at the cabinet. "I don't see how I'm ever going to fit in there."

He grins. "Well, you *are* my best stuff. Maybe you should have a drawer all to yourself."

"Oh, a whole drawer?" I pat his very fine ass as I walk past him to the bedroom door. "Thank you so much, kind sir. You're so generous."

He grabs me around the waist and hauls me against him for a hot, hard kiss that sweeps a tingle clear down to my toes.

"Oh, I'm generous," he murmurs against my lips. "If you're lucky, you'll find out later tonight just *how* generous."

I smile and squeeze him around the waist, any lingering irritation fading at the thought of indulging in a sexy night before he leaves for Italy again tomorrow morning. Absence has never made our hearts grow fonder—because they couldn't possibly be filled with *more* fondness—but maybe we can use the separation as a way to keep things hot and tense.

Yes! Redirection, like I do with Nicholas when he's on the verge of a tantrum. *Look, here's your shiny train set, why don't we make the tracks go around the kitchen table, isn't this fun...*

Whoa. Redirecting myself back to the anticipation of a sexy night, I press up against Dean and kiss him again.

"I'm already lucky," I tell him, rubbing my breasts against his chest. "You just need to show me *how* lucky."

We indulge in another kiss that makes my tingles tingle. It's so easy to fall into the pleasure of us that at times like this, I can't figure out how we ever disconnected in the first place.

Dean spreads his hands through my hair, angling my mouth so he can kiss me more deeply. My blood heats, my nipples stiffening against the planes of his chest. Only when I start to hazily think I could quite happily fall into bed with him right this second do I ease reluctantly away.

"Later," I promise, nipping at his lower lip.

"Damn right later," he mutters, giving my breasts a quick groping as I back away from him toward the door.

Happy anticipation rises in me as I head downstairs. It's not the romantic weekend I'd planned, but sending my husband off with a much-needed hot night will be a reminder of just how good we are together. And it will set the stage for his return.

I head back to the kitchen and check on Nicholas, who has lost interest in the xylophone and moved on to his toy fire station. Dusk is falling outside, the picture windows revealing the garden and trees thrown into shadows. I put a pot of water on the stove to boil and preheat the oven for the roasted cauliflower dish I plan to serve with crispy chicken.

I'm halfway through dinner preparations when a chill breaks over my skin. I go to check the thermostat when I realize the sliding glass door in the sunroom is open, letting cold evening air into the house.

My heart stutters. "Nicholas?"

I glance around the sunroom. His toys and books are strewn over the floor, but my son is nowhere to be seen.

"Nicholas?" I shove my feet into my shoes and hurry out to the garden. "Nicholas!"

Birds squawk and a light wind rustles the trees. I squint into the growing darkness, telling myself to be calm. It wasn't that long—I don't think it was that long, at least, but I was focused on the stupid chicken—so he can't be far.

He's probably digging for worms or waiting for birds at the birdbath or…oh, Jesus, the *birdbath,* which I just filled with water this morning…

"Nicholas!" I run over the flagstone paths, fear spiking in my blood.

The circular, cement birdbath looms ominously in a corner of the garden. I come to a halt, panting.

"Nicholas, where are you?" I shove aside a rising panic and rush to check every part of the yard—the bushes where we play hide-and-seek, the lawn where we toss balls back and forth, the garden where we'll plant vegetables this summer…

"Nicholas…" I stop, my heart hammering so hard I can hear it inside my head.

Beyond the garden lies an acre of land thick with trees and undergrowth. The border isn't fenced yet, and Nicholas isn't allowed to go there, which is just one of the reasons Dean and I never leave him in the yard by himself…

"Dean!" His name rips from my throat. I run back into the house. *"Dean!"*

I barely make it to the stairs before he comes hurrying down, alarmed at the panic in my voice.

"It's Nicholas." I grab his arm, fisting my hand into his sleeve. "I can't find him. I was cooking dinner, and then I noticed the sliding glass door was open, and…Dean, I *can't find him!*"

He's already pulling on his shoes and heading outside before I finish. I run after him, terror swelling into my throat. My breathing is too fast, shivers erupting over my arms.

"Nicholas!" Dean's deep voice resounds through the thicket of fir trees and evergreens.

"He's not in the garden." I'm starting to shake. "I looked everywhere."

Dean looks again. He races around the sides of the house,

checks behind the garage and in the front yard, calling for Nicholas the whole time.

"Stay here," he orders, heading toward the trees. "In case he comes back. Run down to the basement and grab a flashlight."

I careen to a stop as he disappears past the tree line, sinking into the depths of the woods. I struggle against the fear threatening to engulf me, my mind flooding with images of Nicholas hurt, lost, or worse…

I hurry back to the house. Dean's voice echoes behind me as he calls for our son, the sound laced with a panic I've never heard from him before. My stomach wrenches. I grab two high-powered flashlights from the basement and return to the garden.

"Dean?" My voice fades into the growing darkness.

His footsteps rustle on the leaves and undergrowth before he appears at the tree line, holding out his hand for one of the flashlights. He turns and disappears back into the woods.

I switch on the second flashlight and tread another path around the garden. It occurs to me that despite the door having been opened, Nicholas might not have gone outside.

I hurry back inside and search all the rooms upstairs and down, calling his name. A deafening silence fills the entire house. By the time I make my way back outside, I'm shaking so hard my teeth are rattling.

I go down the steps of the back porch toward the woods. A sudden noise from behind me jolts my heart up into my throat. I turn and hurry back to the porch.

"Nicholas?" I shine the flashlight around the base of the porch. There's a narrow opening on the side skirting, one I hadn't noticed before. I crouch down and push aside a loose board, trying to peer inside. "Nicholas?"

I aim the flashlight beam under the porch, illuminating nail-studded boards, cobwebs, a growth of scrubby weeds…and our son crouched in a corner, his hands and face streaked with dirt.

"Nicholas!" The cry escapes me before I can stop it.

He jerks his head up, takes one look at me, and crumples up his face to cry.

"Nicholas, no, no, it's okay." Forcing my voice to even out, I try to crawl through the opening toward him, but the board is too tight. "Honey, it's okay, I'm sorry. I didn't mean to scare you. I was just worried...Nicholas, come here, please..."

He opens his mouth and lets out a howl. My heart is hammering—I can't tell if he's hurt or not.

"Nicholas, *please!*"

He cries harder, his face streaked with dirt and tears in the beam of the flashlight.

"Liv!" Dean's voice rumbles through the cold air.

Relief floods me. I push away from the opening and wave the flashlight.

"Over here!" I call. "I found him!"

Leaves and twigs crunch as he runs toward us, his hair messy from the wind, his eyes still dark with panic.

"I can't reach him." I move away from the porch, my breath rasping in my throat. "I think I scared him when I called his name. I don't know if he's hurt."

Dean moves to yank at the loose board, pulling it away from the skirting. He shoulders his way through.

"Hey, buddy." He greets Nicholas in a calm, measured tone. "What're you doing under here? You okay?"

Nicholas hiccups and gives a waning sob. Dean shoves his way farther under the porch, his voice a low, steady stream of reassurance as he inches his way closer to our son. When Nicholas's crying lessens, my relief blooms stronger—if he were hurt, he wouldn't be easily calmed.

I shine my flashlight under the porch as Dean crawls toward Nicholas, finally getting his hand around Nicholas's arm. Slowly, he pulls backward.

"Come on, buddy. Let's go inside. Maybe Mommy will make us some hot cocoa."

Nicholas scrubs at his eyes and moves toward Dean. I almost hold my breath as they make their way back, Dean guiding the boy out ahead of him.

I grab Nicholas and pull him close, holding on tight. I bury my face in his hair and close my eyes, a thousand words of gratitude spilling through me like a rainbow.

Dean pushes the board over the opening behind him and gets to his feet, holding out his arms. I move closer so he can embrace Nicholas. Dean meets my gaze over the top of our son's head, the last remnants of panic fading from his expression. We walk back to the house and spend the next half hour getting Nicholas cleaned up and ensuring he isn't hurt.

When I return to the kitchen, I'm still shaking. The pot on the stove is boiling over, drops of water hitting the burner with a sizzle. I turn it off and push the pot aside.

"You okay?" Dean comes up behind me and settles his hands on my shoulders.

I nod, even though everything inside me is shouting, *"No! No, I'm not okay! I left my two-year-old son alone, for god's sake. Alone. I wasn't paying attention. Anything could have happened to him. Anything."*

I inhale a ragged breath and concentrate on the weight of my husband's hands on my shoulders, like he's securing me to the earth.

"Nothing happened," Dean says gently. "He's fine."

This time.

The ominous warning blisters in my head. You hear stories all the time of children who escape their caregivers and end up hurt, or parents who get distracted by something for *just a few minutes,* and then—

Guilt scorches my chest.

"Liv, it wasn't your fault."

"Of course it was my fault." The words break like glass in my mouth. "It was my watch. Whose fault was it, if not mine?"

Dean doesn't respond, but pulls me toward him and kisses me. Then he goes to read a picture book Nicholas is holding out.

The black thought of *what might have happened* hovers over me like a cloud as I finish getting dinner ready. It makes no sense to blame myself for things that didn't happen to my son. But good sense has nothing to do with the guilt and fear that gnaw at me for the rest of the evening.

Long after Dean and Nicholas have gone to bed, I sit on the sofa and look out the picture window at the garden enshrouded in darkness. In addition to the self-blame, I'm upset by the fact that Nicholas found a hiding place *in our own home* I didn't even know existed. What if this had happened out in the park or playground, or a place that was totally unfamiliar to me? I wouldn't even know where to begin looking.

Slowly I make my way upstairs and crawl into bed beside my husband. I huddle up against Dean's warm, strong body, which moves in the steady rhythm of sleep. Everything about him has always made me feel so safe, but a feeling of safety is no guarantee of anything.

Our home aside, what if I'd lost track of Nicholas tomorrow night, when Dean is gone, rather than tonight? What if Dean hadn't been here? I might not have heard the noise from under the porch, and certainly I wouldn't have known to even look there. Or what if I hadn't noticed Nicholas was missing until…

I shove the oil-black thoughts aside. I'd once told Dean to stop thinking *what if* and to focus on *what is*. I only wish I could take my own advice.

I press my body closer to his and rest my hand over his heart, which beats ceaselessly against my palm. Despite our ups and downs, I know to my bones this man, at least, always *is*.

CHAPTER 13

OLIVIA

J'm reluctant to be apart from Nicholas after Dean leaves again. It's irrational, I know, and my reluctance only seems to intensify Nicholas's clinginess, but it's also part of the overall unsteadiness I've experienced ever since Dean told me about the new job opportunity. Ever since I started thinking it would be perfect for him.

Not for us, but for him.

I have to disentangle myself from my crying son when I leave him at daycare—a process that brings a lump to my throat and elicits sympathetic murmurs from Christine as she gently separates Nicholas from me.

Just a phase, I tell myself as I drive to the café. *Remember, there will come a time when he won't want you around. A time when he'll go off to college with a "Bye, Mom," and a quick hug.*

I exchange a few texts with Dean during my shift, which

makes me feel better, and Christine sends me a few pictures of Nicholas happily playing with some of the other kids.

Still, deciding more time together is a good thing, I pick Nicholas up early from daycare and take him to the children's museum for a couple of hours, then to the Boxcar Deli for dinner.

As we settle into a booth, I hear a woman say my name. I look up to see Jessica Burke approaching. We greet each other, and she ruffles Nicholas's hair.

"Can you join us?" I ask her, gesturing to the seat opposite me.

"I'm meeting a friend, but I'm early so I can sit for a few minutes," she says, sliding into the booth.

"Any word on possible jobs in the area?" I ask.

"No." She sighs and gives me a rueful smile. "I applied for a visiting professorship in Indiana, so we'll see what happens. How is Dean's trip going?"

"Fine, from what he tells me." I hesitate, then figure she can probably give me a good perspective on this whole assistant director position. "What's your take on the WHC job opening?"

"It's fantastic, and a great opportunity for Dean," she says, accepting a glass of water from a passing server. "He'd have a ton of influence if he were offered and accepted it. He might even be able to get the Youth Experts program started again."

"What's the Youth Experts program?"

"It was started as a program for students around the world to get involved with conservation issues," Jessica explains. "Dozens of students have been interested, but the program hasn't had a leader so it's been something of a disorganized mess."

"And Dean could fix that?"

The answer is obvious, of course. Dean can fix anything.

"Yeah, definitely," Jessica says, shooting Nicholas a smile as he offers her a slobbery goldfish cracker. "If he were assistant director, he could totally allocate funds and hire someone to organize the Youth Experts program. It would make a huge difference to so many young people, since they're the ones who will one day be in charge of the sites."

I'm certain if Dean had the power to hire a leader of the Youth Experts program, that person would be Jessica Burke. And with her looking for a job right now...

She waves at a curly-haired young man who enters the deli.

"Sorry, Liv, I gotta go." Jessica slides out of the booth. "Let's have coffee soon, or let me know if you need a babysitter for the cutie over here."

"I will, thanks."

We say goodbye, and I turn back to the menu. Knowing that Dean taking the job could also lead to a prominent position for Jessica and opportunities for students around the world is an unexpected thorn in my side.

I shake my head to dislodge the dreaded sense that I could be the one preventing so many opportunities for others because I don't want anything to change.

I pull a few coloring books out of my bag and turn my attention to Nicholas. Most of the time, I love being alone with Nicholas, except this time I feel Dean's absence more acutely than I have before. With his new responsibilities over the past couple of years, I've gotten used to him being away, but only now do I realize I don't like being *used to* a separation from my husband.

Later that night, after Nicholas is asleep, I call Dean. His phone goes to voicemail.

"Hi, it's me," I say. "Just wanted to see how things are going. I'm about to go to bed, so I'll try you again tomorrow."

As I end the call, I remember when he first went to Italy a few years ago. For the two months he was in Altopascio, we had a standing phone date every night at ten sharp. Not once did either of us miss our nightly calls.

I slide into bed, rolling over to press my face into his pillow, which I still often do when he's not here. The faint scent of his shaving soap clings to the cotton.

I inhale deeply and imagine the two of us closing the door of a hotel room and turning toward each other. Shutting the rest of the world out, the way we used to do so often, even in the early part of our relationship when we were utterly captivated by each other.

I still remember those days so clearly. I woke one morning alone in Dean's bed, absorbing the warmth still lacing the sheets, the lingering smell of lust. I listened to the sound of the shower and imagined him naked under the hot spray, soap sluicing over his muscular body...heat coiled through me as I reached for my robe.

After tugging it on, I went to use the guest bathroom. When I returned, the main bathroom door was half open. Dean was standing at the sink, getting ready to shave, a towel wrapped around his waist.

Fragrant steam coated the bathroom and fogged the mirror. I paused in the doorway, allowing my gaze to travel over the contours of his bare shoulders and chest still damp from the shower.

He was such a beautiful man. A shiver ran down my spine as I recalled the previous night when I had traced the slopes of his pectoral muscles, his rigid torso, following that line of hair down to...

"Keep looking at me like that," he said, "and I'll have you on this counter in two seconds."

"Promises, promises." I leaned my shoulder against the door-jamb and continued to watch him.

I had never seen a man shave before. I'd lived my childhood with my mother, and despite her numerous men I'd never become accustomed to their rituals or behaviors. I'd spent so much of my time trying to hide from them that they'd been like alien creatures—vaguely menacing and fearsome.

Dean was the one who proved I had nothing to fear, not from him. He was all warmth, heat, and tenderness.

"How often do you shave?" I asked.

"Once a day at least. Twice if I'm planning to take my lady out." He took a razor out of a drawer and turned on the water faucet.

"You don't use an electric razor?" I asked.

"Not a close enough shave." He rubbed his whiskery jaw. "Prefer it the old-fashioned way. Soap, not cream, and a good double-edge razor."

"Soap?"

"With a brush." He extended a small bowl with a disk of soap and a shaving brush.

I took them both and swirled the brush into the soap, creating a frothy lather. The spicy scent rose to my nose, filling me with memories of that scent clinging to Dean's skin.

"Can I put it on you?" I asked.

"Sure."

I stepped closer and reached up to slide the brush over his jaw. Before I could, he took hold of my waist and lifted me onto the counter beside the sink. My heart thumped at our nearness. He slid his hands to my thighs, the heat of his palms burning through my cotton bathrobe. He pushed my knees apart so he could move into the juncture of my thighs.

"I thought you wanted to shave." I was close enough now that I could see the water still beading on his chest and shoulders.

"I do." He took hold of my hand and lifted the brush toward his face. "But I did say I would have you on the counter."

My breath caught in my throat as I stroked the soap-covered brush over his cheek and down to the underside of his chin. I swirled the brush into the soap again and covered the other side of his face and around his mouth. With my finger, I wiped away the excess soap from his lips. By the time I was finished, my pulse was pounding.

Dean reached beside me and picked up the razor. I eased to the side so he could see himself in the mirror. He took my hand again and closed my fingers around the razor handle.

"Dean, I can't…"

"I trust you," he said.

I looked at him for a moment, struck by the intense light in his eyes. It had taken me a long time to realize trust didn't come any more easily to him than it did to me. But every time we were together, it felt like an undeniable acknowledgment we'd both crossed that barrier. I knew everything we did together, every act in which we engaged, would serve to either strengthen our trust in each other or prove that it was warranted.

He brought the razor to his face, his hand still clasped around mine. "Sideburns first. Downward stroke."

I smothered the worry about nicking him as I positioned the razor and drew it downward. It was a rather thrilling sensation to slide the sharp blade over his face, whisking away the lather and stubble and leaving a smooth patch of skin.

Dean took his hand from mine. I rinsed the razor and lifted it to his jaw again, using my other hand to pull his skin taut before I positioned the blade.

"Okay?" I whispered.

He nodded, his gaze on my face as I stroked the razor down to his cheek. The air between us was still fragrant and steamy from the shower. I rinsed the razor between each stroke, shaving each of his sideburns, then his cheeks, wiping away traces of soap with a towel.

Beneath my thick robe, my skin was getting damp as I became increasingly aware of Dean's body between my legs, the movement of his breath, the heat of his skin. I adjusted my legs around his hips and turned to rinse the razor again. As I did, I felt his finger trail down the open V of my robe.

"I'm holding a sharp blade," I reminded him, trying to ignore the tickling sensation of his finger over my skin.

"Mmm. Now you're not only sexy, but dangerous too."

I shot him a look from beneath my lashes. "If you want me to finish this, you can't touch me until I'm done. It's not safe."

He held up his hands in a gesture of surrender. I lathered up the brush again and swept it across his neck. He lifted his chin so I could reach underneath. My hand trembled as I eased the razor over his throat. Slowly I scraped the coarse stubble away. He didn't touch me, but he shifted his hips closer, and the ridge of his erection brushed my inner thigh.

A few traces of soap lined his neck. I wiped them away with my fingers before setting the razor aside. I studied his face, ensuring I hadn't left any patches of roughness. He looked gorgeous with his face clean-shaven and his hair still damp, the delicious scent of soap rising from his hot skin.

"Okay." My heart was thumping slow and heavy. "You're done."

Dean slipped his hand beneath my chin, lifting my face toward his.

"I was done the second I first saw you," he murmured the instant before his lips touched mine.

With a sigh of pleasure, I parted my legs as he deepened the kiss, one hand moving to the nape of my neck. I loved how he gently angled my head, as if he were intent on fitting me against him exactly right and locking our mouths together without a seam. I parted my lips to let him in, heat unspooling inside me as his tongue probed deeper. He slid his hands to the front of my robe and tugged at the lapels.

"You'd better be naked under here," he warned against my lips.

My pulse throbbed. "I...I have panties on."

"Not for long, you won't."

A moan escaped me as he opened my robe and slipped his hands inside to my breasts. His chest rumbled with a groan. He lifted my breasts, cupped them in his palms, and rubbed his thumbs across my nipples.

I squirmed, aching for him to touch me between my legs. He stepped back, pushing the robe off my shoulders. Still loosely belted, it fell around my waist and left me naked from the waist up.

A flush rose to my cheeks as Dean raked his hot gaze over me. He reached for the shaving brush again and swirled it into the soap, then brought it to my breasts. I drew in a breath when the soft, warm bristles touched my nipple. I watched, mesmerized, as he ran the brush over my breasts, painting them with lather, the white foam slick and shiny against my damp skin.

The sound of our breathing filled the air as he loaded the brush again and painted lather between my breasts, across my chest, down to my belly. The spicy scent filled the air, tinged with the aroma of eucalyptus.

"Too bad it's not whipped cream," I remarked, my voice thick with arousal. "So you could lick it off."

His eyes darkened with heat. "I'll put that on the list for tomorrow."

I could hardly wait.

I wiggled closer to him, tightening my knees around his waist, sharply aware of the heavy bulge pressing against the towel. I trailed my fingers over his washboard torso and down to the front of the towel. His breath escaped on a hiss when I closed my hand around his cock.

"Christ," he whispered, moving his lips across my cheek to my mouth. "One touch from you, and I want to come like you wouldn't believe."

My heart raced. I tightened my grip. "If I keep touching you, would you…"

"I'll do anything you want." He lifted his head to press kisses over the side of my neck, pushing his hips forward.

"Anything," he repeated, running his hands over my slick, lather-coated breasts.

I shuddered, arching my back to press my breasts into his hands, moving my lips closer to his ear.

"Would you come on my pussy?" I whispered boldly.

"Fuck, Liv." A shudder racked his body, and his shaft pulsed in my hand. "You sure as hell don't have to ask."

I shifted, releasing him momentarily to push the towel off him. The sight of his big, erect cock sticking straight out from his groin elicited a hot throb of longing.

We both watched as I stroked my hand up and down his shaft. As much as I loved the feeling of him inside me, on top of me, driving both our pleasures, now I wanted to be the one in control. I wanted him helpless at my touch.

I used my other hand to scoop up a handful of shaving lather from my breasts, then spread it over his erection and continued to work my hand up and down. He gripped my hips, lowering his head to my neck again and licking a path from my collarbone to my shoulder.

"You make me crazy," he said, his breath hot against my skin. "You're so damn sexy and so fucking sweet. Whenever I look at you, half the time I can't decide if I want to hug you or rip off your clothes and pound into you until you scream."

"You...you could do both."

His husky laugh vibrated against my shoulder. "Then I will. Indefinitely."

My heart thumped at his use of the word *indefinitely*. Now that we were together, that word had never sounded more powerful and significant.

Dean lifted his head to look at me. "Did I say something wrong?"

I loved that he was concerned, even with both of us half-naked and me still stroking his hard cock. I leaned forward and pressed my lips against his neck.

"No," I assured him. "You never say anything wrong. You say everything right."

In response, he glided his hands over my slick breasts again and down to unfasten the loose knot of my belt. After pushing it open, he rubbed me through my panties. I squirmed closer to encourage him to press harder, my grip on his erection loosening.

"Look at that," he murmured, his gaze on the cotton stretched over my sex. "So hot and wet you're soaked right through your panties."

A shudder rocked me. "God, Dean."

He shot me a wicked smile. "Why is that, beauty?"

"Because of you," I whispered, faintly aware I was no longer exactly in control. If I ever was to begin with.

He grasped the waistband of my panties, and I obediently lifted my hips so he could pull them off. He tossed them on the floor and put his hands on my inner thighs, pressing them farther apart.

A waft of still-steamy air brushed my folds. I shivered again, tensing with the eager expectation that he would position himself between my legs and thrust into me. Instead he reached for the shaving brush again.

My breath stuttered in my throat. I watched as he rinsed the brush in warm water, then brought it between my legs. The instant the wet bristles touched me, I gasped.

"Oh, god…"

He cupped my chin again and captured my mouth in a hot, deep kiss as he swirled the shaving brush over my cleft. Urgency built inside me with volcanic force. I gripped his biceps and moaned against his mouth.

He lifted his head, his eyes dark with lust. Without a word, he adjusted the brush, and then I felt the smooth, wooden handle press against the opening of my body. I gasped, my gaze flying to Dean's. Sweat glistened on his cheekbones, beads of water still coating his chest.

I shifted forward, easing myself onto the wooden handle,

feeling it slide into me. It wasn't long, but it was wide at the base with a shaft that narrowed before flaring into a thick knob in the middle. By the time I'd wiggled myself up to that point, my entire body was throbbing with need.

"Dean." A strain threaded my voice.

He edged his fingers between my thighs. I closed my eyes as tension coiled through me, heightened by the handle pressing inside me. Two strokes of his adept fingers and I came with a shriek, vibrating around the brush handle as if it were his erection.

Before the tingles had begun to ebb, he pulled the handle from me and set the brush aside. He took my hand and guided it back to his cock.

Trembling, I rubbed his shaft, the smooth, warm flesh gliding in and out of my fist. He pushed his hips forward and, with a groan, shot over my spread pussy. We both watched, our breathing hot and heavy, as I continued slowly stroking the final pulses from him.

His breath escaped in a rush. He gathered me into his arms and pulled me against him, the shaving lather still slippery on our skin.

"We need to take a shower," I murmured.

"Mmm. I take no responsibility for what I might do to you in the shower."

A pleasurable tingle of anticipation ran through me. There was still so much I wanted to do with him. I didn't even know if a lifetime would be long enough for us.

I snuggled closer and wrapped my arms around his waist. I could do everything and anything with him. I trusted him with my heart, my soul, my life.

"You're going to need a new shaving brush," I remarked.

"Are you kidding?" He pressed his lips to my temple. "That's the only brush I'll ever use again."

Part II

CHAPTER 14

DEAN

*M*y trip passes in a blur of work and activity as we hurry to get the proposal in order. We meet with Italian officials, seismologists, scientists, and historians. We take photos, ensure the site meets all the WHC criteria, review the comparative analysis, and provide details of the quake damage.

Simon Fletcher, my old friend from grad school days who has been directing the Altopascio excavation for years, is jittery with nerves over the impending protection vote. He's a big, no-bull-shit guy, most at home when he's crouched in the dirt digging up an artifact.

We take the train to Paris, loaded down with files of reports and photographs. A UNESCO car and driver takes us from the de Gaulle airport to the Four Seasons Hotel.

"Since when do a couple of ordinary scholars get royal treat-ment?" I ask Simon as we check into the rooms that have already been reserved for us.

"Not for me, boss," he replies. "You're the king around here."

I glance at him. "What's that mean?"

"We know the WHC is courting you big time," Simon tells me, reaching down to heft his ratty rucksack. "And you're the reason the UN Assembly is voting on the site. If it weren't for you, we'd already have lost the project completely."

"That's not true. You were working on the site long before you asked me to come on board."

"Yeah, but we were scrambling for funding back then." Simon punches the elevator button. "You're the one who got us in with the IHR and the Conservation Committee. You're the one who got the seismologists in after the quake and put together the damage report. You're the one who got the proposal pushed through the WHC so the Assembly can vote on it. And that's a lot of fucking bureaucracy and red tape to cut through. You get shit done, man. It's a beautiful thing."

He extends his fist. As our knuckles bump, I can't help thinking that getting shit done for the sake of the archeological team has been one of the most rewarding parts of my career. And it all came about because Liv insisted I work on the dig in the first place.

"You'd better plan on going to the UN Assembly," Simon tells me, as we get into the elevator. "You're the man we need to convince the delegates to give us their vote."

"Any one of us can give the presentation." I scroll through the calendar on my phone, double-checking the UN Assembly dates, which are a two-week period in July. "I can't go anyway. I promised Liv I'd help out with a festival she's planning."

"Can't you still do that?"

"The festival is on a Saturday right when the Assembly is meeting. You're going, right?"

"Sure, but I'm not as high-powered as you."

"So many compliments." I narrow my eyes at him. "You're not going to try and kiss me now, are you?"

"You should be so lucky."

With a grin, Simon gives me a salute and lumbers down the hall to his room.

I spend the next few days meeting with program directors at the World Heritage Center headquarters, a seven-story building designed in the shape of a three-point star, with a panoramic view of Paris from the rooftop.

In addition to Altopascio, there are questions about UNESCO, my opinion on the heritage sites, goals, and programs. It's clear to me the exchange of ideas is also a thinly disguised series of interviews. I tell myself to stick to the path of political navigation, even as my brain processes the details of all the initiatives.

On my final night in Paris, after an evening dinner honoring the UNESCO goodwill ambassador, I finally return to the hotel close to midnight. My flight leaves at noon the day after tomorrow, so I'll be home by evening. Just in time to read Nicholas a few stories before he goes to bed.

I call Liv and leave a message on her voicemail. While I wait for her to return my call, I pull a loop of string out of my pocket and twist it around my fingers. And I think. Hard.

The possibility of the World Heritage job makes me wonder what I'd been striving for before I met Liv. I knew I'd wanted a tenure-track position with a respected university. After a year of caring for my sick grandfather and writing my dissertation, I wanted to solidify my career.

But had there been anything else?

After Liv, it was easy—I wanted to know her, love her, give her everything she wanted. I wanted to excavate my way through the maze of her secrets and desires. I wanted to free-fall into her.

And my career became about more than my love for history and my drive to be the best—it became about Liv too. What jobs or postdocs would work for both of us. What university town would she want to live in, what would make her happy, where could she find a path of her own.

Not for a second do I regret that, especially seeing how she's blossomed in Mirror Lake. She's become everything she always was, yet hadn't known.

But I can't remember what else I'd wanted. My attraction to Liv, and then my love for her, had been so blinding and intense it obliterated anything that didn't affect her.

What had there been before her? With my father's incessant pushing me to succeed, I find it hard to believe—even now—that a quiet, medievalist professor career was the endpoint of my professional ambitions. Maybe I'd even once dreamed of pursuing a position like assistant director of the World Heritage Center.

I shake my head. Stupid to think further about the challenges of the job. No sense looking at a door I can't walk through.

"I don't want you to take a new job, Dean. Certainly not one in Europe. But I also don't want to be the reason you turn down an amazing opportunity."

So what did that mean? Liv doesn't want me to consider the job, but she also doesn't want me *not* to.

I call her again. This time she picks up, her voice warm and smooth like melted syrup. The sound of it settles something inside me.

"So how are things going there?" she asks.

"Fine. Busy."

I push aside the curtain to look at the street below. It's raining, so the nineteenth-century buildings and boulevards are all cast in a damp, gray sheen.

I remember a day during our honeymoon. A rain shower drove us indoors to Angelina's café where my new wife and I spent a couple of hours together, watching the rain and passing pedestrians as we ate lunch and drank cups of thick, hot chocolate piled with cream. Even when I'd kissed Liv later that after-noon, she'd still tasted like chocolate.

"Tell me about the room," Liv says. "The Four Seasons is no travel hotel."

"Lots of satiny stuff," I reply, glancing around. "Blue and yellow. Nice big four-poster bed with a million pillows. I'd love to get you spread out on that bed."

"I'd love to be spread out on it, from the sound of things," she says, a smile in her voice. "Will you have time to do any sightsee-ing? Louvre or the Orsay?"

"I doubt it. Wouldn't want to without you here, anyway."

"One day we'll be in Paris together again," Liv promises. "Hold on, I'll put Nicholas on."

"Hi, Daddy!"

The knot in my chest both loosens and tightens at the sound of my son's voice.

"Hey, buddy. How's Fred?"

"Fed noogie."

I grin, picturing Liv rolling her eyes with disapproval that our two-year-old son knows words like *noogie* and *wedgie.* I make a mental note to blame Archer.

After Nicholas tells me about Clifford the Dog's fire-fighting abilities ("Dog Fed!"), Liv gets back on the phone. After discussing the rest of my plans, we exchange goodbyes and promises to talk tomorrow.

I stretch out on the bed and look at the ceiling, the pale blue crown molding edged with gilt. I'd intended to stay in a place like this for our honeymoon, but Liv hadn't wanted to. For her first trip to Paris—her first trip out of the States—she'd asked if we could stay in an apartment.

"That's how you and I started, right?" she'd said, tucking her hand into mine. *"In your university apartment, just the two of us. Exploring the city. Exploring each other. I want our honeymoon to be the same way."*

And, of course, because that was what my lovely, soon-to-be-wife wanted, that was what I gave her.

For the two weeks of our honeymoon, we stayed in a little apartment off Boulevard Montparnasse, a former artist's atelier with worn hardwood floors, and a wrought-iron balcony overlooking a maze of rooftops punctuated by orange chimneys and antennae.

We explored the city. We explored each other. I'd loved showing her hidden parts of Paris, the things I'd learned as a medievalist—the dimensions of Chartres Cathedral, the stories embellishing Notre Dame's rose windows, the place where Abelard and Heloise fell in love. I took her to my favorite cafés and restaurants, introduced her to the pleasures of French pastries.

One morning I woke and felt the warm weight of her curled against my side, and I was filled with renewed gratitude for us, for her. Olivia West. My *wife.*

As soon as I thought that word, Liv turned, her long hair sliding like silk over my chest. She pressed a line of slow kisses from my shoulder to my neck. The fragrant scent of her, peaches and sugar, filled my head.

Her lips reached my jaw, her fingers tracing my mouth. Her wedding ring gleamed in the early morning light. I stroked my hand over the arch of her back, never able to get enough of touching her.

With a little moan, she shifted, draping her body over mine, her full breasts crushed against my chest. Her nipples were already hard. She had always been easily aroused, even if she tried to resist it in the beginning, but over the two years of our relationship she'd become increasingly uninhibited. Free.

I fucking loved it. And even more, I loved that she was *mine.*

I stroked my hands over her ass and between her thighs. She tightened her legs around my hands, the soft heat of her skin jolting me with lust.

I couldn't get enough of her. Every night when we returned to the apartment after dinner or a walk, the pent-up urgency of the day unleashed. I grabbed Liv, she fell against me, and then we were kissing and groping like love-struck teenagers as we made our way to the bedroom.

She was always ready, always eager. So was I. I slipped my finger up to her clit and circled it slowly. She gave a muffled groan and shifted her hips. My dick stiffened against her thigh.

Liv lifted her hands to my face and moved closer. She probed her tongue into my mouth, bit my lower lip, kissed the indentation just above my chin.

My wife. My *wife.*

Need boiled up inside me. As if sensing it, Liv rolled onto her back, all soft, yielding flesh and warmth. So perfect with her round hips and tapered waist, her full high breasts with tight nipples begging to be sucked.

I got to my knees, fisting my stiff cock as I pushed between her thighs. As always, I battled the urge to make this last forever with the urge to plunge into her as fast and hard as I could.

"Oh, Dean." She moaned, stretching her arms over her head. "I'm already close."

I put my hand on the side of her face, turning her toward me. She stared at me, flushed and hot. I felt her body straining, almost vibrating with need.

"Look at me." I commanded gently. "You look at me the whole time, beauty. I want to watch you when I push inside you, when you take my cock nice and deep. I want to see your expression when I start to fuck you. I want to look into your eyes and know you're feeling every goddamned inch of me filling you. I want you breathless, overwhelmed, taken. And I want to see you when you come, when you clench your sweet pussy around me so tight I can't fucking hold back anymore."

Liv stared at me, her lips parting and her eyes widening with shocked arousal. "God, Dean."

She slid her hands under her thighs to hold them farther apart for me. I eased into her slowly, my jaw clenching as her hot slickness closed around my shaft.

"Ah, fuck." I inhaled a ragged breath. "So goddamned tight."

"Please." She panted, pushing to her elbows so she could keep her eyes fixed on mine. "Oh…*oh!*"

I thrust, sinking fully into her. She groaned, her eyes glazing over. My muscles strained with the effort of trying not to push too hard, too fast. I didn't want it to be over soon, but Christ in heaven, she was so hot and sweet…

"I'm…oh, hurry," she whispered. "I want to come with you inside me, to feel you…so deep…ah!"

I surged inside her, forgetting to be gentle, the sensation of my wife crashing over me. I thrust hard, harder…fucking *harder*. Her body writhed under mine, her breasts bouncing with every thrust, her long hair clinging damply to her face and shoulders.

"Dean." Her voice cracked, her eyes suddenly filling with desperation and the glitter of tears. "I need it so badly. Please…"

Her pleas became a low chant, a stream of fire straight into me. Even as I felt her striving for release, she didn't take her eyes off mine. A thousand emotions filled her expression—need, lust, urgency, love. Heat crackled between us, sparks like the strike of flint against steel.

I drove into her again, wanting to bury myself inside her for days, sinking into all her goodness and warmth.

"Oh!" Liv inhaled sharply. "Dean."

My name was a choked gasp, trailing into a moan as her body shook, hard vibrations trembling through her. Then it was too much, and I sank into her the instant before an orgasm ripped through me. I gripped the sides of her head as I filled her, flooded her. She stared at me in a daze and then our lips crashed together, a sudden explosion of emotions too complex to unravel.

Dean. Dean…Dean.

My wife's voice echoed through me, her tears dampened my skin, and her body stayed wrapped around mine until we finally pulled ourselves out of bed. The rest of the world came slowly back into focus, even though neither of us wanted it to.

CHAPTER 15

OLIVIA

*T*his time, I don't try to prepare an elaborate, welcome-home dinner for Dean—which turns out to be a good thing when he calls to tell me his flight is delayed. Nicholas and I end up going to bed before Dean even gets home, and I find my husband sleeping in the guest bedroom the following morning.

Though Nicholas is initially thrilled with his father's return and the presents of wooden knight and dragon puppets, he launches himself back at me within two hours. He whines when Dean hugs and kisses me, he doesn't want to be put down when I'm holding him, and he won't let Dean help him dress or brush his teeth.

Any hopes I might still have had of a wild return to Sexyland with my husband disappears as I contend with Nicholas's continued bout of intense neediness that is only soothed by the apparent magic of clinging to me like a barnacle whenever the three of us are together.

The third night after Dean's return, I manage to get Nicholas to sleep by seven, but Dean is working late and by the time he comes to the bedroom with a gleam in his eye, Nicholas is calling for me.

I don't know how other women do it all. Then I remember they very likely don't do it all—not if my conversations with The Moms is anything to judge by. I can't even offer to give Dean a close, sexy shave these days because by the time he gets out of the shower in the morning, I'm in the kitchen making Nicholas oatmeal and bananas.

I also haven't yet come up with a viable Plan B to revive our sex life, mostly because my energy is going in so many different directions.

Get my groove back.

The statement stares at me from the pages of the beautiful Italian notebook Dean brought back for me. I've spent a lot of time learning about the importance of setting and keeping goals —and also about how effectively the craziness of working parenthood can thwart even the best of intentions.

A renewed sense of purpose strikes me when I realize Dean has been home for three days, and we haven't managed to progress any farther than a couple of heated, interrupted kisses.

One morning Archer stops by the Butterfly House to drop off the chair he has painted for the Chair Fair. As I'd expected, it's incredible—a detailed, cartoon drawing of Blue, the superheroine with blue-streaked blond hair who derives her power from the weather. Painted tornadoes twist up the legs of the chair, and a villain crawls over the back.

"This is beautiful," I say with admiration, walking around the chair. "Has Kelsey seen it?"

Archer shakes his head, a shadow crossing his expression. "She's been really busy."

Though I suspect Kelsey is keeping herself crazy busy partly to avoid having to deal with the issue of marrying Archer, I keep that thought to myself. Instead I reach out to squeeze Archer's arm.

"You know, I've always thought Kelsey and I were so different," I tell him. "But turns out we have a lot in common. We both know when something is so good it would be foolish to change it."

Archer shakes his head, his mouth compressing. "If you don't change, you stagnate and start to rot. My parents didn't change for twenty-five years, and look at how miserable they were."

I don't have an answer to that because it's the truth.

"It wasn't until they got divorced a few years ago that they were finally happy," Archer continues, turning and heading back to his truck.

"But their relationship wasn't good," I tell him. "It took them awhile, but they had to change to find freedom."

"So do I." Archer slams the open back of the truck and walks around to the driver's side. "Marriage to Kelsey is my freedom."

My heart clenches with painful understanding. Marriage to Dean had freed me too, in so many ways.

"Does she know that?" I ask gently.

"If she doesn't by now," Archer says, pulling his keys out of his pocket, "then the past two years have been a waste."

I realize I can see his point of view on this issue as clearly as I can see Kelsey's. As much as I don't want anything to change about our lives now, if I hadn't been willing to take a risk with Dean almost ten years ago, we'd never have dated and gotten married. I can't even imagine that.

"Archer, she'll come around eventually," I say, aware it's a painfully inadequate reassurance.

"Yeah, well, I'm not going anywhere whether she does or doesn't." Archer shakes his head with a laugh. "Marriage or not, that woman is stuck with me for life. I love her more than I love...*air*, you know?"

"I know."

Archer shakes his head again, looking faintly embarrassed by the confession. He opens the truck door and hauls himself into the driver's seat.

"So, you need my help with anything else?" he asks. "Take care of Nicholas or something?"

An idea sparks in my mind, intensified by my knowledge of Archer and Kelsey's own relationship problems and the undeniable fact that I have to work harder to nurture my marriage.

"Actually, now that you mention it, could you pick Nicholas up from daycare tonight?" I ask. "Maybe keep him until around eight thirty or so?"

I'm not much good after eight in the evening for anything except watching TV and sleeping, but Dean gets home around five thirty, and that will give us three full hours together.

"Yeah, sure," Archer agrees. "I'll take him to the park and food court. He likes that noodle place."

"Wonderful, thank you so much."

I go inside to get him Nicholas's spare diaper bag before he heads off. I spend the morning with Nicholas before leaving him at daycare and going to the café. At four, I finish my shift and walk to Avalon Street.

I make a stop at my favorite downtown lingerie shop and purchase several ruffled chemises and two sets of lacy bras and panties. At home, I go upstairs to the bedroom and open my notebook.

Chair fair underway.
Birthday party orders placed.
Auction donations confirmed.
Daycare payments made.

Café schedule done.
Bills paid.
* Sexy stuff purchased.

I have absolutely nothing else to think about since my entire To Do list has been completed. I'm all about getting sexy tonight.

I set the notebook on my nightstand and strip out of my dowdy work pants and shirt. I put on a pink-and-black sheer chemise whose open front is held together by a little bow. Then I slither into a pair of matching V-string panties that are hardly the most comfortable thing in the world, but I don't expect I'll be wearing them for long.

I do a quick primping in the bathroom, admiring how the chemise looks both pretty and sexy draped over my breasts and hips. Aside from making an effort to lose my pregnancy weight and go to the gym regularly, I haven't paid much attention to my body since I had Nicholas.

A year of breast-feeding, which was both painful and difficult, combined with the unexpected physical demands of a new baby then a clingy toddler, have often made me feel more like a work-horse than a sensual woman.

I turn, still studying myself in the mirror and thinking I look pretty good. All the more reason to stoke the fires again. And even though I do want to know about Dean's fantasies, it's also true I haven't indulged in fantasies of my own in recent months. So this isn't just about him. It's about me too. It's about *us.*

I pull my old, padded bathrobe on over my chemise and belt it closed, then busy myself fluffing up the pillows and smoothing the sheets. I pick up a romance novel by the side of my bed and, to get myself in the mood, I read a few pages of a love scene in which Renaldo is penetrating Lissa's silken petals with his turgid manroot.

"Liv?" Dean's deep voice echoes from the foyer.

"Up here!" I call, adjusting my robe over my lingerie.

I hear his footsteps on the stairs before he comes in, rumpled from a day's work but handsome as the devil in gray slacks and a hunter green shirt, his tie loose around his neck. He stops in the doorway and eyes me in my ragged old padded robe.

"What're you doing in your robe already?" he asks. "You feeling okay?"

"Just fine." I smile.

"Where's Nicholas?"

"Archer wanted to take him to the park. They're going to grab dinner at the mall."

"Oh." With a shrug, Dean goes into the bathroom.

I hear the water running. I know his routine, and sure enough —a few minutes later he emerges, unbuttoning his shirt to change into jeans and a T-shirt. As I admire his chest and the smooth musculature of his shoulders, a ribbon of lust uncoils inside me.

Yes!

I watch him strip down to his boxers. The muscles of his back shift and flex underneath his taut skin. When he turns away to grab a pair of jeans from the dresser, I slither out of my robe and drop it to the floor. By the time I scramble to kneel in the middle of the bed, I'm tingly with anticipation.

Dean turns, his eyes widening at the sight of me.

"Hi," I say breathlessly.

"Well, hello." He skims his gaze over me, his expression sparking with heat. "Is that new?"

"Just bought it today." I stroke my hand over the bed sugges-tively, my fingers brushing against the book.

"You're incredible," he murmurs.

"I thought we could finally have some uninterrupted fun." I pick up the romance novel and show him the cover of a buxom lass with long, red hair about to be ravished by a hunk whose billowy, open shirt exposes his ridiculously impressive abs. "My book gave me an idea."

"Yeah?" Intrigue sparks in his expression as he approaches the bed, erotic tension already lacing his muscles. "What kind of idea?"

"A fantasy about you *ravishing* me."

"Now that," he says, sliding one hand to the back of my neck and dropping his other hand to the waistband of his boxers, "is a fantasy I can get behind. And on top of. As long as we get right down to the ravishing."

"Well, of course, but you know, sharing fantasies is really supposed to…oh!"

Dean shoves his boxers down, his half-hard cock appearing right in front of me. His grip tightens on my nape as he pulls me forward so I'm sitting on the edge of the bed. Without thinking, I part my lips obediently, a bolt of arousal shooting through me as he nudges his cock into my mouth.

I put my hands on his hips, my blood heating as I feel him grow harder. I squirm, pressing my thighs together, a throb of urgency already starting.

He slides his hand over my body and underneath my chemise, his palms sending tingles of electricity racing over my skin. A noise of appreciation rumbles from his chest. I slacken my throat muscles, letting him pump in and out. The salty taste of him floods my tongue, and before long his breath starts to intensify.

"Ah, fuck, Liv."

The low murmur floods me with heat. I move away from him to unfasten the bow holding the chemise together. The chiffon opens, exposing my breasts topped with stiff nipples and the curves of my belly and hips. Dean's eyes darken.

"You are so damn sexy," he murmurs, putting one knee on the bed and pushing me backward.

His lips come down on mine with surprising gentleness—

especially considering that I can feel his pent-up lust ready to snap open. He strokes his tongue into my mouth, smooth and deep, his hands palming my breasts. I twitch underneath him, and when he starts playing with my nipples, electric sparks shoot through me.

I maneuver us both around and fall back against the pillows, gripping his arms to keep him close, our mouths sealed in a hot, wet kiss. With a gasp of pleasure, I wrap my legs around his thighs, my heart kicking into overdrive as his cock rubs against the stretched satin of my panties.

He slides a hand down my abdomen, his fingers twisting in the thin elastic string at my hips before moving around to my rear.

"Hmm." His deep growl vibrates through me. "Not much here."

"It's a little small," I admit, sliding my lips over his jaw to where his pulse is pounding at the hollow of his throat.

"Lemme see." His voice is a gruff order as he pushes away from me.

He sits back, making a circling gesture with his forefinger. I lick my lips, my heart hammering as I turn to show him the skimpy lace-and-satin back that barely covers my bottom.

"Damn." The curse escapes him on a hiss as he covers my ass with both his hands, rubbing and squeezing. He moves his hand between my legs, probing at my damp cleft.

I gasp, arching my back. "Dean!"

"Jesus, you're soaked down here." He pushes a finger into me and strokes it back and forth.

I swear to god I'm already close to coming, and we've barely gotten started. With a moan, I push my rear backward, seeking deeper penetration, my nerves tingling with pleasure.

I twist to look at him over my shoulder. He's gazing at my lace-covered ass, one hand slowly stroking his big cock. The sight of him sends a fire-bolt straight into my blood.

"Dean." I lower my head onto the pillow.

He pulls the panties over my hips and ass, pressing his erection against my bare thigh. I experience an instant of self-consciousness—after all it's not like we've been doing much of this lately—but then he slides his shaft right between my cheeks, and shock obliterates my embarrassment.

He gives a muffled laugh and rubs his cock up and down the cleft of my bottom, slipping lower to my sex before sliding back up again. I grip the headboard with both hands as hot sensations sweep up the length of my spine.

"You're so fucking perfect," he mutters, easing two fingers slowly inside me again. "Spread your legs wider for me, beauty."

I fumble for another pillow to put beneath me and spread my legs apart. I'm quivering with anticipation and need, perspiration damping my skin, my tight, aching nipples rubbing against the pillow.

I shift, feeling his muscular legs pressing between mine, his broad hand coming down to rest on my lower back. The panties are still tangled around my thighs, the constriction an erotic contrast to the pressure of Dean's erection nudging at my slit.

"Do it, please," I gasp. "Fuck me."

With a grunt, he pushes forward, gripping my hips. I sink onto his shaft, crying out with pleasure when he fills me. I tighten my hands on the headboard and brace myself as he starts fucking me with slow, deep strokes that make my whole body quake.

"Move your pretty ass," he orders hoarsely. "Come on, fuck yourself on me...that's it..."

I start to thrust myself back onto his shaft. I squeeze my breasts, playing with my nipples, fiery currents shooting like stars through my blood.

Oh, I could kneel here for hours, letting my husband stroke his cock in and out of me. His fingers tighten on my hips, his breath rasping through the air as our bodies slam together again and again...

"Dean, I'm going to come." I bite down hard on my lower lip as the spool of lust winds tighter and tighter, pulling me closer to the explosion of bliss I haven't felt in longer than I care to remember.

But I want to come while looking at my husband, and he wants to watch, because he pulls out of me and eases me around to my back. His expression is rigid with lust and restraint, his eyes smoldering as he rakes his gaze over my sweaty, naked body.

He rubs his hands in circles over my midriff and hips, bending to press warm kisses over my breasts. He slides his hands between my thighs to spread them apart again.

He enters me with one deep plunge, bracing his hands on either side of my head. My gaze locks with his in a fiery heat of urgency and need that belongs to us alone and that we haven't shared in so long...too long...

"It's going to happen," I whisper thickly, sliding my hands around to grip his muscular back. "I can feel it...oh, yes..."

Born to be Wi-ild...

The song breaks through my fierce, spinning storm of heat and desire.

Born to be...

My cell phone buzzes on the nightstand. Archer's ringtone. I squeeze my eyes shut and try to ignore it.

Dean's breath is hot on my neck, his chest is rubbing against my breasts, his cock throbbing inside me...

Oh, it's incredible, powerful and hot, I'm going to come so hard and feel him shoot deep inside me...

The phone keeps ringing, the stupid song a mind-numbing screech of nails on a chalkboard. I don't need to answer it. I trust Archer implicitly—Nicholas is safe, nothing is wrong...

No! Stop thinking about Archer and Nicholas.

I reach up to grab the headboard, focusing on Dean's burning gaze, the sweat trickling over his temple, the rigid set of his jaw as he fucks me harder and faster…

Head out on the highway…

"Shit." I shove him away and grab for the phone.

Dean groans and rolls off me, the sudden loss of his weight leaving me feeling bereft and raw with guilt. I fumble to accept the call, shoving my damp hair away from my face.

"Hello?" I gasp.

"Hey, Liv."

"What?" I try to control my breathing, my racing pulse. "Is everything…everything all right?"

"Yeah, fine. You sound weird."

"I'm…" I press a hand to my throat and close my eyes. My heart hammers. "I'm fine."

"What does he want?" Dean growls, his chest heaving.

"Oh, shit," Archer mutters. "Uh, sorry, Liv."

"Never mind." I close my eyes, not sure if I want to laugh or cry. "Why did you call?"

"Well, I ran into a friend at the park and told him about the chair thing—hope you don't mind—and he said he knows a guy who owns a used furniture store, if you want a contact for more chairs."

A bubble of pained laughter rises in my chest. "Sure. That would be great. Thanks."

"Also, Nicholas just had spaghetti for dinner and asked for a chocolate ice cream, but I wanted to make sure it was okay with you first."

"Yes, that's fine."

"Okay, thanks. Sorry to have bothered you. Really."

"Not as sorry as I am," I mutter.

I throw the phone on the nightstand and turn back to Dean, but the air between us has cooled and cracked again, the sharp edge of reality blunting my urgency. I know there's no way we can get back to where we were now that chairs and chocolate ice cream have invaded my mind.

I flop onto the pillow, my body still aching with the ebbing tide of unfulfilled lust. Dean shoves up from the bed, his skin slick with sweat and his erection still half-hard, and goes into the bathroom.

Now it's no longer an uncertainty. I definitely want to cry.

CHAPTER 16

DEAN

*S*omething has to change. And in ways that have nothing to do with another job, no matter how impressive. Yeah, I can secure funding for a medieval site. I'm prominent enough to be a frontrunner for an international, diplomatic position. I can write reports, collaborate with scientists, navigate bureaucracy and politics.

I can get shit done. So why the hell haven't I figured out how to revive my relationship with my wife?

I unlock the front door, my muscles still burning and chest heaving from a morning run. The exercise did nothing to ease the frustration that, thanks to last night, now feels like a volcano on the verge of erupting.

I call out a hello to Liv and Nicholas as I pass the kitchen, then head straight for the bathroom. After stripping out of my clothes, I turn on the shower and step under the spray. I lower my head into the hot water and shut my eyes.

I get that Liv is trying. I love her wildly for it. Just thinking about her in that silky little gown, her gorgeous breasts pushed into pillowy cleavage, her hips and thighs all soft and round...fuck.

My dick hardens. And though I'm sick of jerking off, I grab my shaft and stroke. Pressure builds in my groin. As usual, the images flash through my brain with no effort whatsoever—Liv spread out in front of me, her pussy open and glistening, her breath coming in short, little gasps.

"Oh, god, Dean...hurry, please..."

She's all ripe lust and heat, her tight nipples begging to be sucked, her pale thighs tense with strain. My blood surges. I tighten my grip and stroke faster, picturing myself sinking into my wife, her legs winding around my hips, her breath puffing against my neck. I can feel her closing around me like wet, tight silk, gripping my cock, pulling me into her...

"Would you like a piece of pie, sir?"

The image shifts, and then she's wearing a little pink waitress outfit with the buttons unfastened low enough to reveal the curves of her tits. She turns and hikes the skirt up over her hips, showing me her perfect ass as she bends over the counter and spreads her legs. She gives me a hot look over her shoulder, her eyes glazed with lust, her long hair spilling over her back.

Without a word, I grab a fistful of her hair and position myself at her slit, driving into her so hard and fast she lets out a shriek of surprised pleasure. Her ass smacks against my stomach, the wet, slapping sound of fucking filling my ears as I plunge into her again and again...so hot, so fucking good...

"Ah!" A groan rumbles from my chest as I come, shooting all over my hand.

The shower spray beats onto my lowered head and neck as I catch my breath, lust still throbbing in my veins because of course my goddamned hand is no substitute for my wife.

I grab the soap and spread lather over my chest. I'll try again to get Liv to come away with me, though it probably still won't work out with her schedule. At least, her schedule has always been her excuse for declining. I suspect it's also because she's worried about being away from Nicholas, but she won't admit it.

Maybe I need to get on board with her fantasy thing, if it'll help her focus. But no way am I going to tell her about pie and a pink waitress outfit.

Even though she'd be insanely cute in one.

Hmm...

I shut off the water and grab a towel.

Think, West. Figure it out, or you'll be rubbing your dick so much you'll summon a fucking genie.

I'm surprised I haven't already.

A snort of laughter escapes me. Apparently I could use a genie to help get my sex life back. I wouldn't even need three wishes— just one would do. I get dressed in a gray suit and knot my tie while looking in the mirror. Unsurprisingly, my expression is tense and rigid.

I'm not an asshole. At least, I haven't been before now, I don't think. I've always tried to give Liv whatever she wants, whatever she needs. I waited months for her to be ready for me when we were first dating, and damned if I wouldn't have waited longer. I'd have waited as long as it took. Olivia Rose Winter was a woman you'd wait an eternity for. And then you'd sit back and wait even longer.

When she told me to go to Altopascio after the miscarriage, because she knew I had to stay away from King's or risk my career, I went. I'd hated being away from her for months, but I'd done it. Like now, I'd spent most of my nights jerking off like a teenager, waiting to get back to her. Same thing after Nicholas was born, though I'd been expecting that. I waited it out again, knowing it would take awhile.

While we've had brief resurgences of great sex, this drought has now lasted longer than *a while.* And while I would gladly become a monk in exchange for keeping my family safe and happy...well, my family *is* safe and happy.

And I'm no monk.

My cell buzzes with a text from Liv. *Coffee's ready.*

I text back: *Be right there.*

I pull on my suit jacket and shoes, then walk up the spiral staircase to my tower office to get my briefcase.

Sometimes I miss our little two-bedroom apartment on Avalon Street. Proud as I am of the work we've done on the Butterfly House, it's a damn big place. When we're not in the same room, Liv usually calls or texts me from the kitchen or living room so she doesn't have to leave Nicholas alone or climb the stairs to the tower.

On Avalon Street, I used to be able to hear her rattling around the kitchen, humming, or I'd walk out of my office to find her reading in a chair by the French doors or watering plants on the balcony.

I used to be able to come up behind her, wrap my arms around her, bury my face in her long hair. Slide my hands between the folds of her robe and fondle her gorgeous breasts...

I stop the direction of that thought or I'll end up in the shower again.

After setting my briefcase on the foyer table, I go into the kitchen. Nicholas is at the table in his booster seat, eating cereal and a banana.

"Daddy!" He gives me a wave, his round-cheeked face breaking into a smile.

"Morning, buddy." I stop to ruffle his hair. "Sleep well?"

He nods and holds up a piece of cereal. "Cheerio."

"Yum." I let him put the Cheerio in my mouth, which makes him laugh before he goes back to chewing on the banana.

I return to the kitchen, where Liv is at the stove cooking scrambled eggs. She's wearing her old padded robe, her hair pulled back into a messy ponytail. She turns to smile at me, though her eyes are wary.

"Morning." I press a kiss to her cheek, inhaling her sweet, vanilla scent that goes straight to my blood.

"Morning," she murmurs, lifting a hand to the side of my neck. "Sorry about last night. Again."

"Me too."

After Archer's phone call, he'd brought Nicholas back home, and then our evening shifted into our usual routine revolving around dinner, picture books, and bedtime. Any faint hope I'd had about finishing what Liv and I had started disappeared when I came back from putting Nicholas to bed and found Liv asleep on the sofa.

I rub my cheek against the top of her head. I know my wife. She'd been jacked up hard last night too. I'd felt her body straining and pulsing, the heat of her clenching around me so damn tight...

I step away and look at her. She blinks. Amazing how she can still sometimes look so innocent.

"What?" she asks.

I glance back at Nicholas, who is dropping Cheerios onto the floor. I take Liv's arm and tug her into the living room, away from Nicholas's line of sight.

"Dean, what...oh!"

A shocked gasp catches in her throat as I push her up against the wall and plant my hands on either side of her head, penning her into the cage of my arms. I bring my mouth down on hers— hard and fast. She moans, her lips parting, her hands coming up to clutch the lapels of my jacket. A tremble rocks through her.

I reach for the belt of her robe and yank it open, lifting my head to gaze down at her plain pink nightgown. Her nipples are dark circles against the thin cotton. My cock starts to stiffen again. I grab a fistful of her nightgown and pull it up to expose her hips. She gasps again, twisting toward the kitchen.

"Dean, we can't…"

I push my hand between her legs, edging one finger under her panties. Heat bolts through me. She's wet, still aroused from yesterday.

Liv curls her hand around my wrist, her breath coming faster. "What are you…oh…"

Her eyes glaze with need as she thrusts her hips toward my hand, like she wants me to fuck her with my finger.

Of course she does. Before I fuck her with my cock.

I circle my thumb around her clit, ignoring the lust burning through me. When I feel her start to strain harder, her grip tightening on my wrist, I pull my hand away and tug her nightgown back over her hips.

She stares at me, her breasts rising and falling with the force of her breath. "What…what was that about?"

I put my hands on the wall behind her again, caging her in, and brush my lips gently across hers.

"Still hungry from last night?" I ask in a low voice.

"Oh, yes," Liv says, putting her hand on my chest. "That was so hot and felt so good."

"Have you touched yourself lately, my beauty?"

Her breath catches. "God, Dean."

"Have you?"

"N-no."

I narrow my eyes. "You sure? All that talk about fantasies and buying your sexy little lingerie. You're not diddling your pussy when you're alone, are you?"

"No," she whispers, her brown eyes fixed on mine with both wariness and heat.

"You promise?"

"I promise."

"Good. And you won't either." I slip my hand between her thighs again, over her nightgown, and rub her clit. "I've done a lot of waiting for you, Mrs. West. And I'm getting tired of being left out in the cold. It's about time you learned a lesson about not finishing what you start."

She stares at me, her full lips parted, her breath coming in quick little pants.

"Um...what kind of lesson?" she breathes.

I slide my hand up to squeeze her breast. "A lesson about control."

"Control?"

"Uh huh." I pinch her nipple. "You're not allowed to get me jacked up and leave me unsatisfied anymore. In fact, you're not allowed to do a damn thing unless I say you can."

"Um..." Her slender throat ripples with a swallow. "What does that mean, exactly?"

"You'll find out. In the meantime, you don't think about sex. You don't fantasize about pirates or gladiators or anything else. And you sure as hell don't touch your pretty pussy. Got it?"

Liv nods, her eyes still wide and faintly shocked.

"Good." I push away from her, tugging the folds of her robe closed, my gaze on hers. "Now go make me some bacon, woman."

Without a word, she starts back to the kitchen, pausing only to give me a rather dazed look over her shoulder.

Satisfaction fills my chest. I fucking love a good plan.

CHAPTER 17

DEAN

The abandoned freight and passenger line of the Electric Railroad Company once ran from Mirror Lake to Wessington Springs, South Dakota before it folded due to lack of profits. The tracks are still in place, though overgrown with weeds and brush now, and the Mirror Lake Depot—now fallen into disrepair—is a Gothic Revival, brick building with arched windows and a bell tower.

After parking near the depot, I open the passenger side door for Florence Wickham. As she gets out of the car, Archer's motorcycle rumbles up the road. He comes to a halt, pulls off his helmet, and approaches us.

"Well, I can certainly see the resemblance," Florence says brightly, after I introduce her to Archer. "You're brothers through and through, aren't you?"

Archer shrugs, looking away from me to the station. A knot

pulls in my chest because we both know it's not true. We're half-brothers, not brothers "through and through."

"Archer, Liv showed me the chair you painted for the auction." Florence claps her hands. "It's just incredible. I can't thank you enough. I'm thinking of bidding on it for my grandson. Oh, yoo hoo! Mr. Jenkins!"

I look up to see an elderly man emerging from the train shed, which is a wooden barn-like structure a short distance away. Florence waves and smooths down the front of her powder-blue suit.

"Over here, Mr. Jenkins!" she calls.

The old guy shuffles over to us. Dressed in greasy overalls and a hat bearing a Electric Railroad Company logo, he extends his hand and introduces himself as president of the Historic Railroad Association.

"Dean has offered to be the project director," Florence tells him. "He's a professor of medieval history at King's."

"Medieval history?" Mr. Jenkins looks at me askance, as if wondering what the hell a medievalist is doing heading a train restoration project.

I wonder that myself. I don't have the time—or frankly the knowledge—I need to devote to the project, but I also don't want to let Florence down.

"Dean will do an excellent job," Florence tells Mr. Jenkins, patting my chest.

"He'd better," Mr. Jenkins remarks, throwing me a look of warning. "We've been trying to get this place protected for years. Thank heavens for the good Ms. Wickham here, because if the Historical Society hadn't gotten involved, the transportation company would have sold it off to developers. Now we stand a chance of saving it. Don't need any pansy-ass professors mucking things up."

Archer snorts with suppressed laughter.

"I won't muck it up," I assure Mr. Jenkins gravely.

He doesn't look convinced. I'm not either.

"How many trains are there?" Archer asks.

"An old steam engine and a few cars," Mr. Jenkins says, leading us toward the shed. "I'd love to get that engine restored. It'd be a beaut."

"Archer, Dean tells me you're very knowledgeable about engines," Florence says, as Archer takes her arm to help her over a rocky patch of grass. "How to oil them up and all. Get the pistons moving nice and smooth."

"Yeah," he admits. "I know a thing or two."

"Oh, I don't doubt it, my dear." She smiles at him. "I'm just delighted you've agreed to help us."

Archer shoots me a look that tells me he agreed to no such thing. I shrug, like I don't know anything about it.

Mr. Jenkins opens the shed door, and we go inside. An old steam locomotive and train cars loom like monsters in the dim light. The smells of coal, oil, and grease hang in the air.

"Whoa." Archer stops, his eyes widening. "This is incredible. Dude, you need to bring Nicholas to see this."

"I believe the cars were all original to the railway," Florence says. "Isn't that right, Mr. Jenkins?"

"Sure enough."

"You can still see the train numbers." Archer points to the Great Midwest Railway logo and number 3457 on the side of the engine. "Whyte notion of engines based on wheel arrangement."

"You know your trains, son," Mr. Jenkins says, his eyebrows lifting.

Archer starts talking about the engineer he once worked for who taught him how steam engines were classified. Not for the first time, I'm impressed with my brother's knowledge, which proves again that his years on the road shaped him in ways I'd never considered.

We look around more, with Archer and Mr. Jenkins getting deep in conversation about what it would take to fix the engines.

"This is really cool, man," Archer tells me as we leave the shed. "Thanks for bringing me on board."

"Thanks for agreeing to do it."

I'd never imagined Archer and I could find common ground and work on a project together, but maybe this is it. The combination of his mechanical knowledge and my research skills could be a good partnership.

"You remember the bandits from the Castle train robbery?" he asks.

I almost smile. Sometimes our tree house was an Old West train, usually carrying newly minted gold eastward, that we had to defend against masked bandits.

I hadn't remembered the train robberies until now. Makes me wonder how many other memories I haven't managed to preserve. It's easy to look at a dilapidated place like this or the Butterfly House, to imagine restoring a property to its former glory, to see the value in saving it. It's easy for me to look at a historic castle, a cathedral, a fortress, and advocate for its preservation.

It's not so easy to do that with your own life. To know what's worth saving and what's faded enough to let go.

CHAPTER 18

OLIVIA

A lesson about control.

Well, all right then, Professor West. *Teach me.*

Curious thoughts buzz around my mind like bees in a hive as I work my shift at the Wonderland Café. I'm still aroused from both this morning and last night's thwarted lust. And I feel a little raunchy for having lascivious thoughts while I serve heart-shaped jam tarts and cucumber sandwiches to a group of ladies from the Historical Society.

"Thank you, Olivia, my dear," Florence Wickham says. "I'm sorry I missed you at the Historical Society meeting. How are you?"

Horny.

I stifle a laugh as I imagine how the ladies would react if I actually said that. Florence would probably tell me to go right home and put Dean to work.

Except I can't do that. Because I'm not *allowed* to.

A little tingle of excitement goes through me. What on earth *will* I be allowed to do? And when?

I clear my throat and place a tiered tray of tea sandwiches on the table.

"Very well, thank you," I reply. "I hear Dean and Archer are helping you with the railroad."

"Yes, and we're anticipating great things from the auction," Florence says. "Did you ever secure an auctioneer?"

"Didn't I CC you on the email?" I take out my phone and scroll my messages. "Patrick Hartford from Hartford Pharmacy is a licensed auctioneer, but because he's been out of the auction gig for a while, he agreed to do it for a nominal fee."

"Oh, lovely." Florence smiles at me. "What would this town do without you, Olivia?"

Hopefully this town will never have to find out, I think, as I pick up their empty teapot and return to the kitchen. I bring the ladies a fresh pot of Earl Grey and ring up a customer's bill. After I help a couple of teenagers at the counter, my cell phone buzzes with a text.

DEAN: Go into your office and call me.
LIV: I'm working.
DEAN: Do it.

My stomach flutters. As soon as Sheryl returns to staff the front counter, I mutter something about needing to do some "stuff" in the office. I hurry in and lock the door behind me—Allie and I sometimes change out of our work clothes in the office, so she won't wonder why the door is locked. I dial Dean's number.

"I'm here."

"Door locked?" he asks.

"Yes."

"Good. Put your hand between your legs and tell me how wet you are."

I draw in a sharp breath, a shiver raining down my spine. My heart hammers as I slip my hand under my apron and unzip my pants. I'm unfortunately wearing boring cotton underwear, but clearly that has no effect on my arousal.

"God, Dean," I murmur. "So wet. I really was turned on last night…and this morning."

"I know you were." His voice drops an octave. "I'm going to tell you a fantasy, beauty. And when you get home, you strip off your clothes, put on your bathrobe, and lie on the bed with your legs spread. You're going to touch yourself and think about what I'm going to tell you. But you're not allowed to come. Understand?"

My pulse is beating so hard I can hear it in my head.

"Yes," I manage to whisper.

"You're wearing an apron."

An apron?

Since I wear an apron every day, this is not a particularly sexy start. And given Dean's lack of imagination when it comes to fantasies…

"Um, okay," I say, keeping my voice husky. "An apron."

"And nothing else."

"Oh…"

"It's a little red checkered apron with a ruffled hem that just comes to the tops of your thighs and covers your breasts."

Oh my.

Maybe he does have a sexy imagination after all.

"What are you wearing?" I ask.

"You're not allowed to ask questions."

"Oops. Sorry."

"Pay attention. You're only wearing red heels and this little apron that exposes your pretty ass. And you're aroused. Every time you take a step, you feel your clit throbbing and your wetness dripping down your thighs. Your nipples are hard, rubbing against the apron, your breasts bouncing every time you move. You're so tempted to reach under that ruffled hem and touch yourself, but you know that if you do, you won't get fucked.

"And you want to get fucked, beauty. Badly. You want to spread your legs and feel my cock pounding into you. You want to writhe and moan and scream. You want to beg to come, and when I let you, the fucking earth will shake."

"Oh my god, Dean." I grip the desk and close my eyes, sweat breaking out on my forehead. "I'm about to come right now."

"No." His voice steels. "Get back to work."

Seriously?

"Wait," I gasp. "I still have two hours left in my shift."

"I know."

"I'm bringing tea to the ladies of the Historical Society."

"Say hello to them for me," he remarks, his tone now laced with amusement. "Remember what I told you. Be ready. I'll be home at five."

Holy shit.

I stick my phone back into my pocket, trying to compose myself as I walk back out to the kitchen. Figuring I can attribute my flushed skin to the heat of the stove, I manage to get through the rest of my shift with a reasonable degree of composure—even if I do find myself looking at the raw carrots with a perverted interest.

By the time I get home, I'm almost shaking with need. I take off my clothes and pull my robe on over my naked body before stretching out on the bed. Images flood my head of me walking around in the little red apron and heels, the bow tickling my ass, Dean's hot gaze raking over me.

I wonder where we are. Am I working in a bakery? Is he the boss?

Maybe I'm a housekeeper and he's the master of the mansion.

And maybe he catches me stealing a doughnut and decides to punish me by making me strut around half-naked *for his pleasure.*

Ooo. Doughnuts.

Focus, Liv.

I stretch out on the bed, lightly running my hands over my bare thighs through the opening in my robe. I picture myself maybe walking around with a feather duster, dusting Master West's collection of...um, priceless Greco-Roman antiques, when he grabs the duster from me and starts flicking it over my naked body, the feathers tickling my skin...

"Good girl."

Dean's deep voice falls over me. My breath catches as I push up to my elbows, our eyes clashing hot and intense across the room. His tie is loose around his neck, but otherwise he's still fully dressed in charcoal-gray slacks and a navy shirt that fits beautifully over his broad chest and shoulders. I let my gaze wander hungrily down to his groin, where sure enough a heavy, tempting bulge is all too evident.

I lick my lips. He mutters a curse, pulling off his tie.

"Watch it," he growls. "You're also not allowed to seduce me."

"I'm just looking at you."

"You looking at me is a seduction," he says, jerking a thumb toward the door. "Downstairs."

"Downstairs?"

"Go."

I scramble off the bed and pass him in the doorway, making certain to nudge my breasts accidentally against his arm. He frowns.

I hurry downstairs, stopping halfway with the question I can't help asking because it *was* Dean's turn to pick Nicholas up from daycare.

"Where's Nicholas?" I ask.

"With Archer. Who is under the threat of death not to call unless it's a dire emergency."

"Oh." I stifle a giggle. "He must really be wondering what we're up to."

"Kitchen," Dean orders. "Now."

I go into the kitchen, stopping at the sight of a folded, red-checkered apron sitting on the central island along with an array of baking ingredients. There's a pair of red, pointed-toe heels beside the counter.

I pause. "What..."

Dean stops behind me, rubbing his big hands over my ass. "Put on the apron, beauty. And bake me an apple pie."

I turn to stare at him. "You're serious?"

"Never more." Though his expression is stern, amusement flickers in his brown eyes.

"This is your fantasy? For me to bake you a pie half-naked?"

"While I watch," he adds, lifting his hands to fondle my breasts. "If the pie is good, I'll fuck you nice and hard and let you come."

A bolt of heat shoots through me. "And...and if it's not?"

"I'll still fuck you, but you won't be allowed to come."

"Well, that's just mean."

"Better make it a good pie, then."

With that, he sits down on a kitchen chair, crosses his arms, and waits.

And since I really want what's behind door number one, I strip out of my robe—slowly, as his heated gaze rakes over me—and put on the ruffled apron. The skirt is too small, leaving my cleavage exposed on the top and sides, and the little hem barely covers my pussy. I slip my feet into the heels and fasten the thin straps.

I walk over to Dean and turn, flicking the apron strings.

"Could you tie it for me, please?" I ask breathlessly.

I can almost hear his jaw grinding with restraint as he takes the strings and ties a bow right above my bare bottom. Then he gives me a light spank.

"Bake, woman," he orders.

I set to work making the pie crust and peeling apples. And though this is unconventional for us, it's also fun. And pretty smoking hot. Every time I glance at Dean, he's watching me with a smoldering gaze, his muscles leashed with self-control, his erection straining against his fly.

For the fourth time, I drop an apple peel on the floor.

"Silly me." I turn, bending over to pick it up, feeling Dean's gaze on my upturned ass.

I'm sure he's imagining exactly what he wants to do to me. And he was right—with every step, every movement, even rolling out the pie crust, I'm acutely aware of my arousal. My nipples rub against the cotton apron, and I have to fight the urge not to tense my thighs to ease the ache of need.

Apples, cinnamon, nutmeg, sugar, butter. I stir everything up into a nice, creamy mess, load the filling into the pie, and make a quick lattice-work crust before putting the whole creation in the oven.

I close the oven door and glance at Dean. I'm warm not only from arousal, but also the work and heat of the oven.

"It'll take at least an hour to bake," I remark, hoping he'll amend the rules about exactly what needs to happen before we get down to business.

He shrugs. "I can wait."

Of course he can.

With a sigh, I perch on a kitchen stool and drum my fingers on the central island. The clock ticks. I'm not about to risk my pie being anything less than *good*, but I struggle to hold on to my patience as the clock moves at a snail's pace and my body hums with the simmering need for my husband.

I cross my legs. My clit is pulsing. A little tightening of my thighs, and I could totally bring myself off. Dean frowns at me. I swing my leg and smile innocently.

"Believe me, professor," I say. "If I were about to come, you'd know it."

"Indeed I would."

The timer on the oven dings. I hop off the stool and hurry over to take the pie out, pleased that the crust is golden-brown, the filling bubbly and soft.

"Perfection!" I set the pie on a rack.

Dean pushes to his feet and approaches me. "So far so good."

"Well, now you have to wait for it to cool," I say.

He scowls. Hah. Two can play at this game.

But because I don't want to play for much longer, I get out a plate and cut a slice of pie after only a few minutes of cooling time. The steam smells heavenly, curling up from the apples in little whorls of sweetness and spice.

I fork up a generous portion of filling and crust, glancing at Dean as I purse my lips and blow on the pie to cool it further. He lets out his breath, his gaze on my mouth. I hold the forkful of pie out to him. He takes the bite and chews, his expression growing thoughtful, like he's one of those chef judges on a cooking competition show.

Finally he swallows and says, "It's not good."

My heart sinks. "It's not?"

"No." He advances, backing me toward the counter. "It's delicious."

Before I can respond, he plants his hands on the counter behind me and pushes me right up against it, his mouth coming down on mine in a kiss of swift, hot possession.

I melt, gripping the front of his shirt, my lips parting on a moan. He shoves his erection against me, the heat of his stiff flesh burning through his trousers. I fall into him, tasting apples, sugar, and Dean, my head spinning with lust and love.

He grasps my waist, lifting me onto the counter and moving between my spread legs. I slide my hands over his shirt, my fingers trembling as I unfasten the buttons slowly. To my embarrassment, I can't remember the last time I undressed my husband.

Has it really been *that* long?

"Oh, you're so gorgeous," I breathe, sliding my hands over the sculpted planes of his chest and abdomen, down to the tantalizing line of hair leading right into his trousers.

I unbuckle his belt and slide it off, leather rasping against cloth. His breathing quickens. I smile and stroke downward, cupping the bulge pressing against the front of his trousers. I lean in and press my lips against the warm hollow of his throat.

"How am I doing with keeping control?" I whisper.

"Not bad, beauty." His voice is thick with growing lust. He lowers his head, his sandpapery cheek scraping deliciously against mine as he kisses my neck. "Now let's see if I can make you lose it."

Before I can start unfastening his trousers, he slips his hand between my thighs, his fingers delving into my cleft with easy assurance. He knows exactly how and where to touch me, and before long I'm panting and writhing against the pressure of his hand.

I spread my legs wider, squirming to the edge of the counter so I can hook my legs around him. He slips his other hand up to cup my breast over the material of the apron, his thumb flicking my nipple. Sparks fly through me.

Dean moves away only long enough to unfasten his trousers. He shoves them and his boxers down, and my mouth goes dry at the sight of his long, stiff cock poking out from under the hem of his open shirt.

I close my hand around him, my sex clenching at the thought of all that hard flesh filling me. I slide my hand up and down a few times, brushing my thumb over the damp head in the way I know he likes. He moves closer, positioning himself, and my breath catches as he begins a slow, tight entry into me.

"Ah, fuck, Liv…"

His breath stirs the tendrils of hair at my temple. When he's fully inside me, he stops, tightening his grip on my hips. Urgency scorches me from the inside out. I flex my hands on his arms, aching to feel him pump deep inside me.

"Hurry," I whisper, my head filling with the fog of desire, the eucalyptus scent of Dean's shaving soap mixing with the lingering scents of apples and cinnamon.

He presses his lips in a line over my cheek to my mouth, his tongue flickering out to taste my lower lip.

"You want it?" he murmurs, his voice husky.

"Oh, yes…"

"How badly?"

"So badly," I say against his lips, tightening my legs around him. "God, Dean, I had no idea baking you a pie would turn me on this much."

A smile tugs at his mouth, his eyes filled with heat. "Imagine what'll happen when I order you to bake me a cake."

"I'll come before I get the damned thing out of the oven," I gasp, shivering when he slips his hand between my thighs to my clit.

"Wider," he says.

He drags me to the very edge of the counter, half sliding out of me before driving back in, so powerfully that I cry out. I part my legs wider, and he thrusts so deep I feel the jolt all the way to my core. The world around us dissolves, replaced by hot breath, deep thrusts, and the rhythmic cadence of our movements that we still fall into so easily.

"Dean…" My voice is strained tight, like a wire about to snap. "I'm going to…I want…"

"Come on, beauty," he murmurs, his voice rough against my ear. "Come all over my cock. Let me feel it…good and hard."

I moan, squeezing my eyes shut, feeling my body climbing toward the explosion of pleasure I haven't experienced in too long. The instant the pressure breaks, Dean's mouth descends on mine, his tongue sweeping across my lips as light bursts through my body.

Bliss consumes me, a combination of freedom and a renewed anchoring of myself to my husband. I cry out his name, clenching around his shaft as he plunges into me again.

"Do it," I gasp, gripping his shoulders. "Come inside me. I want to feel you."

He clutches my hips, slowing his pace to a long, hard glide in the instant before he comes with a heavy groan. The sensation of him filling me elicits a new wave of pleasure.

Gasping, I fall against him, pressing my forehead to his chest as we struggle to catch our breath. A sheen of sweat dampens my skin, the scent of sex rising from our bodies.

I shiver, pressing my thighs together as Dean slips out of me and reaches for a napkin to clean us both up. He gives me a lazy, satisfied smile—so beautiful with a flush cresting his sharp cheekbones, his dark hair messy, his eyes warm and sated.

Without letting go of me, he turns and takes a chunk of apple from the pie and holds it to my lips. I open my mouth and accept the warm, sugary slice, redolent with cinnamon.

"I love you," I breathe.

"I'm really glad to hear that, beauty." He lowers his head to kiss me, his mouth sweet and sticky. "Because you're the apple of my pie."

I smile and wind my arms around his neck to deepen the kiss.

The phone rings.

Dean tightens his grip on me. "You are not allowed to answer that."

"Good, because I don't want to." I slide my tongue across his lower lip.

The machine clicks on. A man's voice breaks into my haze.

"Liv, it's Roger Jameson calling about the Airstream trailer you were looking at for your party truck. I think I can work out a deal for you. Give me a call if you're still interested."

I suppress a flicker of interest and concentrate on kissing my husband, but the intrusion of the call has cooled our heat. With a resigned sigh, Dean pulls slightly away from me.

"Now you're taking on another project?" he asks.

"Allie and I have been talking about it for awhile. A birthday party truck that—"

"Yeah, you told Archer. And Archer told me."

"Well, he offered to do the engine work, if we can find a used pick-up," I explain. "We have enough for a deposit, but we're also hoping for a loan to help buy the trailer. Except I'll have to increase the amount to include the restoration."

"And who's going to do the restoration?"

"Allie and I." I wince inwardly at the disapproval flashing over his face. "In our spare time. It'll be cheaper than hiring someone else to do it."

"Liv, for the love of god, would you please let me buy you the truck and hire someone to restore it for you? If you take on one more project, I'm putting my foot down."

I run my hand over his jaw. "Well, I do kind of like it when you put your foot down."

He frowns. "I'm serious."

"So am I."

"Let me buy you the damned truck."

"We already applied for the loan." I shift closer to him, not wanting to remind him that he also just took on a new responsibility as director of the train project. "Besides, even if it does work out, we won't get started until later this summer, and I'll be done with the festival by then. So it's not like I'd be trying to do it *right now* along with everything else."

He doesn't look terribly mollified. I can see him bristling with the urge to argue, but to his credit, he only gives me a grudging nod.

"I'm watching you, Mrs. West," he mutters. "And I'll give you this one, but it's clear you haven't yet learned your lesson."

"Maybe I need a time out." I slide my hand down his muscular torso. "A big, thick, *long* time out…"

Renewed heat flares in his eyes as he lowers his head to slant his mouth across mine. Cinnamon, sugar, apples, and Dean. Again, I let the rest of the world fall away.

CHAPTER 19

DEAN

$\mathcal{T}$here's one thing better than a good plan. A good plan that *works.*

And though I haven't yet devised a plan for getting Liv to let me buy the birthday party truck, my other plans are working out very well. So well, in fact, that I divide my time during the next few days between fielding ideas from architects and seismologists about how to stabilize the monastery and thinking of ways to keep my wife hot and needy.

This is not, as it turns out, nearly as much of a disconnect as one would imagine.

I plan another erotic encounter, breaking up the day by calling Liv a couple of times and warning her not to touch herself. I swear, the order alone gets her going, like she's been told she can't have a bite of a fresh-baked cookie—tempting, mouth-watering, and off-limits.

"Are you in your office?" I ask, lowering my voice an octave.

"Yes." The word comes out on a breathless sigh that makes my dick twitch. "Are you?"

"Uh huh. Door's locked?"

"Just a sec." A pause fills the line before she says, "It is now. I'm working on payroll."

I can see her sitting at her desk, her eyes starting to darken with need, her skin flushed and lips parted. She's wearing a purple Wonderland Café apron, but beneath that her nipples are pressing against her white shirt, and any minute now she'll start to squirm...

"Unbutton your shirt," I tell her.

There's a rustling noise beneath the sound of her breath. "All the way?"

"Just enough so you can reach into your bra and fondle your breasts."

"God, Dean."

"Do it."

A small moan escapes her, followed by heavy silence.

"You'd better not be touching your pussy," I remark.

"I'm...I'm not. But I want to so badly." She pulls in a breath. "We're working with this band called Slice of Pie for the festival, and I was listening to some of their songs earlier so we could come up with a playlist and—"

"You're really not allowed to talk about work."

"No, this isn't about work...I mean, I was listening to this song about *cherry pie, in the sky, hoping it will drop from high, juicy and hot, gimme a lot*...and oh my god, Dean, it's so wrong but I was getting incredibly aroused thinking of baking you a cherry pie and imagining what you'd do with all that sweet, drippy filling..."

Hmm. Now I know what she's baking for me this weekend.

"And what were you imagining?" I ask.

"What?"

"What would I do with the cherry pie filling?"

"You'd spread it over my nipples and lick it off," Liv says

breathlessly. "And you'd feed me the gooey cherries with your fingers and make me suck them clean. And you'd scoop up spoonfuls and eat them, then kiss me all sticky and hot while you pushed your cock into my pussy…oh…"

I give a muffled laugh, rubbing the front of my pants. Doesn't take much from my wife to get me hard. Just picturing her with pie filling smeared over her round tits, her lips glossy with cherry juice…

Ah, fuck. My dick is starting to throb.

"Take off your panties," I tell Liv.

"What?"

"Reach under your skirt and strip off your panties. Now."

Her breath catches. There's a rustling noise on the other end of the phone before Liv's voice comes through again.

"Okay," she says. "They're off."

"Now go back to work."

"Without any underwear?" She sounds faintly shocked, as if her customers will somehow know she's naked under her skirt.

"Without any underwear." I lower my voice. "I want you to feel your wet pussy rubbing together with every step. I want you to think about spreading your legs for me, taking my cock in, bending over to show me your pretty, naked ass. I want your nipples to be hard for the rest of the day, so you can imagine me sucking them after I rip your clothes off. I want you to think about how fucking good it's going to feel when I plunge inside you deep enough to make you scream."

No response, aside from her heavy, panting breaths. Finally she whispers, "Okay."

Despite my throbbing cock, I can't help grinning. "Okay."

"I love you."

"I love you, beauty. Don't you dare put your panties back on."

I end the call and spend the next few minutes thinking about medieval arms and armor to get my mind off all the dirty things I want to do to my wife *right this second.*

When I have myself under control again, I pull out my cell phone and send Liv a text: *Be good, and I'll fuck you again tonight.*

A response comes a few seconds later: *That would be lovely, dear, but I don't think your wife would approve.*

What the…?

I check the number and groan. I push the call button, a burn of embarrassment crawling up my chest. "Florence, I'm so sorry."

She laughs. "Don't be. You gave me something to…think about."

"This is why I hate texting."

"I believe that was called *sexting*," she replies. "Not that I know anything about that, although Mr. Jenkins did send me a message about engine drivers the other day."

"If he's hitting on you, let me know and I'll set him straight."

"Actually, if you could give him some pointers, I'd be most grateful," Florence replies rather wistfully. "I asked him to come over one evening to discuss tie plates, but he refused because he didn't want to miss the early bird special at the World Buffet."

"Does he already have a girlfriend?"

"Seriously, Dean? You think a man that clueless has a girlfriend? He clearly lost his game along with most of his hair."

"So why do you want to go out with him?"

"He's a widower who was married for forty-three years," she replies. "He likes to garden, doesn't talk too much, and has a hobby to occupy his time so he won't get on my nerves. Speaking of which, have you contacted engineers about the train restoration yet? Or gotten blueprints?"

I curse inwardly and scribble a reminder to myself on a notepad.

"Not yet," I tell Florence. "I'll get to it soon."

"Let me know as soon as you do," she replies. "I'll speak with you later, Dean. Tell Liv she's a lucky girl, though I'm sure she already knows that."

After we say goodbye and end the call, I turn to my computer and hammer out a few emails to railroad associations. I should be working on a paper about feudal social relationships, but I spend two hours looking for information about engine restoration, the details of which I don't understand anyway.

By late afternoon, I'm ready to get away from my desk. I grab my duffle bag with the intention of going to the gym. Instead I find myself driving to Archer's garage.

He's crouched beside a Harley, checking the tires. He glances up when my shadow falls over him.

"Hey, man." He stands and reaches for a greasy rag. "What're you doing here?"

"You want to go out for a beer?"

"With you?"

"Yeah, with me." Discomfort flickers in my chest. "Who else?"

"Uh, sure." Archer tosses the rag aside and jerks his thumb toward the office. "Just gotta finish a few things."

I follow him into the office and sit on the worn sofa, noticing the half-eaten sub sandwich on the desk.

"You remember those weird sandwiches you used to like?" I ask. "Swiss cheese and ketchup. Peanut butter and mayo."

Archer chuckles, his attention on the computer. "I was a weird kid."

"I was a ten-year-old expert on the Crusades and King Arthur," I remind him. "That didn't make for great small talk with other kids on the soccer field."

"You never had a problem with anyone."

Except me.

The unspoken words hang in the air. Though Archer and I have patched things up, we've never talked much about the old slings and arrows that broke apart our relationship in the first place—the fight when I told him our father wasn't Archer's *real* father.

It's a memory still corroded with regret. I'll never know how different things would have been if I hadn't revealed the secret my mother wanted desperately to keep. If Archer hadn't discovered he wasn't a true West.

Or if he'd known how often I'd wished I was the one with a different father—not because I was ungrateful for what Richard West had done for me, but because I'd never been able to deviate from my set path. Archer had spent his life veering off paths. Making his own.

"Hey, I was doing some research on the steam locomotive." Archer pulls a stack of papers out of a drawer. "Looks like I can order the parts from a dealer in Tennessee. He also put me in touch with an engineer who built one of the engines."

Relief rises in me as I take the papers. "That's great, man, thanks. I didn't know where to start with the engine stuff."

I look through the papers as Archer finishes his work, then goes into the other room to change.

Again, not for the first time, I wonder if things would have been different if my brother had followed his mechanical inclinations toward engineering or a white-collar job that would have made our father proud. Then I think there was probably little Archer could have done to make our father proud—through no fault of his own.

"Where should we go?" He comes out of the backroom, pulling a T-shirt over his head. "I could go for some food too."

"Pizza?"

"Always."

We head out to my car, and I drive to a combination pizza parlor and arcade that has both classic and new video games. Wooden tables line the place, filled with teens and older, beer-drinking guys.

I get us a table, and Archer goes to the counter to order. He returns with two beers and a bag full of tokens.

"Challenge," he says, sliding into the booth across from me. "Lowest overall score buys the tokens, pizza, and beer."

"Challenge accepted." I click my bottle against his.

ADORE   185

When the pizza arrives, we divide it up and eat. Thankfully, our conversation isn't as strained as I'd thought it would be. Archer and I can still talk about sports, cars, politics, and music, even if we have different opinions.

"Hey, I'm taking Nicholas to the downtown fire truck parade next weekend," I tell him, reaching for another slice of pizza. "They let the kids sit in the trucks at the end of the parade. You want to go with us?"

"Sure, but only if I get to turn on the siren."

I grin. "I'll make arrangements."

He grabs the jar of pepper flakes and shakes some onto his pizza. "Liv hear anything about the loan for the party truck?"

I shake my head, still not liking the idea of her tackling a new venture right now—and not liking that I don't like it. Much as I want to support everything Liv wants to do, I'll be damned if our marriage is going to get derailed because she can't keep her mind off one project or another.

"I have a lead on another pickup they could use," Archer says. "I'll check it out before Kelsey and I go to Texas."

"Thanks. When do you leave?"

"After the festival. Liv asked me to help out at the children's stage, and Kelsey is organizing the art booths. What did you get roped into?"

"Nothing yet. I'll probably hang out with Nicholas." I take another swallow of beer. Don't know if it's the alcohol or what, but I say, "So Kelsey said you want to marry her."

Archer's jaw tightens. "Yeah."

"She's independent," I say. "Likes to run her own show."

"You don't need to tell me anything about my girl," Archer says. "I know her."

"She tell you why she doesn't want to get married?"

"Just that everything's so great...which it is...that she doesn't want it to change." He shrugs. "Makes no sense. She drives into storms, man. She travels all over the country. Hell, all over the world. She studies tornados, which are always changing."

"Maybe that's it," I suggest. "When everything else changes, her relationship with you doesn't. Security, you know?"

Archer doesn't respond. A shadow crosses his face, one I recognize all too well. The lingering sense that he's still not good enough for a woman like Kelsey March.

"Let's do it." He pushes his bottle away and grabs the bag of game tokens. "Pac-Man first. You're going down."

We spend the next couple of hours moving from one video game to the next, breaking only for more beer before firing at asteroids, speeding down a NASCAR track, battling street fighters, and dodging Donkey Kong. I keep track of our scores in my notebook, which makes Archer laugh.

We return to our table to finish the cold pizza. After I tally our scores, I push the notebook across to Archer with a grimace.

"You win by eight hundred points," I say. "Centipede put you over the top. I never did like that game."

"Excuses, excuses." He tears the page out of the notebook and puts it in his pocket. "Souvenir. I can't remember the last time I beat you at a game, so I'll take what I can get."

We clink our bottles. I glance at my watch.

"I should go in about half an hour," I say. "I told Liv I'd be home by nine. She took Nicholas to a kids' concert at the museum."

"So how's it been?" Archer asks, chewing on a stale crust of pizza. "Parenting."

I wonder if he wants me to tell him it's incredible, phenomenal, all that I dreamed it would be. In some ways, it is. In other ways, not so much.

I pick at the label on my beer bottle and don't answer.

"Dean?"

"Sometimes it's great," I finally admit. "Other times it's tough. Or it's even great and tough at the same time."

Archer remains silent, like he's waiting for me to continue.

"I mean, Nicholas is amazing," I say. "And Liv is an incredible mother. It's fucking insane how much I love them. There's stuff that's beyond anything, like Nicholas saying 'Daddy' for the first time or taking his first steps, or watching him laugh. Times like that I feel like even if I had a million hearts, it still wouldn't be enough."

I continue picking at the label. The noise of the video games drifts from the arcade.

"But?" Archer asks.

"Man, it's rough sometimes." I shake my head. "When he's tired or cranky and can't tell you what he wants. Or when Liv and I can't do things the way we used to. Or when Nicholas won't sleep. One time last year he got sick overnight, like burning up with a fever and having trouble breathing, and he ended up in ICU.

"Longest night of my life. I started imagining what might happen to him, and I wouldn't be able to do anything about it. It was so fucking terrifying. Then when we knew he'd be okay, I almost hit the floor with relief."

I concentrate on peeling the label off the bottle, not sure where this is all coming from, but not regretting that I'm telling my brother.

"I fell in love with Liv fast," I say. "Hard too, like *bam*. And I figured that was enough, like I didn't need or want anything else for the rest of my life. I'd won the lottery. All I needed was her.

"Then we had Nicholas, and suddenly there are two people in the world I can't protect from everything bad. I can't fix all their problems, right all the wrongs done to them, always make it better. And no matter how often I tell myself it's not rational to want all that, I still do. I always will. But I have to live with the fact that I can't. And that sucks."

I sit back, sweeping the litter of paper on the table into a pile. Then I shake my head, embarrassed by the confession.

"You remember when Liv had the miscarriage?" Archer asks. "And you had it in your head I'd upset her in some way?"

Shame scorches my chest. "I remember. Sorry, man. I was messed up."

"Yeah. But I got it. Why you'd think that, I mean. Why you expected me to screw up or didn't trust me. I worked hard at baiting you my whole life. I wanted you to think the worst of me because it was what I thought of myself. Until I met Kelsey."

I glance at him. He's staring at his bottle, his forehead creased.

"It's the same thing," he says. "I thought she was all I'd need. But I want more. I want to give her everything, you know?"

"Yeah. I know."

"But what do you do when the woman you love doesn't want everything?" Archer asks.

"You wait."

"Wait?"

"Until she's ready."

"Well, how do you know how long that'll be?"

"You don't," I say. "But you wait anyway. You wait for as long as it takes because you know there's no other choice."

I get up from the booth and take out my wallet, dropping a few bills onto the table.

"And I promise you, Archer," I say. "The wait will give you the biggest damned prize of your life. And you'll know you'd do it again, a thousand times over. You'd wait longer than an eternity for her. That's how *worth it* she is."

CHAPTER 20

OLIVIA

Yes!

I'm making a comeback. I'm like Cher in the 1990s. I'm Martha Stewart after she got out of prison, and Justin Timberlake after he left NSYNC. I'm the Boston Red Sox in the ninth inning of the 2004 World Series.

I am *on top.*

Or, in this case, being on the bottom is just fine with me too. Not even work or a fancy job opening can deter Professor and Mrs. West from getting their groove back, good and hard. *With apple pie.*

I hum a little tune as I get breakfast ready a few days after our hot kitchen encounter and Dean's continued *lessons*, which have me on edge pretty much all the time now. Between that and remembering how it felt to sit on the counter and let him drive into me…I shiver. My heart thumps.

Oh, yeah. I still got it. Hot mama. Yummy mummy. MILF.

"B'nana!" Nicholas calls from the table.

My little fantasy breaks apart. "Just a sec."

I grab a banana and slice it in half, removing the peel as I bring it to the table and set it on Nicholas's plate. Dean left for campus early this morning, which is sort of a bummer since Nicholas is scheduled for daycare this morning. I could have dropped him off, then come back home and...

"Oat," Nicholas remarks, digging into his cinnamon oatmeal.

A bolt of embarrassment hits me as I gaze at my beautiful, innocent son.

Good heavens, what kind of mother am I for being anxious to drop my kid at daycare so I can get sexy with my husband?

This isn't an issue they've covered in Mommy and Me class.

I sit down and help Nicholas scrape up the last of his oatmeal before I get us both ready for the day. After running errands in the morning and working the afternoon shift at the café, I grab a takeout salad for dinner and head to City Hall to meet with the festival planning committee.

Things are falling into place, with Edison Power still reviewing my package for a high-level sponsorship, the food vendors secured, and the art booths organized.

I have a short list of things I'm going to ask Dean to help with. I'm happy about the idea that he and I will be doing something together that will benefit the town. We've always worked together for each other, our son, our marriage, and we restored the Butterfly House together, but we've never worked together for a greater cause, as it were.

It's close to eight by the time the meeting wraps up, and I drive back to the Butterfly House. The porch lights are on, but the house is dark.

I go inside and turn on the kitchen lights. There's a white covered box on the central island, with a note beside it.

BEAUTY'S ORDERS

Put these on. Come to the bar at the Wildwood Inn and await further instructions.

P.S. Nicholas is with Archer and Kelsey. He has Binky Bear, a million building blocks, and a double-chocolate brownie. He might not want to come home.

I smile and pull the lid off the box. Nestled in tissue paper is a black lace baby doll edged with purple ribbon, sheer thigh highs, a black G-string, three-inch black pumps, and...a long beige raincoat.

I stare at the items in confusion for a second before shock hits me.

I'm supposed to put these on and go meet Dean at a hotel bar *wearing nothing else.*

How wrong.

How wicked.

How *scandalous.*

Excitement ripples down my spine.

I've never been scandalous before. Heck, I've never even been risqué, unless you count the time Dean and I got hot and heavy on the seventeenth-floor balcony of an LA high-rise. Of course, the chances of anyone seeing us at that height were slim, but still, it was definitely a sexual adventure.

And while Dean's and my sex life has always—*mostly*—been fantastically satisfying and explosive, we've never swung from the chandeliers, experimented with exotic sex toys, played kinky games...

Well, then. Maybe we should start.

My heartbeat kicks up a notch. I can't imagine it.

Olivia West—thirty-three years old, the mother of a toddler, a respectable businesswoman and owner of a birthday party café, planner of the Mirror Lake Bicentennial Festival—getting kinky with her husband.

On the other hand... Why not?

Adventure awaits, right? This is certainly an adventure.

I grab the bag and hurry up to the bedroom. I take a quick shower and rub lotion all over my body before slithering into the skimpy panties, black stockings, and baby doll, which pushes my breasts together into a plump, deep cleavage before draping over my hips to the tops of my thighs.

Nice.

I brush my hair until it shines, leaving it loose around my shoulders because that's the way Dean likes it. I apply more dramatic makeup than usual—smoky eyeshadow, red lipstick, black mascara—and slip into the black heels.

I go back downstairs to put on the raincoat. As I belt it around my waist, a wave of anxiety crashes over me.

No way. I can't do this. What if I get a flat tire or a speeding ticket and have to deal with a police officer? Even if I do make it to the bar safely, I can't sit there in a raincoat, knowing I'm half-naked underneath.

Or can I?

I take a deep breath and check my phone. No message from Dean, but a text from Kelsey appears. *N's playing drums w/Archer. Movie later. He's having a ball. Enjoy your night w/o worry.*

I send her a quick thanks and tuck the phone into my purse. I give myself a firm nod in the mirror. Sure, I'm a mother, a businesswoman, festival coordinator, member of a mom's group, et cetera...but I'm also a *wife*.

More specifically, Dean West's wife.

As I drive downtown to the Wildwood Inn, I remember the storm of emotions rolling through me when Dean and I got married. Excitement, overwhelming love, joy, pride, astonishment—and a deep, abiding certainty that every part of my life had been leading me right to the moment when Dean closed his hand around mine and told me he would never let go.

But I'd already known that. I'd known since the instant his fingers brushed the sleeve of my ratty gray sweatshirt the day we met. Once Professor Dean West takes hold of you, he doesn't let go.

I pull into the hotel parking lot and spend about five minutes gathering my courage before I get out of the car. It's a little chilly out, so at least the coat isn't completely out of place.

I walk to the hotel entrance, making sure my belt is double-knotted and the coat is buttoned up to my neck. The doorman smiles at me and opens the door.

My stomach tightens with nerves. The lobby is hushed and quiet, a few guests sitting in the carpeted area near the oak staircase. Across from the reception desk, voices rise from the bar—an elegant, Old World-style room with stained-glass windows, plush chairs and couches, and glittering lamps.

I am not accustomed to frequenting such stylish places alone —much less wearing nothing but sexy lingerie under my coat— but I straighten my shoulders and enter the bar like I know exactly what I'm doing.

I look around quickly, hoping to spot Dean seated in one of the intimate, shadowed booths or at least waiting for me at the bar. He's nowhere to be seen.

I glance at my watch. It's nine-fifteen. Dean didn't give me a specific time to be here, though I can't imagine he'd expect it to be much later than this. In our normal routine, we do tend to be in bed by ten…sleeping.

But this is hardly our normal routine.

I walk to the bar, my heels clicking against the hardwood floor. Well-dressed patrons sit at the tables, sipping fancy cocktails, their conversations punctuated by low laughter.

I maneuver onto a barstool as the surfer-boy handsome,

blond bartender glides over to place a napkin in front of me. He smiles, his teeth as white as peppermints.

"Good evening, miss," he remarks. "You can leave your coat at the front rack, if you'd like."

A blush scorches my face.

"That's okay." I give him a bright smile. "I'm a bit chilly."

"A drink to warm you up, then?" he asks, letting his gaze slip over me.

I figure I'd better limit my alcohol intake. Even though I'm not sure what Dean has planned, I do know I want to be entirely lucid for it.

"Club soda with lime," I say. "Or can you make me something without too much alcohol?"

"I can make you anything you want," the bartender replies with a wink. "Should I surprise you?"

"Okay. Just not too much alcohol."

"Are you under twenty-one?"

I laugh. "You're closer to twenty-one than I am."

"I don't know about that." He leans his elbows on the counter. "I'm going to have to see your ID."

I shake my head in amusement, thinking he's joking, but he doesn't move, his gaze holding mine. With a shrug, I dig into my purse for my wallet and show him my driver's license.

"Olivia," he says, studying my license. "Pretty name."

"And plenty old," I add.

"Not so much." He hands my license back. "You're five years older than me. That doesn't make you a cougar."

A bubble of laughter rises into my throat.

"My drink?" I ask.

"Yeah, sorry." He pushes away from the counter. "One low-alcohol surprise cocktail coming up."

Still smiling, I turn to scan the bar again. The clientele is mostly men, though several women in shiny, sheath dresses and elegant gold jewelry sip martinis and cosmopolitans.

No sign of Dean yet. An older gentleman at a corner table catches my eye and raises his glass.

It takes me a second to realize that—aside from being conspicuous as the only woman in the bar wearing a *raincoat*—the coat has parted at the fold, exposing a significant length of my stocking-clad leg.

The man's attention makes me wonder what would have happened if Dean and I had met like this—in a hotel bar with me showing off my assets, rather than outside a university registrar's office with me picking myself up off the sidewalk.

"Professors have a lot of power," he said.

I almost smiled. "Even medieval history professors?"

"Especially medieval history professors," he assured me.

"Knights on horseback and all that?"

A responding smile tugged at his mouth. "And damsels in distress."

Ours wasn't a romance of cocktails and silk sheets. Ours was a romance of library call numbers, coffee cake, rainy weekends, history textbooks, and boring foreign films. *We* might not have happened any other way.

Some things, I think, were clearly meant to be.

A shiver of awareness ripples over my skin.

I glance at the entrance to the bar. My breath catches in my throat. Dean is walking toward me, his stride long and assured, his muscular body sheathed in a navy tailored suit that fits him to perfection.

He's not just in full professor mode; he's in full Dean West mode with his perfectly knotted tie and air of complete authority. Other patrons glance at him as he crosses the room. The overhead lights burnish his hair and cast shadows on the masculine planes of his face.

My heart gives a wild, spinning leap. I turn on the barstool to watch him—my breathtakingly beautiful husband who commands attention like a king holding court, but whose eyes remain unwaveringly fixed on me.

Oh, Dean. I've missed you.

He stops in front of me and extends his hand. "Dean West."

I smile. "Well, I *know* that."

He raises an eyebrow, his hand still extended.

Oh!

"I'm Olivia...Winter." I slip my hand into his. "Pleasure to meet you."

"Olivia Winter." His deep voice envelops my name like dark chocolate spilling over a ripe cherry. "Pretty."

"Thanks." I'm getting a little breathless.

His fingers close around mine in a warm, secure handshake that sends a tingle clear up my arm. The scent of his shaving soap tickles my nose. I slip my hand slowly from his and gesture to the barstool beside me.

"Would you like to sit down?" I ask.

"Only if I can buy you a drink."

"Okay." I glance to the other end of the bar, where the bartender is still making my drink. "I just ordered."

"And so will I." He sits beside me, his sleeve brushing against mine.

My heart thumps with a slow, heavy beat. A hint of nervous excitement winds through me—as if he really is a strikingly handsome stranger whom I know nothing about except that I'm captivated by his presence.

"May I take your coat?" he asks, slanting his gaze over my body.

"Maybe later." I give him a sultry, sidelong glance. "Mr. West."

"You can call me *sir*."

Yes, I most certainly can.

"Maybe later," I murmur. "Sir."

The bartender returns, faltering slightly when he sees Dean sitting beside me.

"Here you go, miss." He sets a pretty, pink drink garnished

with a cherry in front of me. "Grapefruit juice, sparkling wine, a touch of syrup."

"Put it on my tab," Dean says.

"Yes, sir."

"And I'll have a scotch on the rocks."

"Yes, sir." The bartender hurries to get the drink.

"So." I shift, letting the raincoat display a bit more of my stocking-clad leg. "What do you do, *sir*?"

"I'm a venture capitalist and businessman," he replies. "I own an international conglomerate of companies branded under the name the Beauty Group."

"I think I've heard of that."

"We have about five hundred companies," he continues, nodding his thanks as the bartender sets the scotch in front of him. "Travel, multimedia, entertainment, finance, hotels."

"Impressive," I remark. "You must be quite wealthy."

He shrugs, like he can't be bothered to consider his billions-of-dollars net worth.

"And you?" he asks. "What do you do, Miss Winter?"

"I'm an actress."

"Really?" He turns to face me, resting an elbow on the bar. "Stage or screen?"

"Stage, of course." I toss my hair back over my shoulder. "Movies are so pedestrian. Stage acting is so much more intimate and challenging. There's no room for error when you're on stage in front of a live audience."

"Hmm. A risk-taker, are you?"

"Under the right circumstances, I can be."

"Interesting." Dean puts his warm hand beneath my chin, turning my face toward his. "And what are the right circumstances?"

"Maybe…" I glance up at him from beneath my eyelashes. "You, Mr. West."

"Ah." He brushes his thumb across my lips, his eyes gleaming with something dark and dangerous. "Right or wrong, make no mistake, Miss Winter. I'm not a circumstance."

"What are you, then?"

"I'm your goddamned destiny."

He lowers his mouth to mine. All the breath escapes my lungs. But instead of the hot, hard kiss I'd been expecting—*anticipating*—his lips are gentle, caressing, a tease rather than an onslaught.

And yet the effect on me is devastating—my blood goes into full boil, heat pooling in my lower body. By the time Dean lifts his head and eases away from me, I'm dizzy with longing.

"Another drink?" The bartender's voice slices through my haze as he plunks a bowl of salted nuts in front of us.

"Not for me." Dean glances at me, his expression simmering with heat. "Miss Winter?"'

"No." I pull in a breath. "No, thank you."

The bartender nods and walks to the other end of the bar to assist another customer. Dean puts his hand on my thigh beneath the counter and finds the opening of my coat. His fingers brush against my leg, his touch sending heat shooting across my skin.

"So why the raincoat?" he asks, gliding his fingers discreetly up and down my leg. "Is that part of the risk-taking?"

"I…I just came from the theater," I reply, making an effort not to squirm on the barstool. "I'm still in costume."

"What kind of costume?"

"One I can't show a stranger."

"Too sexy?" He moves his hand up my thigh far enough to reach the edge of my stocking.

My breath shortens. Dean slips his fingers into my stocking. His eyes darken with growing heat.

"Too…*slutty*," I murmur.

"Tell me," he orders, easing off the barstool to stand beside me, blocking me from view of the rest of the room.

"It's a black lace baby doll with purple ruffles," I whisper, tensing a little when his hand glides toward my inner thigh.

"It's…well, it's a little tight around my breasts, but I kind of like that because it feels really good on my nipples. And I'm wearing a flimsy little G-string, and thigh-high stockings."

"Hmm." A faint growl rumbles in his chest. "What role were you playing?"

"The wife of a medieval history professor who acts out all her husband's dirty fantasies. It's called *The Secret Life of Professor West*. You should come see it sometime."

"Maybe I will." Amusement sparks beneath the heat in Dean's eyes as he slips his hand between my thighs, urging them slightly apart.

A gasp catches in my throat. I curl my hand around his wrist, glancing nervously past his shoulder to see if anyone notices exactly what we're doing over here.

"You shouldn't do that, sir," I say.

"I'll stop if you unbutton your coat and show me your breasts."

Desire bolts through me, centering in my core. I swallow, tightening my grip on his wrist.

"I don't think I can do that."

"Not all the way. Just a little."

He nudges his groin against my thigh. He's already half-hard. I almost moan aloud, suppressing the urge to slide my hand down the front of his gorgeous suit and cup his growing erection in my hand.

I glance around again to make sure no one else is paying attention to us, then I quickly unfasten a few buttons of the coat to reveal the V of my cleavage. Shielding me with his body, Dean gazes at my breasts with hot appreciation before pressing his mouth close to my ear.

"Are your nipples hard?" he asks, his voice echoing deep inside my blood.

"Yes," I breathe, shifting and trying not to press my legs together.

"And are you wet?" He slides his hand over my thigh.

"God, De...sir."

"Are you?"

"Yes. Oh." I writhe a little on the barstool, my clit pulsing with every beat of my heart. "Wet and...hungry, sir."

He smiles. I half expect him to ease the raincoat open farther and start fingering me, but instead he lowers his mouth close to my ear again.

"You're a bad girl, Olivia Winter," he whispers, his breath stirring the tendrils of my hair. "And you're the hottest, sexiest woman I've ever seen in my life. I'd fuck you right here on the bar if it wouldn't get us arrested."

A shudder rocks through me. I flick my tongue out to lick my dry lips. My nipples are so hard they're starting to chafe against the mesh fabric of my bodice.

"Well," I murmur, "is there somewhere else we could go?"

"I'm in the luxury suite." Dean puts his big, warm hand on the nape of my neck. "But I'll only take you there if you agree to do whatever I say. And I should warn you I'm very demanding."

Demanding.

"I'll do whatever you say, sir."

"Yes, you will."

CHAPTER 21

OLIVIA

*D*ean moves closer, his eyes brewing with lust. "Kiss me, Miss Winter."

Before I can take a breath, his mouth comes down on mine again—this time with possessive force. A thousand fireworks explode inside me, my whole being filling with warmth and love. I lift my hands to the sides of his face as he urges my lips apart and delves his tongue into my mouth. Ah, bliss…

He tastes like scotch and sex. The noise of the bar recedes, the lights fading as the world compresses to the movement of our lips together—a warm, lovely kiss edged with the promise of hot passion.

When Dean lifts his head, we're both breathing heavily, and a faint dizziness washes over me. He brushes his thumb across my lips and puts his hand under my elbow.

I slide off the barstool, shuddering as the pulse between my legs intensifies. Dean straightens the folds of my raincoat and tightens the belt.

I slip my hand into his as we cross the room, and I'm distinctly aware of the glances tossed in our direction. I suppress a giggle at the thought of what these people would think if they knew our true story.

But this *is* our true story. Everything we do is part of our story.

We go into the mirrored elevator, and Dean swipes a key card into the reader. The elevator whisks us to the top floor, the doors gliding open right at the foyer of a fancy suite. He steps aside and ushers me to precede him.

I go into the foyer, inhaling a breath of delight and awe at the sight of the floor-to-ceiling windows that overlook the midnight expanse of the lake and the glittering view of downtown. The furnishings are gorgeously elegant—damask wallpaper, sheer taupe curtains, intricately patterned carpet and plush sofas. A carved open door reveals a huge bed piled with silk, tasseled pillows and a bedspread that looks thick and soft as a cloud.

"Oh, Dean." I stop behind the sofa and turn to face him. "This is incredible."

He smiles, his eyes creasing at the corners as he reaches out to tug a lock of my hair. I expect a tender, loving remark or kiss, but he points to a wing-backed chair facing the high windows.

"Take off your coat, Miss Winter," he says. "And sit in that chair."

My heart thumps. Despite his warm gesture, *Mr. West's* iron-clad sense of command is fully intact. And I'm suddenly a little nervous because…well, he's *"very demanding."*

I step away from him, my breath shortening as I walk to the chair. The windows glow with both exterior and interior light, and I can see our hazy reflections in the glass. I stop by the chair and turn to face Dean, who is standing with his arms crossed and his expression unreadable.

I tug at the knot of the raincoat and push it off my shoulders to reveal the skimpy little baby doll that barely covers my breasts and the scrap of lace panties. His gaze rakes over me, slow and heavy.

"Slutty indeed," he remarks.

I curl my hand around the back of the chair, shifting my legs a little because the throb of arousal is becoming more acute with every passing second.

"The outfit maybe," I say, blinking at him. "But really, I'm quite innocent."

A smile quirks his mouth. "Yes, I can tell, Miss Winter. Sit down, please."

I turn and sit in the chair, resisting the urge to squirm again. I can see my reflection in the window, surrounded by the elegant furnishings—my hair long and loose around my shoulders, my body newly sexy in the lacy lingerie and thigh-highs, my feet still clad in the black fuck-me heels. The intimidating, dark shadow of Mr. West behind me.

I shiver. Goosebumps prickle my skin. He approaches, his steps silent on the plush carpet, his tall figure moving ever closer. I watch him in the reflection of the window before he moves to stand in front of me.

My mouth goes dry as I find myself staring at the intimidatingly large erection pressing against the front of his trousers. A fire burns low in my belly, spreading heat outward into my blood. I reach up to touch him.

Before I can, he grabs my wrist.

"No," he says, his voice deep and soft. "You don't get to touch me unless I say you can."

Though I'm not at all certain I can obey that order—after all, touching this man's incredible, muscular body is one of my most favorite pastimes—I nod in agreement. He releases my wrist and reaches into his pocket, producing a length of red silk. Before I can ask what he intends to do with it, he wraps one end around my right wrist.

"Dean, what..."

He shakes his head and loops the silk around the chair arm, then the back, before bringing it around to my left wrist. Next thing I know, I'm lashed to the chair, the silk gentle but secure around my wrists. I move my arms experimentally. There's very little give in the fabric.

"Where did you learn to tie knots like this?" I ask.

He catches my eye for half a second and winks. "Boy Scouts."

Of course.

He reaches into his left pocket and removes another length of purple silk. This time I don't have to ask what he intends to do with it, but my heart stutters when he places the cloth against my eyes and ties it at the back of my head. The world becomes darkness, and a faint fear rises.

Dean spreads his hands over the top of my head, the strong weight of his palms like a beatification.

"Okay?" he asks.

I take a breath and nod. He waits for a minute more, as if ensuring I'm not on the verge of real fear, before slipping his hands away. His lips touch my forehead in a warm, reassuring kiss. Then cooler air fills the space in front of me, and I know he's gone.

My nipples are still so hard, chafing against my bodice, my breasts full and exquisitely sensitive. I wait. And listen, straining my ears for a hint of what Dean might be up to. But all I can hear is the sound of my own breath, quick and heavy in rhythm with the beat of my heart.

He returns, the heat of his presence tangible in the space between us. I arch forward a bit, tensing with anticipation. Then something sticky and sweet-smelling brushes across my lips.

"Open," he commands.

I open my mouth. He slips something inside, and my tongue floods with the taste of sugar and gooey fruit. Cherry pie.

"Mmm." I bite down on the soft cherry, which is almost overwhelmingly sweet and tart, as if my sense of taste is heightened to acute levels since I can neither see nor move. I'm suddenly ravenous for more.

Dean's finger brushes against my lower lip, as if he's wiping away a sticky trace. "Want another?"

"Yes, sir."

"Open."

I open my mouth. He feeds me another cherry. The sweet, sugary flavor goes straight to my blood. Another bite has a bit of crust attached, the flaky pastry a delicious contrast to the gooey filling.

"More?" he asks.

"Yes, please." I think I could eat the whole pie. I *want* to eat the whole pie.

I scoot forward to the edge of the chair and open my mouth. This time when he slides a cherry past my lips, I close my mouth quickly so I can suck the juices from his finger.

He breathes out a mild curse and pulls his finger from my mouth with a pop.

"Behave, Miss Winter," he warns.

I smile innocently, wishing I could see the expression on his face. He holds another cherry to my mouth. I eat a few more offerings before something different nudges at my lips.

And I'm so awash in the taste and deliciousness of cherry pie that it takes me a second to realize it's the smooth, tight head of Dean's cock.

I gasp. "Mr. West!"

"It's bigger than a cherry," he remarks.

I stifle a laugh, my heart hammering at the thought of sucking his cock without being able to touch or see him. For a second, I'm not sure I can do it, but overwhelming that uncertainty is the deep, abiding wish to do whatever he commands, to *obey*.

I inhale a deep breath and open my mouth. His hands settle on the sides of my head, his fingers tightening against my scalp as he pushes slowly forward.

Oh, god...

I have no frame of reference, nothing else to focus on except the aching throb between my legs, the silk tied around my wrists, and the glide of my husband's cock into my mouth. I moan, wanting desperately to reach up and touch him, but all I can do is sit here and take him in.

He pauses, his breath rasping above me. I swallow and move my head forward to indicate it's okay for him to go deeper.

And he does. Filling my mouth. The taste of him mingles with the sweet cherry juice still lingering on my tongue. I slacken my throat muscles and close my eyes behind the blindfold.

When he starts to thrust, I'm ready for him, loving the sensation of him pumping gently in and out of my mouth. His restraint is palpable, as it always is, his care not to thrust too deep, but this time—maybe for the first time—I don't want him to be gentle.

I start to ease back, and he pulls out at the same instant.

"I don't..." I swallow and lick my lips. "I don't want you to be gentle, Mr. West."

"You don't, huh?"

"Not this time." I squirm, wishing he would touch my breasts, rub my nipples. "I want you to fuck my mouth."

A groan rumbles above me. "You're sure?"

"Yes. *Please.*"

His hands tighten on my hair as he pushes forward again. Then the length of his cock is in my mouth as deeply as I can take him. He's still gentle at first before urgency coils palpably through his body and his thrusts increase in pace.

My blood fires with bolts of heat as I sit there, hot and dripping, unable to do anything but suck the cock driving in and out of my mouth.

Dean's breath is heavy and harsh, his fingers gripping my head tightly. I struggle to take him in deeper, breathing through my nose, my wrists straining against the bonds lashing me to the chair.

When he pulls away from me, releasing his hold, a sudden bereftness and fear sparks in my belly.

"Dean?"

"Right here." He puts his hand on the side of my neck, the gesture both reassuring and welcome. "Okay?"

I nod and squeeze my thighs together, desperate to feel him pushing into me down there, so thick and hard…

"Wait," he says, lifting his hand from my neck.

I wait again, forcing my breathing to slow. Then he's in front of me, his hand slipping under my chin. The cool edge of a glass touches my lips.

I open my mouth. The crisp, sparkly flavor of champagne spreads over my tongue. I gulp it down too fast, and a trickle spills down my chin to my neck.

With a soft laugh, Dean lowers his head, his faint stubble scraping my skin as he licks up the stray drops. The touch of his tongue creates a warm, swirling pool of desire in my lower body.

His lips brush against mine. I draw in a breath of relief when our mouths press together in a hot, familiar kiss that reminds me exactly why I've always been so willing, so eager, to let this man alone take me places I've never been before.

The kiss deepens, shifting from familiarity to an edgy lustfulness as he slips his hand down to cup my breast. He grabs the straps of my baby doll and tugs them over my arms, baring my breasts.

I shiver—even though I can't see, I feel his gaze traveling over my body like a touch. I wiggle a little, spreading my thighs in the hopes that he'll slip his fingers into my pussy and stroke me in the expert, precise way of his that makes me crazy with need—

He moves to work the knots of the silk ties. I swallow my questions about what's going to happen next. He doesn't remove the blindfold, instead lifting me up into his arms as if I'm light as a feather.

I wrap my arms around his shoulders and my legs around his waist, loving the solid strength of his body as he carries me across the room. His shirt is smooth and soft against my bare skin. For some reason, the thought of him still fully dressed while I'm half-naked and clad only in skimpy lingerie is shockingly arousing. A few seconds later, he lowers me onto the bed, the comforter plush and pillowy beneath my half-naked body.

"Don't move," he instructs, and he spreads my arms out to fasten the silk around my wrists again—this time, it seems, tying the other ends to the bedposts.

I shift, tugging experimentally at the cloth again, but the knots are as tight as they were before.

"Christ in heaven," he whispers, his voice guttural. "You have no idea how fucking sexy you are."

My pulse hammers. I can imagine how I look—disheveled and blindfolded, my lingerie pushed to my waist to expose my breasts, my messy hair falling in a tumble over the pillows, my skin sweaty, and my inner thighs damp with arousal. I turn my head toward the sound of Dean's voice, wanting the reassurance of his touch.

The bed shifts with his weight. He touches my thigh, the edge of his sleeve brushing against my skin.

"I'm going to fuck you now, Olivia," he says, his deep voice a wash of heat. "And you're going to take my cock as deep as you can, over and over again. You're going to twist and flex your gorgeous body as I pound into your sweet pussy. You're going to scream, moan, and beg for more...and if you're good, I'll give you more. Are you ready?"

My mouth is so dry that for a second I can't even answer. I manage to nod, straining toward him.

"Please," I gasp. "Sir. *Now.*"

A faint chuckle rumbles from his chest. The mattress shifts again as he moves, his fingers adept as he strips off my panties. There's the sound of rustling cloth before he slides his hands against my inner thighs and spreads my legs apart. Obediently, I lift my knees.

I've made love with this man countless times, but this night is so drenched in erotic fantasy it's almost impossible not to feel as if he's a beautiful, domineering stranger who is about to fuck me for the first time ever.

I flex my hands, arching my hips upward. He pushes his cock into me with excruciating slowness, as if he wants me to feel every inch of him. And I do. My nerves fire with sparks as he fills me, stretches me, going deeper, deeper…oh, so *deep*…

I draw in a heavy breath. Sweat trickles between my breasts. He pauses, and his hands spread over my hips, up my torso to my breasts. He pinches my stiff nipples at the exact instant that he plunges all the way into me.

"Please," I whisper, my voice barely audible past the heaviness of my breath. "Fuck me hard, sir."

"I'll fuck you hard." His grip moves to my waist. "I'll fuck you rough."

He pulls back and plunges inside me again, the rhythm edged with lust and the drive toward release. Again, I can do none of the things I would normally do—grip his arms, pull him against me, gaze into his desire-drenched eyes, watch his gorgeous muscles flex and strain. All is darkness, except for the bright, glowing light burning right in the center of my soul.

I twist my hands so I can hold on to the silk ties as his thrusts increase in pace. I draw my legs up, letting him go as deep as he can and knowing I can take as much as he can give.

His breath rasps harshly in the air above me. He pauses once to circle his thumb around my aching clit. I moan, arching into his touch. My eyes dampen behind the silk blindfold.

"I need you so badly," I gasp, pulling ineffectually against the restraints. "Please..."

He pulls out of me, and I feel his fingers working at the knots of my ties. When they're loosened, he grabs my hips and turns me around before fastening the silk back around the bedposts.

Air brushes against my naked bottom. I tighten my hands into fists—this position has always made me feel intensely vulnerable, even at home with Dean, and now that sense of helplessness hits me harder than ever.

I sink my face into the pillow, shivering when his big hands stroke over the length of my back.

"On your knees, Olivia," he orders softly.

I swallow, pulling myself onto my knees, my head and shoulders still lowered onto the pillow. There's enough give in the silk ties that I can rest my arms on either side of my head, but the tension pulls my muscles tight.

"Ah, fuck." Dean's voice deepens. He nudges his knee between my thighs. "Spread them wide."

Oh, how I want to look over my shoulder and see him—all sweaty and muscular, his eyes burning. The head of his cock rubs deliciously against my folds before he sinks into me again. In this position, he's harder to take, impossibly big, his thrusts firing me with both need and apprehension.

"Fuck, you feel incredible," Dean mutters. "Like a tight, hot glove... look at how you spread your legs so well...such a good girl...so fucking perfect."

His words pour over me, flooding me with pleasure, lust, love. Despite my vulnerability, I know I could crouch here forever, letting him drive into me over and over again, but the pressure inside mounts, coiling through me like a whip ready to strike.

"Please, sir," I beg. "I'm so close...I need to come..."

"You don't get to come first," he says, giving my ass a little stinging spank. "I do."

"Then I...oh, I want to feel it, please let me. Come inside me, come on my ass...wherever you want. Whatever you want...please."

He plunges into me once and pulls out, and I know he's stroking his cock. I see him in my mind's eye, his head back and his hand wrapped around his shaft. His shout vibrates against my skin the instant before warm seed splashes over my ass.

"Dean." My voice cracks, on the verge of breaking.

He moves swiftly to unfasten the ties and pull me against his sweaty body, his arms coming around me in the strong, secure haven I know so well. He lowers his lips to my ear and slides his hands over my breasts.

"I love you," he whispers. "You're so goddamned beautiful you break my heart in two. I will climb mountains and cross oceans to get to you. You fill every fucking part of me, my blood, my heart, my soul. I will slay monsters for you until the end of time. And I will make you come so hard you'll see stars."

I can't speak. I'm shaking, trembling, aching. And when he slides his hand between my legs, I explode like a rocket. A scream rips from my throat as I buck against his hand, a torrent of vibrations trembling violently through me.

His voice is a low, deep whisper against my ear, a stream of praise filling me with as much bliss as the physical release. Tears stream down my cheeks and dampen the blindfold. I turn, pressing my face against his chest as the sensations slide from my body.

We lie there for a long time, his arms around me. Then he tugs the blindfold off me and brushes my hair away from my sticky forehead.

I blink, momentarily off-balance as my eyes adjust to sight and light again. The bedcovers are rumpled, the silk ties tangled on the pillow.

Dean cups his hand beneath my chin and lifts my face to his. Love floods me at the sight of him—his beautiful, gold-flecked eyes warm with tenderness, the sharp angles of his cheekbones flushed with heat, his hair tousled and falling over his forehead.

"Hey, beauty," he says.

I smile. "Hi, professor."

He kisses my forehead and pulls me to him. All thought slides away as I relax against his solid strength, and we settle together into the fluffy pillows.

Before long my eyelids start to droop. As the haze of sleep descends, I have the fuzzy thought that I need to call Kelsey and at least say goodnight to Nicholas...

I wake with a start, disoriented and confused until I feel Dean's warm body next to mine. He threads his hand through my hair.

"Midnight," he murmurs, his voice husky with sleep. "Tomorrow is Saturday, your day off. Archer and Kelsey are taking care of Nicholas until late afternoon."

"Oh." I sink against him with a sigh. "You mean we can stay here all day?"

"We're *going* to stay here all day," he replies, skimming his fingers down my spine. "Now that I have you, I'm not letting you go."

CHAPTER 22

OLIVIA

*O*ur night is an echo of the ones we used to spend together. We doze for awhile before pulling ourselves from the allure of sleep and back toward each other.

Our lips meet lazily, I run my hand down Dean's chest, and he tugs my bare leg over his hips. We make love again but slowly, a marked contrast to the rawness of our previous encounter.

In a drowsy haze, the air scented with lust and cherries, I let him pull me on top of him. I slide down onto his shaft, welcoming the faint twinge of pain because it reminds me of how completely I've been *taken*.

I curl my fingers against his chest and ride him until the tension breaks and sends me spiraling into pleasure again. It's so fucking hot—the burn in his eyes, the intensity of his expression, the way he looks as if he wants to devour me. An intense, heady sense of power fills me as I keep moving, feeling his muscles flexing and tensing.

His hoarse groans break through the air. Hot splashes of seed fill me as his body arches upward, pushing deeper into me. There are few things more beautiful in the world than making my husband come so hard that I'll feel him inside me for the next day.

I sink against him, and we fall into another light doze, our bodies wrapped together like the entwining vines of a plant.

We wake again in early morning only to order a delectable room-service meal of coffee, eggs, a basketful of flaky croissants, and fresh strawberries, which Dean feeds to me in bed before we indulge in a hot, soapy shower together.

After another drowsy nap, I look at the clock and almost laugh when I see that it's past noon. Noon on a Saturday, and Dean is still sleeping.

My body feels delicious—warm, sated, and loose, like melted syrup is running through my veins, like I've been soaking in bubbling hot springs and lying naked in the sun.

Or like I've been intensely and exquisitely fucked by my gorgeous husband. I press a kiss to his smooth shoulder and slide out of bed carefully so as not to wake him.

The purple silk scarf falls to the floor. I pick it up and wind it around my neck before going in search of something to wear that isn't my crumpled lingerie or raincoat.

I use the bathroom and tug my hair into a ponytail. There's a travel bag on the bathroom counter. Inside, there's a clean pair of yoga pants, a T-shirt, and slip-on shoes. Of course Dean thought of everything.

I dress and go into the main room. The curtains are still drawn, revealing a bright, sunny sky and the glittering expanse of the lake. I find my purse on a chair near the front door and rummage around for my cell phone, which I haven't even looked at in close to twenty-four hours.

I hadn't even *thought* of checking it. Heck, I hadn't thought of anything except how incredible it was to be alone with my husband again.

A slew of texts runs across the screen of my phone. My heart stutters with fear in the instant before I remember Kelsey or Archer would have contacted Dean if anything had happened to Nicholas.

My initial panic eases a bit and I scan the messages, which are mostly from Allie and Sheryl, the head waitress at the café.

Liv, get over here now. Where are you? She says you approved this... omfg, a police officer is asking for our permit.

WHERE ARE YOU?? Can't reach Dean, cell not working.

Am getting worried!

What the...?

My heart plummets with a sickening sense of dread. I look at the date on the screen. I think frantically, pulling up my calendar and schedule.

Oh, no.

Becky Harrison's birthday party. Becky Harrison's fifth birthday party—*which I assured Allie we could handle and I would take care of*—started at eleven o'clock this morning.

Oh my god.

Not only did I forget, I was thoroughly occupied.

Without even bothering to check my voicemails, I hammer out a quick text to Allie. I have no good excuse, so all I can do is admit to my hideous mistake.

I am so sorry. On my way right now.

I scribble a note for Dean—*Had to run to the café. I love you madly*—then I race downstairs to the parking lot.

I force myself not to speed too much as I drive to the café. All the pleasure of the past fifteen hours disintegrates as the weight of embarrassment, regret, and responsibility crashes over me. I park at the curb and run across the street, yanking open the front door.

A barrage of noise hits me—children yelling and crying, the

clatter of plates and silverware, a customer's angry voice, the stomp of footsteps on the stairs. Parents are clustered around the front counter, apparently trying to collect their children.

I drop my bag and run upstairs to the Castle Room, which is a disaster of raucous children, messy tables, and spilled food and drinks. Allie is standing near the serving station, her hands up in a placating gesture as a blond woman shouts angrily at her.

I hurry over. "Allie."

She turns, her eyes widening at the sight of me. She's red-faced with stress and near-panic. A new wave of regret slams into me so hard I almost can't catch my breath.

"Excuse me." I step between her and the angry woman, feeling the tension tight enough to break. "Are you Monica Harrison? I'm Liv West."

"Liv." Monica's mouth compresses, her furious gaze darting from Allie to me. "Where the hell have you been? You told me you'd be here to run Becky's party."

"I'm terribly sorry." My chest constricts. "I'm…I'll handle everything, I promise."

"It's a little late for that now," Monica replies bitterly, spreading her hand out to indicate the chaos. "This is a disaster. You'd better believe I'm not paying you a dime, and if you don't refund my deposit, I'm suing you."

"Of course we'll refund your money. I'll get things straightened out right away."

Monica hardly looks placated, but she turns to another frazzled-looking mother who is trying to drag a resistant five-year-old toward the door.

I face Allie, whose eyebrows pull together with concern. "Liv, where have you *been*? Is everything okay? Nicholas?"

"Yes." I press my hands to my cheeks and close my eyes. "Everything's fine. I just…I'm sorry. I fucked up. I completely forgot about the party."

Silence falls. I open my eyes to look at her. Her expression hardens with anger.

"You forgot," she repeats.

"I forgot."

"You told me you were planning everything. You told me we could *handle it*."

"I know."

"Where were you?" she asks.

"I was busy," I confess. "I forgot, Allie. I don't have any other excuse."

"Why didn't you answer my calls and texts?"

"My phone was off."

"All morning?"

"Yes." I hold up my hands in surrender. "And Dean got a new cell number that I forgot to give you. Allie, what happened?"

"A fucking disaster, that's what happened," she hisses. "Rachel is outside with the police officer and the band, who refuse to leave unless they're paid even though they haven't performed."

Allie waves her hand toward the window. "You'd better do something about the officer *now*. I've been trying to corral the kids and get them to their parents, not to mention dealing with one seriously pissed-off mother."

I shut off the guilt buffeting me like a storm and hurry back downstairs. Outside, a few children are chasing each other on the grass while their parents watch from the terrace. The band equipment is stacked to one side, five musicians standing with their arms crossed, their expressions sullen and mutinous.

I go to where Rachel is talking to a police officer and a curly-headed young man who looks like the Pieman.

"Excuse me." I take a deep breath and extend my hand to the policeman. "I'm Liv West, officer. I apologize for the confusion."

"No confusion, ma'am." He frowns at me. "Pretty clear you needed a permit for the band, and you don't have one."

"I'm sure we can straighten this out," I tell him, though at the moment I'm not sure about that at all.

"You Liv?" the musician asks, jerking his chin up. "I'm Marty Groman, aka the Pieman. Look, we came here to play and thought you had everything set up. The police officer won't even let me play my guitar, and now we've got a ton of disappointed kids. That's not how we work. Slice of Pie makes kids happy, you know?"

"I know. I'm sorry." If only *sorrys* could fix everything. "Look, could you guys please get your equipment packed up? I promise, you'll be paid the full amount."

"It's not just about the pay," Marty says, hitching his guitar over his shoulder. "I mean, it's bad for our rep if we leave a place with a bunch of upset kids."

"You're also going to need to pay a fine," the police officer informs me, writing something on a pad of paper. "I'm citing you for violation of city ordnance five three one. You'll need to come down to the courthouse and talk to the judge."

Great. Nausea surges in my stomach. The band starts to shuffle their equipment back into their van. I sign the violation notice, write out a check to the band, and rush to help settle the rest of the chaos.

Inside, the noise level is starting to decrease as mothers haul their children toward the door and other customers walk out. I return to the Castle Room, which is now empty.

In addition to the mess of overturned chairs and crumpled paper plates, the murals of black mountains and flying monkeys have been smeared with yellow and blue paint, several of the crystal ball centerpieces are cracked, and there's an entire cake smashed near the stairs.

With my heart feeling heavy as an anvil, I pick up a trash can and start to clean up the plates and cups.

"The Alice in Wonderland room took a hit too," Allie says from behind me. "But this is the worst of it."

I shake my head. "What happened?"

"Everything," Allie says, her voice tight with frustration as we start to straighten the chairs. "First Brent had to go out of town, and Sarah called in sick. Then in addition to the invited party guests, Becky thought it would be fun to tell all her friends to bring their friends. So over fifty five-year-olds showed up, and I knew we couldn't turn them away so we had to scramble to get enough food for them because we hadn't placed that big an order.

"Then the band was late, and they had way more equipment than we'd been expecting, so it took them forever to set up and by then the kids were getting impatient and wreaking havoc in the café because most of their parents had left. A bunch of them were yelling that they wanted cake, which wasn't supposed to happen until after the band, but then Becky saw it sitting on the sideboard and decided to carry it downstairs to the terrace."

She waves toward the cake smashed and trampled on the floor. "Well, of course she dropped it and then got hysterical, but she didn't want any of the café desserts as a substitute. So her mother went out to buy another cake, which meant she wasn't here when the kids started ripping open all the presents.

"I managed to get the band to start, but someone must have complained about the noise, because the police officer showed up asking for our permit—*which you assured me you'd take care of*—and the band had to shut down, which made all the kids upset, and then one little boy thought it would be funny to eat the cake with his hands...and next thing you know, they're throwing cake at each other, Becky is crying, her mother is yelling at me to fix things, the band is complaining about how they came here to play, and the police officer is telling me I have to pay a fine."

She whirls around to pin me with a glare. "And you weren't answering your stupid phone."

"Oh, Allie." Tears flood my eyes, and I sink onto a chair. "I am so goddamned sorry."

"I don't get it, Liv!" She spreads her arms out. "What happened? Where *were* you?"

Embarrassment scorches my face.

"I was with Dean," I admit.

Allie blinks in bafflement. "With Dean?"

"Sort of a date night. Or day. Whatever. We haven't spent much time together since Nicholas was born, and he took me out and…well, I usually have every other Saturday off and I completely forgot about the party."

"I'm not begrudging you a date night with your husband," Allie says. "But it's so unlike you to be so irresponsible."

The word hits me like the tail end of a whip. I've spent my life trying to prove I'm anything *but* irresponsible.

"You were the one who pushed for us to have this party," Allie continues sharply, "and not because you knew we could handle it, but because you were trying to do some tit-for-tat kind of thing with Edison. But you know that's not what the Wonderland Café is about."

"What can I do?" I ask, shame filling my chest. "How can I fix it?"

"I have no idea. I already gave Monica her deposit back. The band is upset because this hurts their reputation for making kids happy, and now we're on record as having been fined. Plus we had to turn regular customers away because we were too busy, and now there are at least three grandmothers out there pissed off because we couldn't provide the high tea they had promised their granddaughters. That's going to mess with our business too, as if our grand opening disaster wasn't enough of a hurdle to overcome."

With that parting shot, she stalks out of the room and down the stairs. I stare at a cracked crystal ball, feeling as if Allie just slapped me. Or as if I just tripped on my own feet and face-planted on a concrete floor. I rest my head in my hands and indulge in a good crying jag.

Of course it was all too good to be true. I finally have everything I've been working for—an incredible husband, a beautiful son, a successful business, a good reputation—and when the final piece of my marriage gets put back into place, all the other balls I'm juggling come crashing down.

I wipe my eyes on a napkin, my insides suddenly aching with longing to see Nicholas. I text Dean that I have to "finish up" some things at the café, then I get back to work cleaning up the mess and trying to patch up the damage I've done.

Allie doesn't talk to me for the rest of the afternoon, and by the time we close the café I'm starting to wonder if I've permanently damaged both our friendship and our business partnership.

"Allie, I don't know what else to say or do," I tell her, as we turn off the lights and lock up.

"Nothing right now, Liv." She turns away from me, her back stiff. "I'll see you Monday."

I watch her walk away, guilt simmering like acid inside me. I get into my car and head back to the Butterfly House.

I leave my purse in the foyer and go into the sunroom, where Dean and Nicholas are building an intricate, towering structure with the blocks Dean brought back from Tuscany. Twilight shines through the picture windows. The song "All Around the Kitchen" drifts from the speakers, loud enough that neither of them glances up from their task.

For a moment, I stop and look at them—Nicholas in a blue sweatshirt with his hair a mess and dried jam on his cheek, and an unshaven Dean, wearing an old T-shirt and jeans, his reading glasses on as he studies what appears to be a diagram of the tower they're constructing. He makes a notation on the picture and hands a triangular block to Nicholas, who places it carefully on top of a stack.

"Mama!"

Nicholas pushes to his feet and waddles toward me, his arms

outstretched. I drop my bag on the kitchen island and crouch to pull him against me, inhaling his toddler smells of baby shampoo, sour milk, and strawberry jam.

"Hey, you get everything done?" Dean approaches, rubbing his hand over Nicholas's head as he bends to kiss me.

"Yes." I lift Nicholas into my arms and straighten, not yet wanting to tell Dean about my egregious mistake.

I lean closer to him, squishing Nicholas between us in a group hug as I breathe them both in. The scents of my husband fill my nose—coffee, laundry detergent, and chocolate mint.

"You found my secret stash of peppermint patties," I remark, rubbing my cheek against his chest.

"You need to work on your hiding skills, lady," he replies. "Did you really think I wouldn't find them behind Nicholas's yogurt bites?"

"Next time I'll hide them behind the organic kale chips."

A chuckle rumbles through his chest. "Well, I guarantee I won't bother to look there."

"Tower!" Nicholas shouts, squirming in my arms.

I lower him to the floor, and he hurries back to the unfinished tower. Dean reaches out to twist his hands around the ends of the purple silk scarf, which I'd forgotten I'm still wearing around my neck. He tugs on the scarf, pulling me to him for another kiss.

"I missed you," he remarks. "I had more plans, you know. Dirty ones."

"Oh, I know." I slide my arms around his waist and squeeze, loving so much the solid strength and heat of his body. "Sorry I had to leave so suddenly."

"S'okay." He rubs my back. "Just gives me more reason to whisk you away again for another night of debauchery."

If only it were that easy...

"Mama, tower!" Nicholas calls.

I pull away from Dean, and we join our son on the carpet. We spend the next hour building, reading picture books, listening to music, and refereeing a toddler fuss that is soothed with a sippy cup of milk.

Our evening routine is a striking contrast to last night, but comfortably familiar—after a dinner of leftover tacos, I get Nicholas ready for bed while Dean cleans the kitchen.

After I return downstairs, I shuffle through the day's mail. There's another postcard from my friend North, this time from Cambodia:

Liv,

Sandcastle temples, sugar palms, monks in saffron robes, crowded markets with pungent scents of grilled seafood and fried insects, brutal scars of the past and yet, when you look, evidence of a bright, serene awakening.

My adventure continues.
North

I join Dean on the sofa, where he's sprawled out watching the news. He extends an arm and I snuggle against his side, letting the warmth of him ease away the lingering tightness in my chest.

"Postcard from North." I hold the card out to him.

"Cambodia, huh?" He reads the card and turns it over to look at the printed photo of the elaborate Angkor Wat temple complex. "I went to grad school with a guy who specialized in Southeast Asian architecture. He spent a year in Cambodia studying Angkor Wat. He invited me to visit any time, but I never made it over there."

For some reason, I don't like the idea of Dean *not* having done something. I stroke my hand under his T-shirt to touch the flat, hard ridges of his abdomen.

"Hey, you okay?" Dean pats my hip.

"Yeah, I just forgot I was supposed to do something at the café, and it sort of screwed things up. I'll straighten it out, though."

"What happened?"

I know he'll find out sooner or later, so I take a deep breath and confess my colossal fuck-up. He listens in silence, his brow creasing with concern.

By the time I'm finished, the tension in my shoulders has eased somewhat. Sharing my burdens with Dean has always made things easier, and I fully expect him to reassure me everything will work out.

"Liv." His expression is somber, his mouth turning into a frown. "I think the universe is trying to tell you something."

I blink. "Like what?"

"Like you've been trying to do too much for too long. Sooner or later, something was going to give."

Though that's exactly what I just told myself, it hurts extra hard hearing it from him—especially considering the reason I forgot about Becky's party.

"You wouldn't have said that when we were getting busy in the hotel room," I mutter, pushing away from him and getting to my feet.

His frown deepens. "I won't apologize for wanting you all to myself for one damned night. You've had every other Saturday off at the café for the past year, and you had it written on the calendar that today was your day off. I'd never have made plans if I'd known you had other commitments, but I can't even remember the last time we were alone together for an entire night. I'm not apologizing for it."

"I'm not asking you to apologize," I retort, tossing North's postcard on a table. "I know I fucked up. But I don't need you making me feel worse."

Remorse flashes in his eyes, but his jaw tightens. "I don't want to make you feel worse. I want you to stop thinking you have to do *everything*. You don't have to tackle every single project on your own just because people ask you to or because you feel you have to. You don't have to prove you can do it all. Everyone *knows* you can."

My insides twist. Why don't I know that by now too? Why don't I believe it?

"Look, I know some people over at Edison Power," Dean continues as he stands and approaches me. "So does Kelsey. Let me call them and—"

I hold up my hand to stop him. I know—I *know*—the easiest way to deal with this mess is to turn everything over to my husband. Just like the night when he effortlessly rescued me and Nicholas from chaos, he would do the same thing now. He'd smooth all the rough edges, negotiate the conflicts, make everything right. He would fix it.

But why shouldn't I be responsible for cleaning up my own messes? I'm the one who wanted to do it all, so I'm the one who has to fix it. Yes, it's a rotten leftover of life with my mother—who never took responsibility for a fucking thing, including her own daughter—but that doesn't give me a free pass. I won't make excuses for myself.

"No." I shake my head. "I'll figure it out."

Dean exhales a sigh of frustration. "Liv, it's okay to ask for help. To accept help when it's offered. It doesn't make you weak or irresponsible."

"I don't think it does."

"Then let me help you, dammit."

I look up at the hard note in his voice. He's standing with his arms folded across his chest, his mouth tight and eyes dark.

I suddenly wonder what it has cost him over the years to

stand back and not intervene in my problems when there is nothing he wants to do more. Being passive, especially in regards to his family, goes against the very core of who Dean West is. He's always been the one to make things happen—to win the game, save the day, find the treasure, lead the battle.

But for me, because I asked him to, he has put himself on the sidelines and watched me try, fail, and try again. He's forced himself not to jump in and rescue me, and because of his restraint, I've grown and changed in ways I'd once never imagined I could.

"Thank you," I say.

"For what?"

"For letting me make mistakes. For not trying to fix things, even though I know you always want to."

He's still frowning. "That sounds like you're going to turn me down again."

"No, I'm not turning you down. I just need to figure out what the fallout of all this is going to be and talk to Allie. Give me a day or two. I promise I'll tell you if I need you."

Dean looks at me for a long moment, his expression shuttered. He reaches over to brush a lock of hair away from my forehead.

"I thought you always needed me," he says.

My heart stutters at the idea he would ever think otherwise.

"Of course I do."

A faint, resigned smile tugs at his mouth. He turns away, picking up a stack of papers from the kitchen counter before he goes upstairs to his tower office.

I have a sudden, sharp longing to return to the hot intimacy we'd had in the hotel room. I want cherry pie and champagne again. I want lacy lingerie, silk blindfolds, the burn of lust. I want to feel Dean's hands sweeping over my naked body. I want to hear his deep voice whispering commands in my ear. I want to close the door and shut the world out so we can focus on each other again.

But even if we could, it wouldn't be the same. All our efforts, both mine and Dean's, to find *that place* again have either failed or created a disaster.

Maybe because that place no longer exists. Maybe we've been trying to recreate something that can't be recreated because it belongs to the past. Maybe it's now just a memory. And if not even Dean can bring it back *to stay...*

My heart aches. I'm tempted to follow him to his tower and curl up on his lap. The sensation of my husband's strong arms tightening around me in a warm, secure circle is, perhaps, the only thing in the world that can banish my sense of hopelessness.

Instead, I turn in the opposite direction, walk up the stairs, and crawl into bed alone.

Part III

CHAPTER 23

OLIVIA

*T*he tension between me and Dean persists over the next day. I know he's frustrated not only by the derailing of our intimacy—again—but also by the fact that he can't jump in to help fix the café's latest disaster.

And though I try to explain I'm not being stubborn—because I'm actually quite willing to let him make calls on my behalf—he doesn't see the point of me wanting to wait for the dust to settle first.

And yet I can't focus entirely on Dean right now, since Allie is the one I betrayed and the one with whom I first need to make amends. She isn't at Wonderland when I arrive on Monday morning, and after getting the café opened, I return to the office and plunge into work.

I leave a message for Monica Harrison with a profuse apology and request to please return my call. I open my email and, with a sinking sense of dread, click on a message from Mike Harrison at

Edison Power.

Liv,

It looks like things won't work out for Edison Power to sponsor the Mirror Lake Bicentennial Festival. However, we're happy to donate two tickets to the Freefall Water Park for the auction. I'll put them in the mail today.

Best of luck with the festival and your future events.
Mike Harrison

My chest constricts. Though I'd been expecting this, I'd also secretly been hoping I still had a chance. I pick up the phone to call Mike Harrison.

"I want to apologize for what happened at Becky's party," I tell him after introducing myself. "It's entirely my fault. We've had so many successful parties at the café that—"

"I'm sorry, Liv, we can't change our decision," he says. "I understand that things go wrong, but at this stage we don't think a partnership between you and Edison is a good idea."

"The festival is a different venture from the café," I continue. "The city council asked me to plan it when the previous director moved away, but—"

"Liv, I'm sorry. We won't be able to sponsor the festival. And we're contracting another restaurant to cater our company picnic in August. We have the sense it might be too much for you to handle, and we need to have complete confidence that the people we hire will be equal to the task."

And that's not you.

The unspoken words ricochet like a bullet inside me.

I manage to mumble a plea about "reaching out to us in the future" and wanting to do something to make up for my mistake. Mike Harrison is polite and gracious, though I can hear the door slamming shut when he hangs up the phone.

I rest my head in my hands. I'd thought we could do everything in one fell swoop—earn enough money for our truck and secure a major sponsor for the festival. Now both of those things are gone because I dropped the ball.

If I didn't know it would put the city council in a terrible bind, I'd resign from the festival director position right now because at the rate I'm going, Mirror Lake's two-hundredth birthday will consist of some balloons and maybe a few grilled burgers from the Boxcar Deli.

And if we don't get enough people to come out to the festival, then the Chair Fair auction will fail, which means I'll also be letting down the Historical Society and the railroad project—

Despair roils in the pit of my stomach. I have a sudden urge to run away.

"Liv."

I lift my head to look at Allie, who has stopped in the office doorway. She doesn't look as angry as she did on Saturday, but she's not exactly her usual cheerful self either.

"Edison turned us down to cater the picnic," I tell her. "And they declined to sponsor the festival, though considering what happened I can't say I'm surprised. I'm so sorry, Allie."

"Me too." She pushes a chair away from the desk and sits down, crossing her arms over her chest. "It might be time for you to take a break, Liv."

I blink. "A break?"

"You're clearly running yourself ragged," she says. "And honestly, you've been overriding me at every turn this past year. We're supposed to be partners, but you've been wanting to do everything yourself. I think we both need to take a step back and reassess how our partnership is working."

Pain tightens my throat. "Oh, Allie, have I been that bad?"

"Not *bad*, Liv, but honestly since you had Nicholas, you've become a serious control freak. And when you steamroll decisions for *our* business, it feels like you don't trust me either as a friend or a partner."

I don't even know what to say to that. But a small, raw corner of my soul knows Allie is right—in my efforts to ensure my son's life, and *my* life, are nothing like my shaky, uncertain childhood, I've totally overcompensated.

"Of course I trust you," I say. "I've been doing everything for us and for the café."

Allie sighs. "Look, I get it, okay? You want to please people. You want to be everything to everyone. But you can't be. No one can be. And I think you need to realize that your family is your priority right now and take a few weeks off."

Hurt and regret twist through me. More than the request itself, I hate that I'm the reason Allie is making it in the first place. That she's reached the point where she needs to stop working with me.

"I don't want to take a break, Allie," I tell her. "Both Dean and Kelsey know people at Edison, and they'd intervene on our behalf. Dean has already offered."

"If Edison already gave us their decision, we're not going to push the issue," Allie replies. "We need to focus on moving forward. I'm already looking into some outreach opportunities, because parents are going to talk, and the Wonderland Café isn't going to come out of this mess unscathed."

"Okay." I fumble through the papers on the desk to find the information about the party truck. "I'll call Roger Jameson about the Airstream and see if we can—"

"Liv." Allie's voice hardens. "We've lost the Airstream. It's over."

"It's not over," I protest. "I just have to finish a few things for the festival and…"

My voice trails off. The despair filling me intensifies.

"You need to step back from the café right now," Allie says. "You're getting the festival and the café way too mixed up. I'm just sorry I didn't try to stop you sooner. Maybe the café wouldn't have taken a hit."

Silence falls between us.

"I had everything under control," I finally say.

"No, you *thought* you had everything under control." Allie pauses and reaches across the desk to touch my arm. "And I'm not going to abandon you. Brent and I will still help with the festival. But you need to leave the café to me."

Her tone indicates that she won't take no for an answer. And if I'm being brutally honest with myself, I can't say I blame her. I wouldn't want to work with me right now either.

"Okay." I push to my feet, feeling as if a black cloud is pressing in on me from all sides. "I want to fix this, Allie."

"You've really done enough." Allie shakes her head. "And I admit I'm partly to blame for not standing up to you sooner. I'll figure this out. If something comes up, I'll call you."

We exchange a hug that isn't as warm as our embraces usually are before I gather my things and leave. As I walk down the porch steps, a mother approaches, herding two young children into the café. The kids climb the steps with a bright, springy excitement, clearly anticipating cupcakes and hot chocolate.

I walk slowly to my car, feeling flattened. I want to cry on Dean's shoulder—because *I need him, dammit*—but he's at the university, probably finalizing things for the United Nations Assembly. It's almost ridiculous how impressive that is.

Cold breaks through me, the old, latent sense of being untethered, adrift. I have the urge to go home and be alone—to curl up with my quilt, a cup of tea, and a book—but I've already let enough people down, and hiding isn't going to help.

I straighten both my spine and my willpower, and head to the Historical Society museum and offices. I still have the Bicentennial Festival to plan, and the entire town is counting on me not to fail.

I find Florence Wickham in her office, peering at a bunch of old railroad photographs spread out on a table. She looks up at me with a welcoming smile, which makes me feel better. At least she still thinks I'm the bee's knees.

"Come in, Olivia, dear." She waves me into the office. "I'm organizing these for Archer to look over. Maybe we can make a display about the history of the railroad to put up outside the auction tent."

My heart lightens a bit at the thought of the Chair Fair. So many Mirror Lake residents have contributed beautifully decorated chairs to the auction it seems like a given we'll reach our fundraising goal. If enough people attend, that is.

"I'm just waiting for four more chairs to be delivered, then we can get the catalog printed," I tell Florence. "I'll send the mock-up to Patrick so he can start studying it."

"Oh, dear." Florence straightens, her forehead creasing. "Did you get Patrick's email? His son just bought a house in Florida, and he and his wife are going down this week to help with some work before they move in. He won't be able to fulfill the auctioneer duties."

Dread pools in my belly again. I take out my phone and scroll through the messages. Patrick's email is buried under all the other ones I missed. I battle back a fresh wave of anxiety and tell myself this is not an unsolvable problem.

"So we need a new auctioneer." I force a light note into my voice, trying to sound like this will be no more trouble than needing a fresh carton of milk. "That shouldn't be too difficult."

"The professional auctioneers charge quite a fee," Florence replies worriedly. "Patrick was doing it as a favor, just to help us."

To help us.

A bright light suddenly flashes in my mind, illuminating the solution to several problems all at once. Not only will this save the auction, but it will also repair the new tension between me and my husband.

"I'll ask Dean," I tell Florence, a welcome relief filling me. "He offered to help with the festival, and he'll be happy to serve as auctioneer."

"Oh, wonderful!" Florence claps her hands. "What a marvelous idea. With his voice, that man will make a metal folding chair sound like a king's throne. The women are going to bid small fortunes."

"I'll talk to him tonight," I say, tucking my phone back into my bag. "I promise, Florence, everything will be fine."

And it will be about freaking time.

CHAPTER 24

Olivia

I pull the blanket up around Nicholas and pick up the baby monitor before heading up the spiral staircase to Dean's office. I knock once and push the door open.

"Dean?"

He's at his desk wearing his pajama bottoms, the phone cradled against his shoulder and his attention on the computer screen. He gestures for me to hold on as he continues the call.

Rather than focusing on what he's saying, I listen to the deep, measured cadence of his voice and admire his sculpted shoulders, the muscles of his chest and back...

A tingle of awareness goes through me. To avoid the temptation of jumping his bones—clearly, my comeback is here to stay, regardless of the fact that everything else is going wrong—I look out the windows and wait for him to finish the call. When I hear the click of the phone, I turn back to him.

He swivels in the chair to face me, his expression one of

distracted concentration. For an instant, I wish I'd come up here with another hot encounter in mind, but Dean and I have a history of using sex as an easy and delicious escape from both reality and our own problems. Unfortunately, the problems are always still waiting when we emerge from our lustful fog.

"I have a favor to ask you." I approach him, reaching out to run my fingers over his corded forearm. "I need a new auctioneer for the Chair Fair, and I was hoping you'd volunteer. I mentioned the idea to Florence, and she's all over it."

Rather than immediately agreeing, which was the response I was hoping for, a shadow passes over Dean's eyes.

"The UN Assembly starts next week in Geneva," he says. "They're going to vote on our proposal to put the site on the protected list."

I nod. "You told me. Simon and Mateo are going to give the presentation, right?"

"Yeah." He leans in to click something on his computer screen. "I didn't think I'd have to go. I'd already told Hans I wouldn't be there."

But...

The unspoken word sparks apprehension inside me. I know the World Heritage Center pushed the proposal through partly because they're courting Dean for a high-level job. And it takes me a second to realize he's telling me something without outright saying it. My heart starts beating too fast.

"But now you do have to go?" I ask.

He nods, turning to straighten a stack of papers on his desk.

"But that means…" *You're going to miss the festival.*

A weighty, thick silence falls between us. A hundred unwanted images flash through my mind. I can see my husband navigating an international convention with his steely self-assurance.

The pictures are crystal-clear—Professor West, clad in his tailored navy suit, his silk tie knotted perfectly, his dark hair burnished by the lights as he shakes hands and extends greetings in French, German, Italian. I hear him discussing Roman aqueducts, building strategies, site management, and cultural landscapes.

I see the United Nations offices in Geneva, a vast conference room with delegate tables arranged in a half-circle before the rostrum where the World Heritage officials sit. I see Dean standing at a podium before fifty diplomats, all identified by plaques announcing their country affiliation. Armenia, Portugal, Mali, Finland, Japan.

They wear identification badges and translation headphones, and their desks are stacked with binders, papers, laptops. There are interpreters' booths, a sound control room, a viewing gallery, a massive screen where renowned historian Dr. Dean West displays photos and maps and explains why the committee should vote to restore and protect a medieval monastery.

My whole body tenses, as if in defense against the images I don't want to see, the truth I don't want to acknowledge.

"You can't go," I manage to say, though of course what he's going to do is far more important than helping me with a chair auction.

"I have to, Liv."

"Why?" I curl my hands around the back of a chair, trying not to shake. "If Simon and Mateo can handle the presentation…"

"Hans called me about an hour ago, asking if I would lead a break-out session on medievalism. And Jessica Burke asked me to talk to Hans about the Youth Experts Program, which is badly in need of help."

I should be so proud. And I am—part of me is, anyway. A part I'm having a hard time finding beneath a sharp, growing apprehension.

I tighten my grip on the chair and tell myself to breathe. I catch the frustrated regret in Dean's eyes as he goes to the table where his briefcase sits open. I know exactly the source of that regret—the push and pull between his loyalty to me and his commitment to his work.

"If the vote passes, it's more than the site being placed on the list," he says, almost as if he's trying to remind himself as well as me. "It means funding to repair the quake damage and support for dozens of people who have been working at Altopascio much longer than I have. It means revenue for the town and government. It means conservation and legal protection for a monastery that's important both historically and culturally. I have to fight for this."

Of course he does. I know that. This is the United Nations. Global education, intercultural understanding and solidarity, democracy, freedom of expression. Dean can't walk away from this fight for anything, not even me. He won't.

I stare at the photographs still on his desk—the images of the dig zones, the tools, a gold disk that was once buried deep in the soil.

"Why…" I swallow hard. "Why didn't you tell me sooner?"

"Because I didn't know." He stuffs some papers into his briefcase. "I knew about the vote, but not about the medieval session. And considering the delegates who are going to be there, plus my work on the Conservation Committee, I have to go."

I cross my arms tightly over my chest, suddenly feeling as if my husband is moving away from me, inch by painful inch, and into the vast unknown of the world where I will no longer be able to reach him.

And that, more than anything, floods me with raw, painful fear. Because Dean has always been so comfortable and secure in the world, so confident, and if that is where he truly belongs, then what happens to *us*?

I take a breath, feeling the start of a fracture. The moment in which I'm forced to admit we might never find our way back to each other, at least not the way we both want to. Too many other things are crowding into the place of Liv and Dean. Separating us.

"Who are you going as?" I ask. "Professor Dean West of King's University or Assistant Director of the World Heritage Center?"

"As a historian trying to save a medieval monastery." He drags a hand through his hair with a sigh. "I don't want to leave again, but this is critical. If the UN votes no, we'll face a huge loss of support and revenue."

"I'm not denying the importance of it," I reply, knowing there is only one weapon I have in my corner, only one way to defend myself against the world that seems determined to lure my husband into exotic, distant places where I can't go.

"I get that it's big and illustrious and not nearly on the same level as a town festival," I say, disliking the strident note in my voice, "but you just gave me a lecture yesterday about asking for help when I need it. And you told me weeks ago you would help us with the festival. That you would help *me*."

"Liv, I'm sorry." He shakes his head, his mouth tightening. "You also told me countless times you have plenty of volunteers, and you didn't have a specific job for me anyway."

"That's not the point."

He straightens to look at me. Because I know him so well, I see the guilt, anger, and frustration warring inside him, right next to his deep-seated certainty that the United Nations task belongs to him alone. No one except Professor Dean West can do this…and he knows it. So do I.

"What is the point, then?" he asks. "You making me feel like an ass for leaving when you've spent the past three years not wanting my help?"

"I haven't—" My voice sticks in my throat.

I'm too late.

The realization that he's right hits me with the force of a blow. I waited too long, tried too hard to do everything by

myself. And now that I'm finally admitting I need Dean's help…
he's already agreed to be there for someone else.

A hot flush of pain sweeps over me. I hate my fear, my desperation, my panic-induced attempt to play this card even though I
know how unfair it is.

"When I told you about the festival, I gave you a chance to say
no," I remind him. "You didn't."

"Damn right I didn't." He turns, anger darkening his expression as he grabs another sheaf of papers from the table. "Don't
you know by now I can never fucking say *no* to you?"

"You're doing it now."

"Because this isn't about you!" he snaps, slamming down the
lid of his briefcase. "I know you like it when I'm at your beck and
call, but believe it or not, I do have obligations to other people."

"You think I don't know that? You think that hasn't been
shockingly clear every time you've gone to Italy or France?"

"I've asked you countless times to go with me."

"And for the first time ever, I haven't been able to go where
you want," I reply caustically. "I know you like it when I follow
you around like a puppy, but believe it or not, I have obligations
to other people too."

"Right." He spreads his arms, his jaw tightening. "So you go
deal with your obligations and I'll deal with mine."

It's not the end of the world. I know that. I'll have to scramble,
but I'm sure I can find another suitable auctioneer for the Chair
Fair. It won't be someone who is as good as Dean, but—as I keep
reminding myself—I've done a lot of things without him over the
past couple of years. I can stage a successful auction without him.

But somewhere deep inside me, in a place where I'm still
captivated by a handsome medieval history professor who came
to the rescue of a girl upset over college credits, I feel as if our
lives are starting to run parallel. We converge around Nicholas
and our home life, but if everything else is *separate*…

I pull in a breath. Maybe this is just what happens when a

marriage stretches and lengthens, when a couple's careers expand, when you realize there are only so many hours in the day and you still have so much to do.

Maybe it's supposed to be this way—my husband and I now putting our other responsibilities first, focusing together on our child and giving each other whatever is leftover.

It doesn't feel right, though. In fact, it feels horribly wrong. Dean and I have never been each other's *leftovers.*

I turn to the door, hating the anger still lingering between us, the discovery of problems neither one of us knows how to fix. Problems that have nothing to do with the United Nations or town festivals.

"What time do you leave?" I ask.

"Flight leaves Wednesday at seven."

"Email me your hotel and flight information."

"I already did."

I pause and turn back to face him. "When are you coming back?"

"I don't know."

"You don't know?"

"Depends on the vote." He doesn't look at me, but his voice is tense with regret. "Simon and I are heading to Altopascio afterward, see if we can start the earthquake repairs. I should know by the end of the assembly."

We're both silent. The resignation and sorrow simmering between us almost breaks my heart in half.

Come back to me. The wish blooms bright and hard in the center of my soul, the place where our unbreakable relationship, our everlasting marriage, has always lived.

I can't remember the last time I'd hoped for anything more desperately. But hope and reality are two very different things. And because there is nothing else I can say, I turn away from my husband and walk slowly back down the spiral staircase.

CHAPTER 25

Olivia

After Dean's departure, the Butterfly House takes on an air of vastness and empty space. Without the secure familiarity of the café to keep me occupied, I'm thrown off balance even more, as if the ground is once again shifting beneath my feet. I try to focus on the final preparations for the festival, even more fiercely determined to make it a success, and spend a great deal of time with Nicholas.

One afternoon, in need of a friend, I find Kelsey in the garage of Archer's shop, crouching on top of a huge, custom-built, storm-chasing truck armored with sixteen-gauge steel plates and a Kevlar coating.

A circular radar device and large antenna sits on top of the vehicle, along with a bunch of little tubes that Kelsey is working at with a wrench. Her hair is covered with a ratty baseball cap, and her tank top and cargo pants are streaked with dirt and grease.

"What are those?" I ask, gesturing to the tubes.

"Cannons." She peers down, flashing me a smile of greeting and pride. "They shoot instrument probes into the tornado to measure and collect wind speed, pressure, and temperature data. This is the first season we're taking Dorothy out, so we'll see how she does."

"Dorothy, huh?" I can't help smiling.

"You and Allie are a bad influence on me. So is the movie *Twister,* which Archer has the poor taste to actually like." She pats the roof of the vehicle affectionately before hopping off and approaching me. "Speaking of Allie, she called me and said something about a birthday party gone wrong?"

I sigh and sit down on a nearby bench. As a silent partner in the café, Kelsey stays out of the daily operations, but Allie and I have always involved her in big decisions and kept her informed when something changes.

I suppose the birthday disaster qualifies.

"It was my fault," I admit. "I'm taking a leave of absence from the café until the festival is over. And speaking of the festival, please tell me you're still going to be in town for it."

"Sure. Archer and I are working at the kids' stage, right?"

I nod. "Did you check the forecast for me?"

"Everything looks great. Nothing on the radar, but I'll check the day before too."

I can see the festival plan in my head. Everything will be situated in Wizard's Park—the carnival rides and game booths, the food trucks, stages, and Chair Fair tent.

And, if I let myself, I can see the townspeople wandering around with their excited children, taking them to the ball-toss game and on the merry-go-round. I hear their squeals of laughter, their pleas for ice cream, their voices accompanying a sing-along.

I don't see Dean anywhere.

"Hey." Kelsey takes off her cap and wipes her forehead with the back of her hand as she sits beside me. "What happened?"

The confession sticks in my throat. I look at the storm-chasing truck and try for the hundredth time to understand why anyone would see a black storm on the horizon and choose to drive right toward it. To go *into* it.

I push to my feet and approach the truck, running my hand over the steel plates. "Why do you do it?"

"Chase?" Kelsey shrugs. "It's hard to explain. It's a rush like no other. Dangerous, exhilarating, thrilling. The realization that you can face down a force of nature is pretty damned powerful."

"And scary."

"Scary is part of the appeal," Kelsey says. "I struggled for a long time with my attraction to danger. I thought it was the reason my father died. I tried to hide in academia and to control everything about my life. But then I met Archer, and I discovered that sometimes being in control can suck. That sometimes I want to let everything go, to give up control and drive into a storm without knowing what will happen."

I turn to look at her. "But you won't marry Archer because you don't want anything to change."

She averts her gaze. "I don't want anything to change about *us*. And I know it's stupid because my parents had a great marriage. They loved each other completely. But then my father died and... well, my mother was alone. Then I lost my mother right when I found Archer. And it's been so good that I feel like I'd be tempting the fates if I married him. What if I lost him too?"

She holds up her hand when I start to speak.

"Don't tell me it makes no sense," she says. "I know that already. But I can't love Archer more than I already do. And I'm not going to marry him just because some bullshit custom says we should or because people think marriage is the only way you can be with someone for life. Because it's not."

"True," I agree. "Swans mate for life, but they don't get married. They just wing it."

A grin tugs at Kelsey's mouth as she climbs back onto the roof of the vehicle.

"You hear anything from Professor Marvel?" she asks, apparently having done enough baring of her soul.

"Yes, he's heading for the UN Assembly meeting as we speak. Being an international diplomat."

Kelsey shoots me a glance. "You don't sound thrilled about that."

"I'm proud of him," I reply, deliberately avoiding her remark. "I'm just sorry he's missing the festival. And I'm worried they're going to offer him the job, which was clearly made for him."

"So why does that worry you?"

"Because I can't stand the thought of moving to different countries, not knowing where we'd go next or how long we'd stay. Hell, Kelsey, I lost Nicholas once in the Butterfly House. What if I lost him in Malaysia?"

I return to the bench and pick up my satchel.

"Liv."

I turn to face her again. She's standing on the roof, her hands on her hips, looking so strong and confident that just the sight of her underscores my recent failures.

"Do you remember when I first hooked up with Archer, and I wasn't at all sure I was making the right decision?" she asks.

I nod.

"You were the one who told me that nothing ever changes if you don't trust your instincts and take risks," Kelsey continues. "And that was exactly what I did with Archer. Turned out it was the best decision I've ever made. Maybe you should take your own advice this time."

"But I don't like what my instincts are telling me," I admit. "I'm worried Dean would be giving up an incredible opportunity because of me. I don't want to live with that for the rest of my life. I don't want him to either."

"Instinct and worry aren't the same thing," Kelsey reminds me. "I still have an instinctive pull toward danger, but I'm not scared of it anymore. And I'm not scared of giving up control because I know I have Archer. He's my rock. He takes my fear away. When you have that, you can do anything."

"Would you get down from there so I can hug you?" I ask.

"Okay." She rolls her eyes. "But only for, like, ten seconds."

She jumps down from the vehicle. We exchange a hug before I walk back to my car. As much as I wish I could "take my own advice," I know Kelsey and I are very different people.

She still controls the entire Spiral Project. She built a vehicle to protect herself from tornados. Archer will never leave her, no matter how many times she turns down his marriage proposal. She'll never leave him either. She chooses to drive into storms. Even when she's not in control, she's still *in control.*

And I am too—at least, for now. Without the Edison sponsorship, I call an emergency planning meeting and ask the festival volunteers to try and secure more funding to make up for Edison's refusal. But after several days of trying, it becomes clear that so many businesses have already donated packages to the Chair Fair they can't take on the added financial commitment of a sponsorship.

After a slew of refusals one afternoon, I bring Nicholas to a park on the west side of the lake where The Moms have arranged to meet for the weekly playgroup. They greet us warmly, though when the children run off to the playground, their mothers turn to me with barely contained curiosity.

"Liv, we heard about the disaster at the café over the weekend," Joan announces, her eyes widening as she leans closer. "What on earth happened?"

I was fucking my husband and forgot about everything else, I think bitterly.

"Just a bunch of mistakes," I say. "All of it was my fault, but we're making amends as best we can."

The Moms blink almost in unison, as if they hadn't expected to hear me admit to blame.

"I heard the kids had a big food fight," Susan remarks.

"There was some cake thrown."

"I heard Slice of Pie almost caused a riot," Joan says.

"They got a late start." I wonder how I can change the subject. "The kids were just eager to hear them play."

"Are they still providing backstage passes for the festival?" Joan asks.

"Uh, I doubt it," I say, suddenly realizing the deeper implications of not having a high-level sponsor. "Honestly, I don't know if they'll even perform at the festival anymore. I don't think we can afford it."

Their mouths drop open in shock.

"Not perform?" Susan repeats. "How can Slice of Pie not perform? I've already told Bailey about it, and she's beyond excited. She told all the kids in her class."

"So did Dylan," Carol adds. "He's been insisting I call him the Pieman for the past two weeks now. He won't stop singing 'Mustard Pie.'"

They swing their gazes to me. My stomach hurts.

"Well, their performance was contingent on me securing a big sponsor so we could afford to pay them," I admit. "So I'd been trying to get Edison Power on board as our one and only diamond-level sponsor. But the man at Edison who's in charge of making sponsorship decisions turned us down."

"He turned down Mirror Lake's Bicentennial Festival?" Carol shakes her head in disbelief. "Aren't they supposed to be all into community support?"

"Yes, but it was his daughter's birthday that was ruined," I say. "Needless to say, Edison no longer trusts me to pull off a town festival. And if we don't have their sponsorship, we can't afford to pay Slice of Pie."

The Moms fall silent. A strange weight seems to lift off my shoulders. We spend so much time trying to prove ourselves and our children to each other, to make it seem like we're totally in control, that we know exactly what we're doing, that all our decisions are the right ones—that it is an unexpected relief to stand in front of a group of mothers and admit to failure.

"Well, Bailey is going to be devastated," Susan mutters.

"I'm sure Bailey will survive the disappointment," Carol replies, eyeing her pointedly before turning back to me. "Do you have other sponsors, Liv?"

"Yes, but not at the diamond level. That's fifteen thousand and over. It was also going to help pay for extra tents and food trucks, plus the carnival rides."

Crap. I need to call the carnival manager now and ask about scaling things back. I'm really running out of time.

"Frank works with the community outreach manager over at SciTech," Carol says, reaching for a cookie from the snacks on the picnic table. "I can ask him to put in a good word for the festival."

"Brian *runs* the marketing department at Horville Foods," Joan puts in. "I'm sure he'll approve some level of sponsorship. And Kathleen still works over at the Blue Shoe Company. They just opened another franchise in Forest Grove, so they'd probably be into some community outreach."

"Sam and I can make a personal donation," Susan says.

They all look at me expectantly again. A faint hope flickers to life.

"In the corporate packages, I mention VIP seating and passes as one of the benefits to sponsorship," I say. "I can give them to you to pass along, if you think people might be interested."

"With Slice of Pie at risk, Liv," Joan remarks, shaking her head, "we're all interested."

Something begins to lift inside me, as if rainclouds are parting to reveal a clear sky. I look at the other women with a dawning realization that for all the hot topics and controversy about advanced schools, organic foods, vaccinations, et cetera, The Moms know how to get stuff done. Not only for their children and families, but for their friends.

"Don't worry, Liv," Susan says. "We've got this."

CHAPTER 26

OLIVIA

Over the next week, The Moms collect close to eleven thousand dollars in sponsorships from various companies. Slice of Pie agrees to perform, and as word spreads of the festival troubles, Mirror Lake rallies to the cause with more volunteers and donations. Allie, Brent, and the planning committee scramble to secure the rest of the entertainment and food trucks.

Florence Wickham tells me her new friend Mr. Jenkins of the Historic Railroad Association will be delighted to serve as the Chair Fair auctioneer. The carnival company sets up rides in a corner of Wizard's Park, while volunteers hang signs and posters in shop windows.

On Saturday morning, the day of the festival, the sun rises into a cloudless blue sky. The grassy expanse of Wizard's Park is dotted with tents where people are selling artwork and various foods. Balloons float from the children's stage, which is surrounded by a bouncy-house and game booths. Folk music drifts from a band at the main stage, and the air is filled with the smells of popcorn, barbeque, and cotton candy.

Armed with a walkie-talkie and my cell phone, I walk around the festival grounds, making sure everything is running smoothly. The volunteers are wearing their purple *Mirror Lake Festival Staff* T-shirts as they help with crowd control, entertainment, and safety.

Earlier that morning, we moved the auction chairs to a cordoned-off area outside the auction tent. The colorful, painted chairs are arranged in perfect rows, like a flower garden drenched in sunlight.

In addition to being thrilled by how everything worked out, I'm incredibly proud of what the townspeople have contributed to the Chair Fair—beautiful, detailed, whimsical, and artistic creations of whatever inspired them. There are chairs painted with teddy bears, rainbows, ocean landscapes, Impressionist artworks, Dr. Seuss characters, and jungle animals.

Taking a break from checking my spreadsheets, I join Archer, Kelsey, and Nicholas for some fun. We have gooey slices of pizza, play beanbag toss, and ride the carousel. I text Dean that the festival is going well, and include a picture of Nicholas eating a cone of cotton candy bigger than his head.

"Forty-five minutes until the auction, Liv." Allie hurries up to me, her ponytail swinging and her glasses askew. "Where's Patrick?"

"He had to cancel." I peer toward the auction tent. "Mr. Jenkins is going to substitute as the auctioneer."

"Mr. Jenkins?" Allie repeats, her expression both surprised and doubtful. "Isn't he, like, eighty?"

"Well, yes, but he's still very agile and spry." I smile to hide my own uncertainty. "It'll be fine."

Just fine, I repeat to myself firmly. I leave Nicholas with Archer and head toward the auction tent, which is starting to fill with patrons. Several people wander around outside looking at the chairs, and their conversations are tinged with admiration and delight.

"Hello, Olivia, dear." Florence Wickham, dainty and pretty in a peach-colored suit and hat, approaches me with a smile. "What a wonderful success this is!"

"So far," I allow, though I won't be entirely relaxed until the festival is over and done with.

"I'm so sorry Dean couldn't be here," Florence remarks wistfully. "But Ronald is delighted to help out. Oh, Ronald! Over here!"

A wizened older man waves and approaches us, leaning on a cane. A fringe of white hair encircles his bald head, and he's wearing a rumpled brown suit and polka-dotted tie. He extends a shaky hand to greet me, and I lead him over to the podium to explain the lot numbers and how the auction will run.

I leave him looking through an auctioneer booklet while I get the volunteers organized handing out paddles and catalogs. As the start time nears, the seats begin to fill up, and before long I realize it's going to be standing room only.

Nervousness twines through me. I've worked hard on the entire festival, but the Chair Fair is especially critical, not only for the Historical Society but for the town itself. If we don't raise enough money to save the railroad depot, there's no telling what developer might grab up the land and possibly ruin the picturesque beauty of Wizard's Park with a strip mall or condos.

I glance at my watch. Five minutes. Mr. Jenkins is standing by the podium with Florence, whispering something in her ear as he pats her rear end. She giggles.

With a smile, I go out to the chair display to ensure they're all lined up in the same order they are in the catalog. A cloud passes over the sun, throwing the chairs into shadow. I do a quick check and return to the tent to get the auction underway.

The crowd quiets down as I introduce myself, thank everyone

who has supported us, explain how the auction will run, and then turn the microphone over to Mr. Jenkins.

He puts on a pair of bifocals and clears his throat, peering at the list of chairs.

"Uh, first item..." he glances at the stage, where a volunteer brings up a chair painted with a rainbow theme "...is a chair."

The crowd smiles indulgently. I move closer to Mr. Jenkins and point to the list.

"Lot number one," I remind him quietly.

"Lot one," he says into the mic. "A really nice chair painted with rainbows. Let's start the bidding at...say, fifty dollars!"

Several paddles wave in the air. I see Archer standing by the edge of the tent, Nicholas perched on his shoulders.

"Fifty dollars, anyone for sixty?" Mr. Jenkins's voice grows louder, excitement appearing on his weathered face. "Sixty dollars for this beautiful, hand-painted chair!"

My tension eases a little. He just needed some time to warm up. I glance at Florence, who is watching from the sidelines and gazing at Mr. Jenkins adoringly.

After the rainbow chair sells for over a hundred dollars, Mr. Jenkins waves to the next, teddy-bear themed chair.

"And who wants to own this adorable chair, perfect for a nursery or children's room?" he shouts into the mic.

A loud squeal penetrates the tent from the feedback of his yell. I wince and gesture to the sound guy to turn it down.

"Who bids fifty bucks for the teddy bears?" Mr. Jenkins calls.

A few paddles rise. I write down the numbers.

"Fifty dollars, right there, lady in the blue, who bids sixty right there man in the red shirt perfect seventy bidder bidder would you bid eighty one hundred would you bid more who bids more would you bid one hundred five..."

His words slur together faster and faster, as if he's trying to whip the crowd into a frenzy of bidding, though the audience is looking at him with confusion.

I step forward and put my hand on his arm, leaning toward the microphone. "We're at one hundred five, ladies and gentlemen. Do we have a bid for one twenty?"

More paddles rise. The chair sells for one hundred fifty, and I write down the winner's number as a volunteer brings up the next chair.

"Hey, Liv!" shouts Mr. Jenkins, even though I'm standing right beside him.

I glance at the audience. Several people are shifting in their chairs, looking vaguely impatient. A cool wind wafts through the tent, the light dimming as if clouds are gathering overhead. I smile nervously.

"Yes, Mr. Jenkins?" I say.

"What do planets like to read?" Mr. Jenkins asks.

"Um, what?"

"Comet books!" he yells.

A few people smile indulgently, but restlessness runs through the crowd.

"And the next lot number, three, is an incredible chair painted by renowned atmospheric scientist Kelsey March!" I announce. "Let's start the bidding at one hundred dollars."

"Who bids one hundred one hundred lady in white do you bid one hundred five one hundred five six seven bidder up batter up seven eight nine…"

His voice lowers again into a garbled, unintelligible monotone that has the audience looking both baffled and impatient. One person in the back row gets up and leaves.

I grab the microphone and yank it away from Mr. Jenkins.

"Hey, Mr. Jenkins," I say brightly. "What did the ocean say to the sea?"

"What?" He cups his hand behind his ear and leans toward me.

"Nothing. It just waved."

"Hah!" Mr. Jenkins thumps the podium and cackles. "Now,

folks, that joke comes free with the purchase of this incredible chair! Does anyone bid two hundred?"

A woman in the back, looking amused, lifts her paddle. I breathe a sigh of relief.

"Two fifty?" I ask. "Anyone?"

No response.

"Come on now!" Mr. Jenkins bangs his fist on the podium again. "Someone bid two fifty or we'll tell another joke."

Three paddles shoot up into the air along with a few chuckles.

"Two fifty!" Mr. Jenkins points at a man who might have raised his paddle first. "Two seventy-five anyone? What do you get when you cross a busy road and a strawberry?"

"What?" I ask dutifully.

"A traffic jam!"

The audience chuckles again as a patron raises her paddle.

"Three hundred if you stop with the jokes!" she calls.

"Sold to the lovely lady in pink!" yells Mr. Jenkins, banging the gavel and pointing at the winner. "Next item is a princess chair complete with crown!"

The volunteers bring up the pink, sparkly chair topped with a glittering tiara. The bidding gets started, interrupted by what turns into the Liv-and-Mr.-Jenkins comedy act as Mr. Jenkins fires off riddles about bugs, animals, and outer space, while I play the straight man and laugh at every joke.

"Lot five, folks," I announce as a volunteer brings up another chair, "a gorgeous Indian-patterned chair with an incredibly detailed mandala on the seat."

The next hour passes in a blur of activity and whirlwind bidding, as the audience gets into the rhythm of the event and Mr. Jenkins and I find our groove. The light grows dimmer as more clouds gather overhead, but at least I'm not worried about rain because Kelsey checked the forecast and assured me the weather would be good all weekend.

Archer's chair is next—the detailed rendition of the comic-book superheroine Blue causing a stir of interest in the crowd. Paddles lift into the air as Mr. Jenkins reads the description.

"We have a bid for three hundred," I announce. "Do I hear three fifty for this incredible work of art?"

"Five hundred dollars," a female voice calls from the back of the audience.

Everyone turns to look at the woman who dared defy the order of the paddles.

Kelsey March.

Of course.

She's standing on the edge of the crowd, the blue streak in her hair glowing like neon, her arms crossed and her features set in that stubborn expression I know so well. She looks exactly like the strong, fierce Blue who can create tornadoes from the palms of her hands.

"We have a bid for five hundred dollars," I say into the mic. "Do we have a…"

"Six hundred!" a deep male voice booms from the other side of the tent.

We all look in that direction. Archer is standing there with Nicholas still on his shoulders. Nicholas is waving a paddle in the air. Kelsey shoots Archer a glower. He responds with a look of pure defiance.

"Six fifty!" Kelsey calls.

"Do we have a bid for seven hundred?" Mr. Jenkins asks.

Several paddles lift.

"Eight hundred," Archer shouts.

Mr. Jenkins and I exchange looks of surprise.

"A thousand?" he asks into the mic.

"A thousand five hundred," Kelsey calls.

People turn to stare at Archer and Kelsey. Though they're on opposite sides of the tent, they're looking at each other with such challenge it's as if they're the only two people present. I can practically see the sparks flashing between them.

"Do we have a bid for a thousand six hundred?" I ask, torn between wanting the money for the restoration and not wanting my friends to go over the top.

"Two thousand," Archer calls.

There's a collective gasp.

"Two thousand five hundred?" Mr. Jenkins asks.

Archer taps Nicholas on the knee. Nicholas waves the paddle in the air.

"Uh, you're bidding against yourself, son," Mr. Jenkins remarks.

The audience chuckles.

"No," Archer replies. "I'm bidding *for* her."

A smattering of applause and laughter rises in the air, and a flush colors Kelsey's cheeks. Mr. Jenkins grins.

"Do I hear two thousand six hundred?" he asks.

I look at Kelsey, who shakes her head. A man in the front row raises his paddle, which causes another ripple of surprise.

"Three," Archer shouts.

In the end, Archer buys his own chair for three thousand two hundred dollars—easily the largest bid yet, and one that brings the audience to its feet in a standing ovation. It takes Mr. Jenkins and me a good five minutes to get everyone settled back down and focused on the next chair.

The frenzy over Archer and Kelsey's bidding has galvanized both the crowd and Mr. Jenkins.

"Lettuce raise the bids, Liv!" he shouts into the microphone.

I smile and rush through the remaining sales pitches, describing a jungle-themed chair, an ocean chair, a Dr. Seuss-inspired chair—all of which bring in substantial bids.

Just as Mr. Jenkins slams the gavel down on a winning bid, a booming noise cracks overhead. I jump a little, startled, as the patrons murmur to each other and glance up at the tent roof.

"Hey, Liv, what does a cloud have on under his pants?" Mr. Jenkins asks cheerfully.

"Um, what?" I realize the sky has grown even darker, almost iron-gray. I've been so preoccupied with the auction I didn't notice before now.

"Thunderwear!" Mr. Jenkins claps his hands and laughs.

Thunder?

Light flashes through the grayness. I turn, looking past the patrons to where the chairs are all lined up on the grass, awaiting pickup from the winning bidders. Another crack sounds in the distance, a rumbling noise like a hungry giant or—

The skies open up. A flood of heavy rain begins to pour down, splashing onto the tent and pooling immediately into puddles of muddy water.

Are you freaking kidding me?

A gust of wind billows against the tent, rippling the cover. Shrieks and gasps rise from the crowd. People push to their feet, clutching bags and purses as they hurry to seek more secure shelter.

I grab Mr. Jenkins' arm, helping him down the steps of the stage to where Florence is sitting.

"The café is open, if you can make it over there," I tell them. "But hurry."

I run outside, thinking of the carnival, the entertainment, if there's enough shelter for everyone. The rain spills down, lightning splitting across the sky. People rush away from the stages, clutching their children's hands or holding event fliers over their heads.

"Save the chairs, man!"

I whirl at the sound of Archer's voice. He's waving frantically at Brent, who is running toward him from the direction of the food trucks. Kelsey is close behind, holding Nicholas. She sees me and swerves, as Brent and Archer rush to pull the painted chairs into a nearby truck.

"Freak storm," Kelsey gasps, her blond hair hanging damply over her face. "It wasn't on the radar, Liv, I swear."

"Can you take Nicholas to the café?" I ask. "Get him changed? There's clean clothes in his diaper bag in my office."

"Yeah, but you need to take cover too."

"I'll be there in a sec. Just want to make sure no one needs help."

Kelsey runs off into the storm. I hurry to the stages to ask if the bands are okay or if they need help with their equipment. In seconds, I'm drenched through, water spilling down my face and soaking my clothes. Another crash of thunder and lightning rents the air.

The rain comes down harder.

CHAPTER 27

Olivia

The festival volunteers rally as best they can, but the lightning is getting closer and being in an open field is about the worst place for any of us. The wind increases, pushing against the tents, tipping over garbage bins and sandwich-board signs.

When a food tent dislodges from its moorings and billows toward the lake, the remaining staff and festival-goers run toward Avalon Street, seeking shelter in shops and restaurants.

Wiping rivulets of water from my face, I return to the auction tent to try and find Brent and Archer, but the place is empty, chairs overturned and auction paddles lying in the mud. I cast a glance over the park. It's now deserted, the wind and rain whipping through the abandoned tents and art booths.

I turn, hurrying to the Wonderland Café. Mud soaks into my shoes. By the time I go up the front porch steps, I'm waterlogged, cold, and starting to shiver. Light blazes through the windows of the café. The air inside is fragrant with the scents of sugar cookies and hot tea.

Because the café was closed for the festival, the only people inside are Florence, Mr. Jenkins, and Kelsey. They're all still in their wet clothes, but somewhat drier thanks to kitchen towels. Nicholas, in dry clothes from his diaper bag, is sitting at one of the tables in his booster seat, eating cheddar crackers and drinking milk.

"You okay?" Kelsey hurries toward me. "Everyone else?"

"I think everyone is okay, but I'll check with the fire department. They were on hand in case of an emergency." My phone is wet but working, so I contact the fire chief and paramedics, who thankfully report no injuries or accidents.

"Have you heard from Archer?" I ask Kelsey.

"Not yet." She checks her phone, her forehead creasing with worry.

I go into the back office, where I keep extra clothes for myself, and change into black yoga pants and a T-shirt. When I return to the front room, a clatter of activity comes from the porch. The door opens, and Archer walks in, carrying the Blue chair.

"We got all the chairs to the warehouse," he tells me, plunking the chair down by the counter. "Doesn't appear to be much damage."

His gaze meets Kelsey's across the room. Energy arcs through the air. She crosses her arms. Her eyes narrow with defiance, as if she's trying to resist the obviously magnetic force between them.

"I wanted that chair," she informs him icily.

"Good, because I made it for you." Archer's expression becomes equally mutinous. "You don't want to get married, fine. But no way are you shutting me out, storm girl. You're *mine,* dammit. You're mine for life, whether you marry me or not. You won't take my ring yet, but you'd damned well better take this chair."

He folds his arms across his wide chest and glowers at her, as if defying her to say *no*. The rest of us are silent, the air tense with anticipation over what Kelsey is going to say or do next.

She walks toward Archer, her gaze never leaving his.

"Ask me," she orders.

He studies her for a second, then goes down on one knee in front of her. My heart gives a little leap. He puts one hand on the Blue chair.

"Kelsey March," Archer says. "Will you accept this chair?"

A slow smile blooms across her face. She reaches out to thread her fingers through his hair. For a long moment, they look at each other, caught in something so intense and private I'm sure they've forgotten everyone else in the room.

"Yes," she says, running her hand down the side of his face. "Forever."

Florence and I clap. We all smile as Archer gets to his feet and pulls Kelsey into his arms for a kiss. Happy as I am for both of them, and their consensus that a lifelong love can bloom bright even without marriage, I still experience a sudden, sharp longing for my husband. For us, our marriage is everything.

Our marriage is everything.

The declaration repeats in my mind, like a comet streaking endlessly across the sky. Something opens inside me, revealing the basic truth that has always been a part of me. But it had gotten buried beneath the chaos of work, responsibilities, parenthood, daily living, and…I admit rather reluctantly…dusty old fears that maybe it's time for me to throw out for good.

"Well, we should get going," Florence remarks, tugging on her damp coat.

"We might need an ark." Mr. Jenkins looks at the cascade of rain falling outside the window. "Good thing I Noah guy who can build one."

Florence rolls her eyes. Kelsey, Archer, and I all chuckle.

"It's still raining pretty hard," I tell them. "You shouldn't drive home yet."

"We'll be fine." Florence waves her hand in a circle. "I'm in the mood for some hot toddies, if you know what I mean."

Kelsey shoots me an amused look and strides to the door.

"We'll drop you both off," she offers. "We need to get home too."

There's a small flurry of activity as everyone prepares to leave. I don't want to go home until I can assess the festival damage, and I promise Kelsey I'll stay at the café until the rain lets up.

After they all leave, I make myself a cup of tea and pick up Nicholas when he starts whining and rubbing his eyes. I turn on some gentle music and walk around the café with him in my arms.

I pass the Mad Hatter tea party, the wacky croquet game where the Red Queen's face is contorted with anger, the Kansas farm where a twister spins from the floor to the ceiling, whisking Dorothy and Toto off on an adventure.

I walk through the Wicked Witch's castle, the poppy fields, Munchkinland where Dorothy took her first step on the Yellow Brick Road. I pass the garden where Alice is talking to the caterpillar, seated on a soft mushroom with smoke billowing above him, and where she dances the quadrille with the Gryphon and the Mock Turtle.

And the Gryphon added, "Come, let's hear some of your adventures."

"I could tell you my adventures—beginning from this morning," said Alice a little timidly, "but it's no use going back to yesterday because I was a different person then."

Nicholas shifts in my arms, resting his head against my shoulder. I return to the office and place him gently in his soft playpen, dimming the lights and turning the music lower.

He sleeps soundly, his mouth slightly open and his hands balled into little fists. I settle my hand on his back, feeling the rise and fall of his breathing. I whisper a few words of thanks, then take my mug of tea out to the covered back terrace.

The rain is still coming down in heavy, gusting sheets. I stop at the railing, looking at the expanse of Wizard's Park, the broken tents lying on the grass like wounded sea creatures, the litter of sodden popcorn boxes and popped balloons, the deserted food booths and overturned chairs.

Tears sting my eyes. The disappointment I've kept at bay now settles heavily around my heart. Despite my stumbles, I'd worked hard for the festival. I'd desperately wanted everything to turn out well. I'd wanted it all to be *perfect.*

I wipe at a drop rolling down my cheek, not sure if it's rain or tears. I can't help feeling as if I let down so many people. Townspeople, sponsors, vendors, artists, entertainers, children, the Historical Society. Myself.

No, it doesn't make sense to feel like this. Not even Kelsey, atmospheric scientist extraordinaire, could have predicted this storm. And I've certainly learned that life hides countless unforeseen catastrophes no one can predict.

Hell, life is messy. Stormy. Uncontrollable. Maybe all you can do is shelter yourself with the people you love most. At least then, you can enjoy the good weather and get through the storms together.

I start to go back into the café when a movement catches my eye. I turn and look into the distance. My breath catches, my heart making a wild, spinning leap up into the stars.

In the rain, the indistinct outline of a tall, broad-shouldered man appears, striding through the flooded wreckage of the park as if he's a warrior crossing a battlefield.

As always, his path is a direct, unwavering line straight to me.

CHAPTER 28

OLIVIA

I walk to the railing of the terrace, curling my hand around a post as I watch my husband come toward me. A thousand emotions flood my heart and soul.

Dean is soaked through, his hair plastered to his head, rain dripping in rivulets over his face. He stops at the bottom of the terrace steps. For a long moment, we look at each other, the rain falling between us, a rumble of thunder echoing over the mountains.

He climbs the steps to where I'm standing, and as he closes the distance between us, the ache inside me softens and disappears. Dean twists a lock of my damp hair between his fingers and tucks it behind my ear.

"Hey, beauty." His voice is a warm, gentle current sliding right around my heart.

"Hi, professor." I reach out to put my hand on his chest. "You came back."

"I will always come back to you."

Fresh tears sting my eyes. Uncaring that he's drenched, I move closer and slide my arms around his waist. He folds his arms around me. Rainwater seeps from his clothes into my T-shirt, but the sensation of his powerful body against mine, and the delicious, familiar warmth of him, burns away the cold.

I feel my world straightening into balance again, a palpable shift beneath my feet, securing me to the earth, to myself, to this man.

Only when a chill ripples over my skin do I lift my head to look up at him.

"Nicholas is sleeping in the office, but there are extra clothes in the backroom. You should find something that fits you."

Dean picks up my hand and presses a kiss to my palm before twining his fingers through mine. We go into the café and I pull on a dry shirt before checking on Nicholas again. Dean emerges from the backroom in sweatpants and a black Wonderland Café T-shirt. He sits at a stool on the counter as I pour him a cup of hot coffee and refresh my tea.

I set the coffee in front of him, gazing at the thickness of his eyelashes, the way his lips close around the rim of the mug.

"What happened?" I ask quietly.

"The Assembly voted to protect the site. There was a unanimous yes vote from all UN delegates."

"Oh, Dean." Pleasure and pride flood me in a wave as I lean across the counter to kiss him. "Congratulations. You must be thrilled."

"Yeah, I'm happy about it." A self-conscious smile tugs at his mouth. "Now we won't have any trouble with funding or repairing the quake damage. Not to mention, we can keep the entire excavation team intact and work on finding out what else is there."

I take his hands in mine and squeeze, unable to speak past the sudden lump in my throat. I forget, sometimes, how much I admire this part of Dean's character—the relentless drive to pursue a goal, to get things done not only for himself, but for other people. For history.

"I gave the presentation on Tuesday, and they voted on Wednesday," he continues. "Then I had the session on medieval sites all day Thursday and Friday. I figured if I hurried, I could get back here in time for at least part of the festival, so when the last session was over, I caught the next flight out. And here I am."

Here you are. Right here. As always.

"I thought you were going to Altopascio after the assembly," I say.

"I told Simon he'd have to go without me." Dean shrugs and takes a sip of coffee. "He was heartbroken, of course."

"Of course. But I'm sure he'll get over it."

"Yeah." He sets the mug down and looks at me, his gaze tracking warmly over my face. "Sorry I couldn't stop the storm for you."

I smile. I suppose it's about time I also accept the fact that not even my husband can prevent certain kinds of storms.

"I know you would have, if you could have," I tell him.

Sometimes I wish there was a way to be prepared for everything. Then I remind myself that I was never prepared for the things that set me on the path of my life. And, like a string of pearls, everything is connected. The endless travels with my mother, all the strangers and friends we met along the way, the path to Twelve Oaks and North, then to my aunt Stella. Then Fieldbrook, North again, the University of Wisconsin. Dean. Our son.

"Did you talk to Hans and Simon about the job?" I ask.

"Yeah, we had a few meetings." Dean rubs a hand through his hair, faint hesitation flashing across his expression before he says, "The World Heritage Center committee did formally offer me the assistant director position."

A sense of inevitability crashes over me, but not in an

unpleasant way. This news isn't a surprise, but it's been an uncertainty. And now, at least, knowing is better than not knowing.

I reach across the counter and put my hand on the side of his neck. The sensation of his heart beating strong and steady against my palm is beautifully reassuring, one of the few things—it seems—that hasn't changed.

"Dean." Saying his name, too, eases my apprehension. It still tastes smooth and richly sweet, like cherry brandy or butter pecan. "Congratulations. I knew they'd offer you the job. They courted you so hard because they wanted you so badly."

A smile tugs at his mouth. "Like the way I did with you, huh?"

I return his smile. "But I didn't turn you down."

"You didn't say yes right away either."

Silence fills the air between us. My heart thumps.

"So what did you say to the WHC?" I ask.

"I said thank you," Dean replies. "But that I couldn't leave King's or Mirror Lake. They told me to look over the employment package and benefits before they accepted my answer. Hans is calling me next week."

"Have you read the package yet?"

"Yeah. It's pretty incredible. Even included an au pair option, if we want one for Nicholas. Rent, expenses, travel. Everything."

I'm not sure what to say to that revelation, much less how to feel. I've spent the past few weeks knowing what an extraordinary opportunity this would be for Dean, yet fighting the very idea of changing our lives so drastically.

What about him?

I look at him, the shadows carving over his face, his thick eyelashes and dark eyes I've lost myself in more times than I can count.

I wonder about the *number*s of us—how many times we've kissed, how many times I've pressed my hand against his chest, how many times he's touched my face or tugged gently at a lock of my hair. How many times he's called me *beauty*.

"Do you know one of the things I loved about you from the start?" I ask. "One of the things I still love most about you?"

"The professor thing."

"Well, that too," I admit. "But I also love how you want to *know* everything. How curious you are...not just about history, but about people, places, and things. And you don't need to travel the world to learn. You were like that before we got married. You read books about religion, art, and politics, you wanted to go to museums and gardens.

"When we were living in Madison, you got involved with the Wisconsin River conservation, and when we were in LA, we ended up in the weirdest places. That mosaic tile house in Venice. The original Bob's Big Boy. The velvet painting museum. No matter where we were, you found something fascinating to learn about."

Dean keeps watching me, his eyes almost glittering.

"I remember one weekend in Madison when we were hanging out in your apartment," I continue. "You were reading a book about the history of cryptography. You were telling me about it, and I totally wasn't getting the point, so you sat down and taught me some nineteenth-century code. Then you wrote me a note in the code and told me to decipher it while you went to make dinner."

"What did I write?"

"You wrote..." My heart gives a happy little knock of reminiscence. *"Come here, beauty. I need to kiss you."*

He smiles, his eyes creasing at the corners. "And did you obey?"

"You don't remember?"

"I remember." His voice deepens. He crooks his finger at me. "Come here, beauty. I need to kiss you."

I go around the counter to where he's sitting. He grips my waist and pulls me into the V of his legs, bringing one hand up to the nape of my neck. With intense pleasure and relief, I let myself fall into the warm pressure of his mouth, edged with the crystalline memory of our past.

"I've always sought knowledge," Dean says, lifting his head. "That's why I was so into the King Arthur stories when I was a kid—I wanted to know more about the knights, the Crusades, the castles. I guess that expanded into other areas as I got older. But of all there is to learn in the world, there's only one subject I've ever wanted to know *everything* about."

I wait, my heart pounding, my gaze locked on his. His expression is warm and tender, a look reserved only for me.

"You, of course," he says. "You're the book I want to open. The story I want to read. The lesson I want to learn, the music I want to hear, the painting I want to study for eternity. If I know nothing else in life except the truth and heart of Olivia West, I'm the luckiest man alive."

"Well, that's just great," I mutter, pressing my face against his shoulder. "Now I'm crying."

A chuckle rumbles through his chest as he spreads his hand over the side of my neck and presses his lips to my forehead.

"I love you, Liv. If you're happy, I'm happy."

"I've always been happy with you."

So why have I been so knotted up at the idea of us ever leaving Mirror Lake?

Dean and I lived in a few other cities before we settled in Mirror Lake. Even though they were unknown to me, I was happy to be wherever we needed to be.

Granted, we didn't have children then, and I didn't own a café or have a strong circle of friends and community, but the idea of *change* wasn't that scary since I knew I'd always have my husband. And now the two of us have our son.

I take his hand and rub it slowly between my palms. "You know my Pinterest boards?"

"Your what?"

"Pinterest boards. It's that site where you make these bulletin boards with different themes. Crafts, recipes, books, fashion, whatever. I have about a dozen of them. One with sexy pictures, but the rest are recipes and stuff about motherhood and raising children."

"What's the point of them?"

"Inspiration. Planning. Ideas. Ever since Nicholas was born, I've had all these intentions of making homemade baby food and gourmet dinners. I have a board of pictures from other cafés and bistros that I thought we could adapt for Wonderland. I was going to spend weekends with Nicholas making sponge towers and spaghetti paintings and walnut-shell boats…"

My voice trails off. An image of Nicholas and I snuggled under a blanket in the living room appears in my head.

"But do you know what, Dean?" I pull myself onto the stool beside him and rest my elbows on the counter. "We haven't yet made spaghetti paintings or walnut-shell boats. And I don't know when we will."

"Ah, well." He tightens his arm around me. "Sounds like a waste of good food anyway."

"I just wanted everything to be perfect, you know? I wanted Nicholas to have all the things I never did. I wanted the café to be this warm, fuzzy place where parents and children can be transported to the land of make-believe. I wanted feather-light lemon cakes and rainbow parfaits. I wanted the festival to be fun and heart-warming, where we all joined together as a community. I wanted you and me to have our hot, explosive sex life back. But not only did everything turn out so *not perfect*, I somehow managed to screw it all up."

I shake my head. "But I think I might have realized that as imperfect as it is, everything is the way I wanted it to be, just not exactly how I envisioned. And what kind of an ass would I be to complain about anything when I have all *this*?"

I wave my hand in a gesture that encompasses Dean and me, Nicholas, the café, our friends, and all the rest of Mirror Lake.

He slides his hand over my back, rubbing the ridges of my spine.

"A very sexy ass," he remarks, moving his hand down to pat my rear end. "And it's okay. You don't need to feel guilty for wanting things to be perfect. You don't need to feel guilty at all. I get where it comes from."

"I guess I totally overcompensated."

"Yeah, you did. I get that too."

I turn to look at him. It's the same reason he spent his life working so hard to be the perfect son—to compensate for the dysfunction of his family and his own guilt over ruining his relationship with Archer.

I straighten, cupping my hand around the back of his neck. A drop of water runs from his damp hair over my fingers.

Our marriage is everything.

"I love you, Dean. And I don't want you to have any regrets."

"As long as I have you, I never will," he says. "I wouldn't change what we have for the world."

"But maybe we should change it for the world," I reply. "You were always meant for more. I know you love working at King's, but I also know there's a reason you've been doing so much internationally over the past few years. And I know this position with the World Heritage Center has sparked something inside you. All those dreams of crusades and adventures you had when you were a boy...well, maybe this is your chance to make them come true."

"Ah, Liv." He shakes his head. "I don't need the job."

"You don't need it, but you might want it."

A sudden gust of wind bangs the screen on the front door. Dean and I both climb off our stools but instead of closing the door, we walk out to the covered front porch and sit on the white porch swing, which is sheltered near the building.

"Moving to Paris isn't like going to the moon," I remark, even though it's certainly felt that way to me.

Damp air brushes against my face. Beside me, Dean is a solid wall of security and strength. He settles his hand on my thigh.

"Paris is one thing, Liv. But already neither of us likes the fact that I have to travel so much. I'd have to travel even more as the assistant director. And you coming along to Malaysia or Cambodia with a toddler…no."

Allie's voice echoes in my head.

"People move all over the world with young children all the time," I say.

"We're not people. We're us."

Silence falls, broken only by the sound of rain pattering on the porch roof. The streetlights along Emerald Street create golden circles glowing wetly on the sidewalks. The town is alive around us—the lake rippling in the wind, the metallic-gray storm clouds gathered overhead, the windows of downtown shops blazing with light.

I once couldn't imagine leaving Mirror Lake. But now, knowing the world wants and needs my brilliant husband, knowing I'm strong enough to share him, that he will always walk a path that leads straight back to me…now I'm starting to believe I can find a home anywhere.

"Do you remember I once told you about Dorothy discovering she always had the power to leave Oz?" I say. "She'd been wearing the ruby slippers the whole time."

"I remember."

"I've done that a lot too," I admit. "I've spent all this time looking for something I already have."

"Ruby slippers?"

"No, professor." I lean my head against his shoulder and close my eyes, breathing in the scents of rain and Dean and our future. "Perfection."

"You had it all along?"

"Of course." I rub my cheek against his shoulder. "It's you. You're my perfection."

"Ah." He pats my hip, his voice warm with tenderness. "Good one, beauty."

I smile, snuggling closer to him. We sit together for a long time, as the rain begins to lessen and the clouds slide away from the sky, revealing a sprinkle of stars and a perfect, spiral moon that will follow us wherever we go or wherever we stay.

CHAPTER 29

DEAN

*A*rcher's motorcycle is parked outside the railroad depot. The doors to the train shed are open, work lights glowing from inside, a radio playing the Stones' "All Down the Line." Archer is crouched by the side of the engine, working something with a wrench.

"Hey." I stop near him, shoving my hands into my pockets.

"Hey." He glances at my suit. "Guess you're not here to work."

"No. You got a minute?"

He nods and pushes to his feet. I sit on the steps of a cargo car, while Archer reaches into a nearby cooler and produces two cartons of chocolate milk. He offers me one. I take it, remembering how chocolate milk was a staple in our Castle tree house. Archer has never lost his love for it.

He sits beside me. I take a drink of the sugary milk, admitting it tastes pretty good. I set the carton down and rest my elbows on my knees, linking my hands together.

"You know that job I told you about?" I ask.

"The fancy European thing." Archer tilts his head back to take a drink. "Yeah."

"When I was in Geneva," I say, "they offered me the job."

He's silent for a minute before he says, "So what did you tell them?"

"They want an answer next week. I have to turn them down."

"You have to," Archer repeats, looking at the engine on the opposite side of the shed. "That's different from you *want to*."

Silence falls. I don't contradict him because he's right.

"When I was a kid, I dreamed of something like this," I admit. "Traveling the world. Going to unknown places, having adventures. But when I met Liv, I thought she was all the adventure I'd ever need."

"Now you think differently?"

"No, that's not it. I could live in a cave with her and be happy. It's more that...she had a shitty childhood and hated moving from place to place, being dragged around by her mother. She's never seen the appeal of traveling, seeing new things, meeting new people. So part of me wants her to know what that's like, and to have more adventures *with* her. With Nicholas. I've always wanted to give them everything, including the world."

"But?" Archer asks.

"But not like this," I say. "If I took this job, I'd have to be away from them more than I already am. And Liv and I have both been spending too much time at work for too long. Something has to give for both of us. So I need to step down as project director of the train restoration."

Archer is quiet.

"Well, damn," he finally mutters.

"I don't want to entirely quit," I continue. "It's a great project, and I still want to help out. I just can't direct it anymore. I was hoping you would."

He blinks. "You want me to lead the project?"

"You're way more qualified than I am," I say. "And Mr. Jenkins respects you a hell of a lot more too. Now that the project is funded, you could hire a few more guys, get the work done faster and better than I ever could. It'd be like running your garage, only with historic trains."

Archer looks somewhat baffled, like he'd never have expected me to ask him something like this. "You're serious?"

"Sure. I can still help out with the research and stuff, but you need to be in charge."

He doesn't respond for a minute.

"If it means I get to tell your sorry ass what to do, I'm on board," he finally says. "Thanks, man."

"Yeah, well, keep in mind you also have to let Florence Wickham squeeze your biceps at least once a week."

He grins. I push to my feet. We hold out our hands at the same time and shake. When I leave the train shed, I feel lighter, like something heavy has been lifted off my shoulders. Something to do with my brother.

I head back to campus and call Florence to tell her Archer is taking over as project director.

"Oh, Dean, what a wonderful idea!" she says, with so much delighted enthusiasm my ego takes a hit. "He's perfect for the job."

"I thought you said *I* was perfect for the job," I mutter.

"Oh, you're perfect for many jobs, my dear," she assures me. "But perhaps not this one."

I grudgingly agree. After ending the call, I spend the rest of the afternoon working on a paper about castle architecture, which is much more familiar territory than old trains. I glance up when Frances Hunter knocks on the open door.

"This just came in for you," she says, handing me a padded envelope.

The stamps are postmarked from Paris, and the World Heritage return address is in the corner. I peel off the packing tape and remove several folders containing reports from the UN Assembly.

"As young people say today," Frances remarks, "they think you're the boss."

"I told Hans I can't consider taking the job." I leaf through a report about how to engage local communities in heritage preservation. "I won't."

"Clearly he thinks you can be persuaded otherwise," Frances says.

"You know I have a life here." I drop the report on top of the other documents and push the whole pile to the side. "Liv owns a business. We have a son, a house, a *lawnmower*. And no way do I want some other medievalist coming to King's and taking over the program *I* started. I still can't believe you think I'd consider saying yes."

Before Frances can respond, there's another knock on the door. Jessica Burke comes in with a worn paperback.

"Sorry for interrupting, but I wanted to return this," she says, handing me the book. "I found a copy online. I have some good ideas based on Chaucer's portraits of knights and merchants."

"Great. I'll look through my bibliography and see if there's anything else I can find for you."

Jessica glances from Frances back to me. "So can I ask what's going on with the World Heritage position?"

"They made an offer." I drag a hand down my face. "But I'm not actively pursuing it, Jessica. I can't leave King's or Mirror Lake."

A flash of disappointment crosses her face. "I figured you'd say that. Did you and Hans talk about the Youth Experts program?"

"I told him the WHC should get it up and running again," I say. "And, Jessica, if you want to spearhead the organization of the program, I'd be more than happy to put in a good word for you."

"Me?" Jessica's eyebrows lift. "I don't want to organize the program."

"Why not? You're the one who's been advocating for it. You'd be great at directing and organizing."

"No way." Jessica shakes her head. "I'm trying to finish my book, teach classes, apply for jobs. Now that my father is gone, my mom really needs me. I want to help with the Youth Experts program as much as I can, but I can't take full responsibility for it right now. I was hoping *you* would."

"How could I?"

"As assistant director, you'd be in charge of a bunch of different programs," Jessica explains. "You could make the Youth Experts a priority."

It's an idea I've found intriguing since she first mentioned it a few weeks ago. Working with students has always been one of the most rewarding parts of my career, and the idea of collaborating with young people around the world to protect historic sites is highly appealing.

But...

"As assistant director, I *might* be able to help the Youth Experts," I tell Jessica. "But you know the job is highly political and involves a ton of negotiations and bureaucracy. Chances are slim I could even get the Youth program funded, let alone involved in specific projects."

Jessica shrugs, not looking convinced. "You're the only one who cares enough to try. Certainly you're the only one with enough influence to make a difference."

"It would be right in your wheelhouse, Dean," Frances adds.

"You saw the assistant director job description," I tell her. "I don't know how I'd get all that done in a day, much less have time to organize the Youth program."

"So there's no way you would take the job?" Jessica asks.

I shake my head, aware of Frances's gaze. "I can't."

That's not a phrase I often use, and they both know it. Jessica and Frances exchange glances and turn to leave. I watch them go, hating the sense that I've somehow deeply disappointed them both.

CHAPTER 30

DEAN

I stop in the kitchen doorway and look at my wife. She's washing dishes, her head bent as she rinses one of Nicholas's cups. Her hair is tied up into a ponytail that exposes the graceful curve of her neck. A few strands are loose, drifting around her face and shoulders.

I let myself gaze at her for a good long time—the shape of her breasts and hips, the length of her legs beneath her skirt, the pretty curve of her rear.

I move into the kitchen and come up behind her, sliding my arms around her waist. She startles before giving a little laugh.

"I didn't even know you were there."

"Nicholas just fell asleep." I press my lips to her warm nape and spread my hands over her torso. "And you look so good doing the dishes."

"Mmm. You should watch me when I'm vacuuming. I'm hotter than a firecracker the way I shimmy my hips around."

"Maybe you could do a private show for me one night." I move my hands around to squeeze her gorgeous ass. "Maybe you could do one *right now*."

Liv flicks soap bubbles over her shoulder at me. "I need to finish these dishes and then work on some festival reports for the town council. I also want to get started on thank-you notes to all the people who painted chairs for the auction."

Clearly this is a challenge. I reach around her to turn off the water and push my groin up against her. Ah, damn, so soft and yielding. There are few things more perfect in the world than my wife's ass.

"Dean." Liv squirms a little and nudges me with her elbow. "I have to work."

"Me too. I have to work my cock in and out of your sweet, tight pussy."

"Dean!" she gasps, her breath catching with that little noise that makes me hot in two seconds flat—as if I weren't already getting hot just pressing my dick against her.

"Come on, beauty." I work my hands underneath her apron and slide them into the waistband of her skirt. Lust fires through me at the sensation of her soft, warm belly against my palms. "Let's fuck."

She gives another breathless laugh and shakes her head, her ponytail swishing against my chest like a swath of silk.

"Later," she promises.

I groan. "I have a conference call in twenty minutes. No idea how long it will take."

"Well, now that I know you wanted a quickie, you can darned well wait until you have time to service me properly."

"Don't I always?"

"Yeah, you do all right." She turns in my arms, her expression amused. "But it sounds like you have more mundane work to do first. Who are you talking to?"

"A couple of the medievalists who were at the UN Assembly.

They're interested in working with me on conservation techniques."

Liv studies me, her eyebrows pulling together. "You know, with all that's been going on, I've neglected to tell you how proud I am of you."

"You don't have to—"

She shakes her head to stop my words. "Really, Dean. It's incredible, what you've done. What you're doing. I've been so caught up in how all the changes would affect me—*us*—that I haven't even told you how extraordinary your work is. The impact you're having on both history and the present...it's beyond impressive. I'm so proud of you."

I brush a stray eyelash off her cheek, thinking that her praise means more to me than anything the World Heritage Center—or anyone else on the planet—could offer.

"Thanks," I say, aware of the painful inadequacy of the word.

But all my wife has to do is look at me to see right into my heart.

"You're welcome." She smiles. "Go take your call, hotshot."

I tug her ponytail, tilting her head back and pressing my lips against hers. "Be ready for me."

"Don't take too long." She brushes her hand over my chest and turns back to the sink.

I head to my office and dial in to the conference call. It's lengthy and detailed, covering conservation techniques for several different sites in Europe and South America. After the call, I check my email, which includes a message from Hans Klasen confirming our phone appointment on Monday.

A knot pulls in my chest. There's never been a question that my family comes first. Always. And I hate knowing that by turning the WHC job down, Liv will still feel responsible for what she thinks is a missed opportunity. No matter how much she doesn't want to change our lives.

I finish up some other work and shut down my computer. I

check all the doors in the Butterfly House to make sure they're locked and turn off the lights before going upstairs.

I stop in Nicholas's room. He sleeps with his fists bunched up on either side of his head, exactly the way he did as an infant. His mouth is open, a faint whistling coming from his nose with every breath.

Makes no sense that we only have one heart to contain all these emotions. I brush my hand over my son's head and pull the blanket up around him before going into the master bedroom. Liv is in bed, a book open on her lap and her head tilted to the side as she dozes.

I put her book on the nightstand and turn off the light. After changing into pajama bottoms, I climb into bed. She turns to me sleepily like she always does, a movement as dependable as the sunrise, tucking her head under my chin and shifting her body against mine. No matter how hard she sleeps, she always turns to me when I get into bed. I wrap my arms around her and pull her closer.

A perfect fit. My head fills with the scent of peaches. Any lingering tension in my chest disappears. I feel her start to wake, to realize I'm there.

"Oh, sorry," she whispers, rubbing her cheek against my shoulder. "I really was waiting for you."

"Yeah, I could tell by the way you were snoring. Very seductive."

She chuckles and pokes me in the stomach. "I do not snore."

"Uh, sure you don't," I assure her.

She pokes me again and lifts her head, her thick hair tumbling over her face. I reach up to brush it back, sliding my hand over her cheek. She shifts upward to press her soft lips against mine. I breathe her in, letting the feel of her fill every part of me.

"Before I fell asleep, I was thinking about our honeymoon," Liv says.

"What were you thinking?"

"I was remembering one afternoon," she murmurs against my mouth, running her hand across my chest. "We'd just been to the Rodin Museum, and we stopped at a patisserie to get some brioche to have with coffee when we got back to the apartment. The second we stepped outside, the skies just opened up with a torrent of rain, like Zeus himself had ordered a thunderstorm. Lightning cracked through the black clouds, and everyone outside started hurrying for shelter.

"I tucked the bag of brioche under my sweater, you grabbed my hand, and we started running toward the apartment like we could somehow escape it. But it was pouring so much that we were soaked within seconds, and then I stumbled on the curb. You stopped to steady me, and we were both absolutely drenched, water streaming into our eyes and ruining our shoes. And do you remember what we did?"

"I remember."

"We looked at each other and started to laugh." Liv presses kisses over my cheeks, down to my jaw and neck. "I can still hear your laugh, echoing against the old buildings and cobblestones, more resonant than the thunder. We were laughing so hard we couldn't move, so we just stood there, getting more drenched with every second. By the time we managed to regain our composure and get back to the apartment building, we were literally soaked to the skin. We left puddles of water all over the stairs until we finally reached the apartment."

She circles her hand over my chest, her warm mouth sliding over the side of my neck, her hair like silk against my skin. Her touch alone fires heat through my blood. When she rubs her full breasts over my chest, my cock starts to harden.

"Do you remember what happened then?" she whispers.

How could I forget?

I fist the length of her hair into my hand and pull her head up. Her brown eyes are heavy with growing desire, her pale skin colored with a slight flush.

"I remember," I say before pulling her into another kiss.

The door slamming behind us. Turning to look at Liv, her hair plastered to her head, her eyes bright with laughter, rain trickling over her face. My mermaid wife.

My *wife.*

Grabbing her shoulders, crowding her up against the door, crushing her mouth with mine. Her gasp of surprise, then her open, eager response as she parted her lips to let me inside. Both of us laughing again as we struggled to peel the wet clothes off each other right there in the foyer. Water evaporating into steam.

"Best storm I've ever been in," Liv remarks, lifting her head with a smile, her breath hot against my lips.

"What happened to the brioche?" I ask.

"They landed on the floor, and we squished them when you rolled me over."

"Oh, yeah."

An image of her *rolled over* flashes in my head—her beautiful, round ass perched right in front of me, her legs spread in invitation. Her desire-dark eyes as she turned to look at me over her shoulder, breathlessly begging me to fuck her.

Lust surges through me. I start to reach for the folds of her nightgown, but she pushes away from me.

"Don't move." She lifts her gown over her head and drops it to the floor.

I groan. The sight of her naked jerks my cock into full hardness. I reach into the waistband of my boxers and grab my dick. Liv rises to her knees, all voluptuous curves, her full breasts topped with stiff, dark pink nipples. I reach out to caress them, palming their weight before sliding one hand between her thighs.

"Oh!" She gasps as I probe into her. Her clit quivers against my forefinger. She grabs my wrist. "Dean, wait. Not yet."

Reluctantly, I pull my hand away, beckoning her closer.

"C'mere," I order. "I want my wife."

"You have your wife," she assures me, lowering her head to

kiss the hollow of my throat. "Every minute of every day. And right now she's going to have *you*."

She trails kisses in a line down my chest and over my abdomen, her breasts sliding over my thigh. When she cups my cock through my pants, heat jolts through me. She glances up at me with a smile before hooking her fingers into my pants and tugging them down.

She murmurs something low in her throat, wrapping one hand around my shaft and stroking. *Ah, shit.* Her cool fingers against my hot skin almost makes me come. I push up into her fist, both wanting her to get me off and wanting this to last for hours.

I inhale a rush of air when she starts taking my cock into her mouth. I grip her hair at the nape of her neck to keep it from falling into her face and concealing the view.

I love watching her lips slide over my shaft, her eyes half-closed with her thick lashes like feathers. She lowers her mouth halfway down before sliding back up.

It's so fucking good that I could come any second, but I want to be deep inside her when I do. I pull her up toward me, grasping her hips to roll her onto her back. Her eyes are glazed with lust, her breath coming in little gasps, her skin flushed. My perfect wife.

I slide my hands over her naked body, pinching her nipples as I get between her legs, spreading her thighs apart. I circle my thumb around her clit before lowering my head to lick her cleft.

"Dean!" She gasps, twining her fingers into my hair as she arches upward.

Her body vibrates with need. I settle between her thighs, sliding my tongue over her. Little moans stream from her throat as she writhes underneath me, her fingers clenching and unclenching in my hair, her legs winding over my shoulders.

Ah, Christ. My dick throbs against the bed sheet. The taste

and scent of my wife fills my head. I spread her open and push my tongue into her, feeling her start to tense.

"Oh, Dean, hurry." Liv grabs my shoulders, trying to pull me up to her. "I need you to fuck me. *Please.*"

I get to my knees, position myself, and sink into her with a groan. Fucking *heaven.* All thought disappears into blinding heat and the drive for release. Liv's cries of pleasure fire into my blood. Her hot, sweaty body jostles beneath mine as she meets every thrust, her beautiful tits bouncing, her hair spilling over the pillow. I edge my hand between us to find her slippery clit. She reaches up to grab the headboard.

"Oh, god," she gasps. "Dean, I'm so close."

"Do it." I rub her harder, gritting my teeth with restraint. "Christ, you feel amazing."

"Wait…just there." She bites her lower lip, her eyes darkening. "I'm going to…please…*oh!*"

She lets out another cry and clenches around my shaft. The sensation of her shuddering is too much to withstand. I thrust hard, explosions firing through me as I shoot deep inside her. So damned good. So damned *perfect.*

Liv wraps her arms around me, her breathing heavy. I roll us both over so I can pull her on top of me. She stretches out, every curve of her body fitting to mine, her breasts pillowed against my chest. I stroke my hands over her back to her ass.

"If thinking about our honeymoon gets you this turned on, I'm going to dig up all our old photos," I tell her.

"Don't need photos, professor." Liv smiles and taps her temple. "It's all up here."

For me too. I still wish we could live it all over again.

Liv kisses my throat and tucks her head underneath my neck. As she settles against my chest and drifts into sleep, everything fades except her.

CHAPTER 31

OLIVIA

I step into the Wonderland Café, comfort descending over me when I hear the familiar sounds of conversation and laughter, the clink of silverware, the bustle emanating from the kitchen. Allie is working at the front counter, her head bent as she organizes the morning's receipts. She glances up as I approach.

"Welcome to Wonder...oh, hi, Liv."

"Hi, Allie." I hold out the potted lantana plant I'm carrying. "Peace offering."

"No peace offering necessary, since you and I were never at war." She comes around the counter to take the plant from me. We exchange a hug.

"I'm sorry," I say. "I know I went over the top."

"We all do sometimes." She shakes her head with a smile. "Just ask my dad about my college days."

She sets the plant beside the register and nods to an empty stool at the counter. "Have a seat. I'll bring you tea and cookies."

Feeling as if I'm being welcomed back into the fold, I sit at the counter as Allie brings me a fresh pot of Darjeeling tea and a plate of Yellow Brick Road cookies. I tell her how the town council is handling the aftermath of the storm and that everyone is hoping we can recreate the festival next year—the Bicentennial Plus One Festival—and maybe turn it into an annual event.

"Are you still in charge?" Allie asks.

"Lord, no. My festival planning days are over. Before the storm, we did do quite well at the auction, raising enough money for the Historical Society to start the restoration. Archer wants to talk to your father about the depot architecture."

"My father would love to get involved," Allie says. "He just finished work designing a modern office building, but historical architecture is his thing."

"Thanks again for all your help with the festival," I tell her. "How's everything been going here?"

"All right. We invited the kids from Becky Harrison's birthday party back with their families—on different days—for free dinners and cake, and we gave all the kids a party gift bag. That smoothed things over quite a bit. I also added guest limits to all the party packages, so we won't have that kind of situation again."

Relief fills me. "That's wonderful, Allie. Thank you so much."

"Hey, Liv, the place looks great."

Allie and I look up to see Jessica Burke entering the café, her curly brown hair pulled back into a bun. I reintroduce her to Allie as she hitches herself onto the stool beside me. I push the plate of cookies toward her in invitation.

"I was heading over to Java Works when I passed by," she tells me, pulling a laptop out of her satchel. "Figured I'd stop here instead. Okay if I just sit and work?"

"Stay as long as you like," Allie offers. "What are you working on?"

Jessica grimaces. "Medieval history job applications."

"Any leads?" I ask.

"Nothing close by, but I'm applying wherever I meet the qualifications," Jessica says. "There's an opening at UC Riverside, but I'm not all that nuts about moving that far away from my mother."

"Does Dean have any ideas for you?"

"Yeah, he's contacted a bunch of people on my behalf, but nothing's come of it yet." Jessica shoots me a rueful smile. "Guess I should have listened to my dad when he said a PhD in medieval history wasn't going to lead to an outpouring of job offers."

"Following your bliss is far more important than multiple job offers," Allie advises sagely. "I was an art major, for heaven's sake. But if I hadn't been, I'd probably never have partnered with Liv to open Wonderland."

My heart lifts at the implication she still considers it good fortune that she and I went into business together.

"And look at Dean," Allie continues. "He's the rock star of the medievalist world. Get that man some leather pants, right?"

Jessica and I exchange amused looks at the idea of Professor West in leather pants.

"Dean is an exception," Jessica says. "I mean, don't get me wrong. I know I'm a good historian, but I harbor no illusions I'd ever be offered the assistant director position at the World Heritage Center. And yet Dean tells me he's going to turn it down."

"Really?" Allie swings her gaze to me. "So you're not going back to Paris?"

"Well, no." I shift, vaguely uncomfortable. "Dean started the Medieval Studies program at King's. He'd never want to leave."

"It's a shame," Jessica says. "The job is made for him. And without him, I'm pretty sure the Youth Experts program is doomed."

Well, great. I can just add that to my cauldron of guilt, which is like a witch's brew I keep stirring. Dean won't take the job because of me, and now I'm not only jeopardizing hundreds of important, historical sites, I'm also dooming the hopes and dreams of eager, intelligent students.

"I should get going." I glance at the clock and climb off the stool. "Good to see both of you."

"You too," Jessica says.

"See you tomorrow," Allie says.

"What's going on tomorrow?" I ask her. "I don't think I have anything on my calendar."

"You're on the schedule for the morning shift." Allie takes out her phone and starts pressing buttons. "I'll email the schedule to you. August is a busy month, so we have some planning to do."

I reach across the counter to squeeze her arm. "I'll be here."

"I know you will."

Happy at the knowledge that we've mended fences, I return home. Nicholas and Dean are out in the back garden, tossing a ball back and forth. I watch them from the big picture window for a few minutes. A bunch of thoughts tumble through my mind like a kaleidoscope constantly shifting and changing, but always bright and beautiful.

Dean and Nicholas stomp into the house with dirty shoes and grass-stained jeans. I make them take off their shoes and shoo them upstairs to change before we sit down for dinner. Afterward we settle Nicholas down with picture books and a cookie while Dean and I clean the kitchen.

"Any word from Hans yet?" I ask casually.

"We're talking on Monday." Dean's expression is pensive as he takes the last dish from me and puts it in the cupboard. "Frances stopped by my office yesterday. She's been telling me for a while how good this offer is for both my career and King's."

As I dry my hands on a towel, I dig for courage and say the words I've felt since Dean first told me he was a frontrunner.

"You want the job, don't you?" I ask. "Your comments about office politics and the WHC not wanting an answer right away are wearing a bit thin."

A faintly sheepish expression crosses his face. "I did want to read the whole salary and benefits package. I had to find out exactly what I was saying *no* to."

I understand that. I'd have expected no less from Professor Dean West, in fact. He never takes action without examining all the angles first, leaving no stone unturned. Of course this would be no different.

Dean takes hold of my shoulders and turns me toward him again. He takes my face in his hands, his gold-flecked eyes fixed on mine.

"But I would never…" His throat works with a swallow. "I would never ask you to give up everything for my sake. Never."

"I know you wouldn't." I curl my hands around his wrists. "But that doesn't mean you can't want what you want."

"I have everything I want right here."

"Wants aren't that rigid," I say, realizing only now the truth of that statement. "They're like water—constantly moving and changing. When I was five, I wanted a pony. When I was ten, I wanted a normal life and home. When I was fifteen, I wanted good grades. When I was twenty-five, I wanted to be with you more than anything. And while that will never change, I now have a whole other set of *wants* that center around our son and our marriage. When life changes, so do the things we want."

I loosen my grip from his wrist and put my hand on his cheek. "So it's okay to want an incredible opportunity. Heaven knows you've worked hard enough for it."

"Liv, I'm not going to—"

"You didn't answer my question."

He's quiet for a moment, his gaze on mine. I can almost see all the wheels and gears clicking through his beautiful mind— assessing, evaluating, thinking.

"I don't know if I want the job," he finally admits. "Yeah, it's a big deal. Probably the biggest opportunity a medievalist could ever have—helping protect sites around the world, working on a bunch of different projects.

"But at that level, there's more politics and red tape than I'd want to contend with…and in dozens of different countries. I'd have to give up teaching and writing. Hell, I'd have to give up my research. I don't even know if I'd have the time to finish the book I'm writing about illuminated manuscripts.

"I'd have to give up working at Altopascio. I'd spend a lot of my time in meetings and navigating bureaucratic mazes. And while I'd love to research the sites, I'd probably have to delegate a lot of that work to other people because I'd be dealing with the bureaucracy and paperwork."

He reaches out to lightly tweak my nose. "Then there's you, Mrs. West. You and Nicholas. Taking you away from Mirror Lake, from the café, from the life we've built. Living in Paris might be an incredible experience, but I don't know how much time we'd have together.

"And I'd have to travel more than I already do. I don't like leaving you and Nicholas at all, but at least here I know you have Kelsey, Archer, Allie, everyone else. I couldn't leave you both alone in a foreign city. I *won't*."

Silence falls between us again, brimming over with the tension between the safety of what we have and the possibilities of risk and chance.

"But?" I ask gently.

He coils a few strands of my hair around his finger and brushes his thumb against my cheek.

"But," he says, "I remember our wedding and honeymoon. I remember staying in that little apartment with you and never wanting to leave Paris. I remember endless hours walking through the Louvre. I remember busy cafés, quiet restaurants, the look on your face when you tasted your first pistachio macaroon.

I remember walking through Notre Dame and telling you everything I knew about its history. Not once did you yawn with boredom. Just the opposite, in fact—you wanted to know everything.

"I remember you sitting on the wrought-iron balcony of the apartment with potted plants around you and the rooftops of Paris behind you, like you were in an Impressionist painting. I looked at you and thought, *God in heaven. That's my wife. Right there. My wife.*

"I thought we could never leave Paris because surely it was too good to be true. If we left the city of lights, the spell would break. And even though it didn't, even though I'm spellbound by you for eternity, I still think about how it was just you and me there.

"And the idea of going back, but this time with both you and Nicholas, to work for an international organization dedicated to preserving history—and to *live there*...It would be another chapter in our great adventure."

Something loosens inside me, like a tangled string slackening, and then a deeply rooted knowledge of my husband surfaces into the light.

"When I first went to your apartment in Madison almost ten years ago," I tell him, "there was a box on the kitchen table filled with loops of string, some of them knotted and twisted together."

His eyes crinkle. "I remember."

"I thought it was so wonderfully dorky that you made string figures," I continue. "And somewhere way down deep, I've also always known how *perfect* it is."

"Perfect how?"

"That you, of all men in the world, are an expert at fastening string together," I explain. "Unraveling it, working out all the knots, and then making intricate, beautiful patterns. You do that in every other area of life—fixing, connecting, creating—it makes perfect sense you'd do it as a hobby."

A smile tugs at his mouth as he pulls me against him.

"You do it with me all the time." I slide my arms around his waist. "You know exactly how to unknot me."

"Hmm." His deep voice rumbles in his chest. "I think we've discovered I also know how to tie you up."

"Oh, yes, you do." I smile, a shiver of remembrance sliding down my spine. "Maybe you can do that again sometime soon."

"There's no *maybe* in kinky sex, Mrs. West," Dean murmurs, moving his hands down to my bottom. "There's only, '*Yes, sir.*'"

"Yes, sir." I stand on tiptoe to press my lips against his.

Warmth floods me, but just as Dean lifts his hands to tilt my head to the right angle, Nicholas shouts, "Milk!"

With a resigned laugh, I give Dean a quick, hard kiss and go to attend to our son. Dean pats me on the rear and mutters something about, *"Not done with you yet."*

With that promise humming in my blood, I take Nicholas upstairs for a bath and bed, while Dean picks up the scattered toys in the sunroom and heads up to his tower office.

After getting Nicholas into his train-patterned pajamas, I squeeze into the toddler bed beside him as he starts to fall asleep. I wrap my arms around him. His little body moves with the rhythm of his breath. I lie back against the pillows and look at the ceiling, where a projection of smiling sea creatures from Nicholas's nightlight floats in a slow circle.

I remember a paper Dean once wrote about medieval monsters—apes with spiked wings, leathery dragons, lion-clawed griffins, dog-headed men, giants, serpents with sharp teeth, and cloven-hoofed demons.

These dreadful creatures existed on the margins of illuminated manuscripts and maps, a dire warning about the terrors that lay beyond the known world. Though the monsters inspired both fear and awe, the pervasive belief in them didn't stop people from launching expeditions and traveling to distant, unknown lands.

And as those explorers sailed right into possible storms and danger, they encountered unfamiliar territories, different people, strange animals, but no horned demons or five-headed serpents. If it weren't for their courage, their curiosity, their sense of adventure, they might never have discovered that the horrific monsters they'd envisioned didn't exist.

Dean, of course, has always been one such daring explorer—at least, in his secret heart—seeking new, exciting experiences, charting new territories, unafraid of imaginary dangers.

I, on the other hand, am the devoted scribe, sitting at my desk believing in scary things outside the boundaries of my own world, but content in the belief that if I stay here, I will never have to confront them.

I'm not ashamed of being that way. I make no apologies for it, not anymore. Because if it weren't for the scribes, there would be no bright, intricately illuminated manuscripts, no textual representations of the past, no rich, detailed illustrations of saints and angels, of flora and fauna, even of imaginary monsters.

And though I know Dean will never admit—maybe not even to himself—that he'd take the job in a heartbeat if it didn't mean leaving Mirror Lake, I don't ever want to be the reason he smothers his longing for risk and adventure.

I pull Nicholas closer. His breath puffs against my neck. Sometimes our son is fearless. When he's climbing the jungle gym, swinging on the monkey bars, running through the park—he has no obstacles, no worries about things that don't even exist, things that are just illusions.

As I slide out of the bed and pull Nicholas's blanket over him, I wonder at what point in life it becomes so much easier to be scared and so much harder to find courage.

Our great adventure. The adventure of Liv and Dean.

I press my lips to my son's forehead, leaving him to sleep in the soft glow of circling fish and mermaids. I take the baby monitor and walk up the spiral staircase to Dean's office.

"Dean?" I knock on the open door.

"Right here." He turns from his computer to smile at me.

My heart gives the same warm, little flutter I'd felt when I saw him for the first time all those years ago. I've spent so long believing it was possible to not only have everything, but to have everything be perfect.

Because if it was all perfect here, in Mirror Lake, then neither Dean nor I would ever need anything else except each other, our child, and our work. We would never have a reason to look beyond what we had already created. We wouldn't want anything to change.

But how dull life would be if nothing ever changed. If it *was* always perfect. If we never tried to create something new.

"Love of my life." I stop beside my husband and rest my hand on his shoulder. "I have an idea."

∾

Over the next few days, a great deal of discussion and persuasion follows the announcement of my idea.

"I've started researching how it would work." I sit across from Dean at the breakfast table with a blueberry muffin. "And it's not actually as unnerving as it sounds. You said yourself that you'd have an incredible benefits package."

"That was for the assistant director position," Dean reminds me. "I turned it down already."

I eye him over the rim of my mug of coffee, knowing well that salary and insurance are not the issue here. Neither is the assistant director position.

"Dean, one of the reasons the WHC wanted to hire you was because of your negotiation skills," I say. "I'm certain they would be more than willing to work with you on a mutually beneficial agreement, especially if you go to them with the entire plan in place."

Which, of course, he would. Professor Dean West, master of rock-solid plans.

"I know part of the reason you turned the assistant director job down was because of me," I continue, holding up my hand to stop his immediate protest. "It's okay. We both know if I didn't have the café, or if I weren't so rooted here, you might have been more interested.

"But I also know there was a lot about the job description you didn't like, which is why you really need to talk to Hans Klasen and Frances Hunter about the Youth Experts program. They might very well say no, but you'll never know unless you try. And I know you would love to work with students from all over the world, especially on the conservation of historic sites."

He sits back and looks at me, his expression both tender and amused. "You know that, do you, Mrs. West?"

"Yes." I approach to sit on his lap, twining my arms around his neck. "Because I know you, Professor West. Sometimes better than I know myself."

"I can't let you do this for me, Liv."

"Yes, you can. Because you have to do something for me in return."

"I do?" Interest sparks in his eyes. "What?"

"I'll tell you later," I promise.

For the next few days Dean does research, writes a proposal, discusses the idea with Hans and Frances, talks to Jessica Burke, contacts World Heritage field offices in different countries, and sends out feelers to various universities.

Slowly the pieces begin fitting together, until a picture begins to emerge of a way in which Dean can still do what he loves to do, but on a more powerful, impactful level. A way that will allow him to mentor international students, work at the World Heritage Center and the Altopascio site, and live in Paris with his family without excessive travel.

And a way in which I have to let go of my fear, take a risk, and trust myself. I know I can do it, too, because everything I have in Mirror Lake will still be here waiting for my return.

That is the crucial difference, the one thing that solidifies my courage. In all my traveling and moving with my mother, I never knew where we were going, but I always knew we were never going back. Because there had never been a place to return to. Never the security of a home waiting for us.

It's not a surprise to me when Hans Klasen and the World Heritage committee are more than happy to accommodate Dean's proposal. They know exactly how good he would be as the director of the Youth Experts program. When Hans and the committee approve the creation and funding of a new position especially for Dean, there is no turning back.

Frances, who has approved of the idea from the start, arranges for Dean's leave of absence from King's, with Jessica Burke taking over his classes and duties as a visiting professor for a one-year term, her contract renewable for a second year.

Dean's contract with the WHC is worded in much the same way—we'll move to Paris for at least a year so he can work on organizing the Youth Experts program, and at the end of the year, he will have the option of either staying or moving back to Mirror Lake.

After all the contracts have been signed and arrangements made, Dean approaches me one evening with a gleam in his eye. He pulls me close and presses a lovely, warm kiss against my lips. Tingles drift through me like snowflakes.

"Now," I say meaningfully, "I need you to do that *something* for me."

"Name it, beauty," Dean runs his hands over my back. "What do you need me to do?"

"I need you to buy a birthday party truck for the Wonderland Café."

CHAPTER 32

OLIVIA

*S*ailboats glide like birds over the sun-bright surface of the lake. Pedestrians walk leisurely along Avalon Street, pausing to look into shop windows. Bouquets of brightly colored balloons wave like flowers from benches around Wizard's Park and the terrace railing of the Wonderland Café.

The air is filled with the sound of children laughing—and occasionally screeching or crying. Three members of Slice of Pie, including the Pieman, are performing at a temporary stage, and the music and lyrics of "Cherry Pie" float over the park.

The Airstream trailer glows bright silver in the sun. The full-time team Dean hired renovated and decorated the trailer in record time—so quickly and beautifully, in fact, that I wish they'd been filmed for one of those before-and-after reality shows.

The sides of the trailer are adorned with a flowing design of clouds, poppy fields, hot-air balloons, and a tree in which the grinning Cheshire Cat sits. A cursive script reading *The Traveling*

Wonderland Café is painted on both sides. A retractable, red-and-white striped awning extends from the trailer, and round tables are set up underneath.

Inside, the décor is exactly what I'd imagined—playing-card patterns, whimsical clocks and tables, plus closets filled with birthday party costumes and supplies. A huge, red ribbon loops around the trailer, ending in a bow fastened to the front door.

"I can't believe it." Allie comes up beside me, looking pretty and summer-like in a green flowered dress that complements her red hair. "It's incredible, Liv."

I nod toward Dean, who is approaching from the direction of the stage with Archer and Nicholas. "He's the one who did it all."

I feel her looking at me.

"Do you remember when we were opening the café and you weren't into using any of your and Dean's money?" she asks.

"I remember."

"So what changed your mind about letting him buy the trailer?" Allie asks.

I learned a lesson, I think as I watch Dean coming toward me. Professor West is a damned good teacher. And though I often have to fumble my way through things, I have always been an excellent student.

Dean's gaze meets mine, a smile curving his beautiful mouth. A pleasurable shiver runs down my spine.

"I learned that sometimes it's okay to take help when it's offered," I tell Allie. "And to graciously accept a gift someone has been trying hard to give you."

Aside from that, I also wanted to leave Allie and Wonderland with a parting gift that will not only compensate for my past mistakes, but that will set the café on an exciting new path. The Traveling Wonderland Café proved to be the solution to several problems all at once. I just needed to get out of my own way in order to see that.

"You both ready?" Archer crouches beside the microphone

and speaker next to the trailer and fiddles with the controls. "Slice of Pie is on their last song of this set, and they're sending everyone back over here as soon as they're done."

The entire staff of the Wonderland Café, all wearing white jackets and purple aprons, gather around the front of the trailer. Parents and children drift over from the stage, and soon a large crowd is standing near the tables.

Archer hands me the microphone. I pass it to Allie. She blinks at me.

"You're in charge now," I remind her.

"Not for good," she says. "You'll always be my partner, whether you're living in Mirror Lake or Timbuktu."

"Aw." I squeeze her arm. "Come on, then. We'll do this together."

We step in front of the ribbon encircling the trailer and face the crowd.

"Ladies and gentlemen," Allie says into the mic. "Boys and girls, thank you so much for coming to celebrate the opening of the brand-new Traveling Wonderland Café. With this venture, we plan to deliver peppermint twist cupcakes, lemon parfaits, and plenty of birthday parties all around Mirror Lake and beyond. With my partner Liv" —she pauses to clear her throat— "leaving on new adventures, we will continue to run the café with the much-needed help of numerous other people."

She introduces the staff members who will be taking on new duties to help her run the café, including Brent, who is stepping up his responsibilities in my absence.

I glance at Dean. He's standing to the side with Nicholas perched on his shoulders, his elbows resting on Dean's head.

"And now," Allie says, reaching for a pair of silver scissors. "Welcome to the opening of the Traveling Wonderland Café!"

She moves aside so I can put my hand over hers. Together, we cut the red ribbon. The crowd erupts into applause, music bursts from the speakers, and three employees bring out huge sheet cakes and tiered trays of cupcakes.

A flurry of activity follows as we slice cake for everyone and hand out cupcakes to the children. I see Archer standing beside the trailer, his hands in his pockets and his gaze scanning the crowd. I bring him a slice of cake and a fork.

"Cake?" I ask, holding it out.

"No, thanks," he replies. "I'm waiting for Kelsey."

Though I don't see why that precludes him from eating cake, I shrug and turn away. Dean is standing near the tables, and he and Archer exchange fleeting grins that seem to carry some brotherly secret.

It's about time, I think.

I hand the cake to Dean, who takes it without hesitation. The thought of leaving Archer and Kelsey causes a sad pang in my chest, especially if Dean and Archer are finally starting to find their way to being brothers again. But Kelsey and Archer have assured me they'll come to visit us in Paris and we'll have regular video calls. Also, as Kelsey reminded me, *"You'll come back."*

And yes, we will come back. For visits, certainly, and someday to live again. We don't yet know when—it could be years, depending on the job and the contracts—but the promise is like a little star.

I look at the expanse of Wizard's Park, the silver trailer gleaming in the sun, the families gathered around laughing, eating, playing on the playground. In the distance, the railroad depot sits behind a row of trees, waiting for Archer and Mr. Jenkins to bring it back to life.

Allie walks around the tables, pouring fresh lemonade into paper cups, her face bright and happy. Florence and Mr. Jenkins are canoodling at one of the tables, eating cupcakes and drinking tea.

Kelsey comes toward Archer from the parking lot. He holds

out his arms, and she walks right into them, her body curving against his like a comma fitting into place.

Nearby, Nicholas lets out a yelp as he runs after a Frisbee Dean has tossed. The red saucer spins in a perfect arc before Nicholas makes a flying leap and manages to catch it in his little fists. His face breaks into a huge grin. Dean gives a cheer and hauls Nicholas onto his shoulders, running around with him in a victory loop. Nicholas laughs and laughs.

I smile, my heart filling with a riotous combination of love and joy. I've learned in life that if you're going to run, you should always run toward something. On the flip side, you should also have a place to run *back* to, if needed.

Mirror Lake will still be here if or when we return. But beyond that, a two-year-old boy and a certain medieval history professor are my safe haven, the place to which I will always return, my home anywhere in the world.

CHAPTER 33

Olivia

Three months later

The facade of the Louvre spreads like wings around a central plaza leading to the vast expanse of the Tuileries gardens. Hungry birds, unafraid, flutter around seeking bread scraps dropped by people who purchased baguette sandwiches from the snack bars.

Dozens of Parisians and tourists wander around the wide pathways, some lounging in the sun and others walking toward one of the museums. Nicholas runs ahead of me, making a beeline for the large fountain that sits like a lake shimmering in the sun.

I catch up with him, huffing and puffing a little thanks to the extra ten pounds I've gained, and pull a small box out of the tote bag I carry with me everywhere.

"*Les bateaux,*" Nicholas announces in—to my ears, flawless—French before taking two walnut-shell boats out of the box.

Nicholas's boat is bright red with a little blue flag attached to a toothpick and a tiny stick-figure sailor. My boat is glittery pink with a striped sail and a heart painted on the inside of the shell.

"Here's the starting line," I say, pointing to the edge of the fountain.

We set our boats in the water and together chant in commanding voices, *"À vos marques."*

"Prêts!" I call. *"Partez!"*

We release the boats and watch as the light breeze pushes them along the water. When we first raced walnut boats in this fountain, we designated "over there" as the finish line, so we follow the boats around the water for a few minutes, each of us cheering our crew on. We mutually agree that Nicholas's boat wins this particular regatta before we take a few more boats from the box and set them racing.

After the races are finished—Nicholas: 8, Mom: 1—we visit the playground and stop for an ice cream. Our afternoon is one of the ways Nicholas and I have spent the past few months in Paris. We've visited many parks, often finding the best ones packed with French toddlers and their mothers or nannies, and had many snacks.

Dean and I have timed visits to museums to coincide with Nicholas's naps, and several times we've been able to stroll through the Louvre or the Orsay, pushing our sleeping son in his stroller.

One of Dean's colleagues has a daughter, Marie-Laure, studying literature at the Sorbonne, and she has become our de facto nanny when I have French lessons or errands to run.

It's not perfect, of course. The number of cars and people make me nervous when Nicholas is walking, but it's cumbersome to navigate his stroller. He's pitched fits in public—once loud enough to get us politely removed from a café—and I'm still too self-conscious to approach any of the women at the playgrounds to try and make friends.

Interestingly, through my French lessons, I've made friends

with a German woman, a Canadian woman, and an American couple who invited Dean and me over for dinner one night. And Dean's colleagues at the World Heritage Center have been exceedingly helpful and solicitous as we navigate our new world.

Nicholas and I take the bus back to the Latin Quarter, where our apartment sits in a nineteenth-century building. We stop at the boulanger, where we buy our bread and croissants daily from Mme Cassin, and greet the grocer who is stocking the fruit bins in front of his shop.

We walk up four flights of stairs to our apartment, a two-bedroom place about the size of the Butterfly House's kitchen and sunroom. It's bright and airy, with a wrought-iron balcony that overlooks the narrow avenue. It reminds me of our little apartment on Avalon Street.

I settle Nicholas in his room with some books and stuffed animals, leaving the door partly open so I can hear him if he calls. No need for a baby monitor here.

While he naps, I get dinner prepped—in a blossoming haze of ambition I've taken to trying recipes from the cookbooks of Jacques Pepin, Julia Child, and Paul Bocuse, albeit with varying degrees of success.

In my most recent Skype call with Allie, she again suggested I take classes at Le Cordon Bleu, and while I laughed the idea off initially, I contacted the school the next day asking about classes. In other words, I haven't ruled it out, even mentioning the idea on my blog *Liv in a Parisian Wonderland*, which elicited dozens of excited and encouraging comments from my mom friends and fans.

Tonight's dinner menu is ham with remoulade sauce, cucumber salad, and for dessert, plum sherbet and cinnamon-lemon cake. Nicholas wakes from a nap just as I put the ham in the oven, and close to six, a key turns in the lock of the front door. Nicholas bolts upright from lounging on the sofa.

"Daddy!" He rushes toward the foyer.

I follow, happy as always at the sight of Dean, so handsome in his tailored suit and five o'clock shadow, his tie loose around his neck. A warm glow lights in his eyes as he picks Nicholas up for a hug. He listens with interest to Nicholas's excited babbling about the walnut-shell regatta before Nicholas squirms to get down.

Dean sets our son on the floor and approaches me, pulling me into the strong circle of his embrace. He spreads one hand across my rounded belly and bends to press his mouth against mine.

"Hey, beauty," he says.

"Hi, professor." I tighten my arms around his waist, feeling a delicious glow of happiness and contentment. "Welcome home."

EPILOGUE

Dear North,

Cobblestone streets, tree-lined boulevards, the Eiffel Tower parting the clouds like curtains. Bustling metro stations, colorful street markets, the endless flow of the Seine. Fresh baguettes.

Paintings glowing like jewels, marble statues captured in time, the sand-castle facade of Notre Dame, the silky sweetness of vanilla mascarpone cream enrobed in white chocolate. Expansive gardens, glittering shop windows, booksellers and street performers. Drinking coffee at a Latin Quarter café with my husband. Watching our son chase birds. Finding a new place.

We have a girl this time. Her name is Isabella. She has just enough hair to wear a little red ribbon.

Our adventure continues.

Love,
Liv

ABOUT THE AUTHOR

New York Times & USA Today bestselling author Nina Lane
writes hot, sexy romances about professors, bad boys, candy
makers, and protective alpha males who find themselves
consumed with love for one woman alone. Originally from
California, Nina holds a PhD in Art History and an MA in
Library and Information Studies, which means she loves both
research and organization. She also enjoys traveling and thinks
St. Petersburg, Russia is a city everyone should visit at least once.
Although Nina would go back to college for another degree
because she's that much of a bookworm and a perpetual student,
she now lives the happy life of a full-time writer.

www.ninalane.com

f facebook.com/ninalaneauthor
🐦 twitter.com/ninalaneauthor
📷 instagram.com/ninalaneauthor
a amazon.com/author/ninalane
g goodreads.com/ninalane

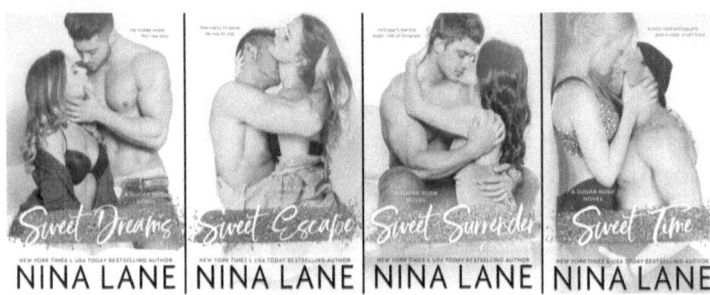

THE SUGAR RUSH SERIES
Sweet is the new sexy.

From the Stone family patriarch down to the youngest
bad boy, follow the lives and loves of the Sugar Rush men and the
women who bring them to their knees.

THE SPIRAL OF BLISS SERIES

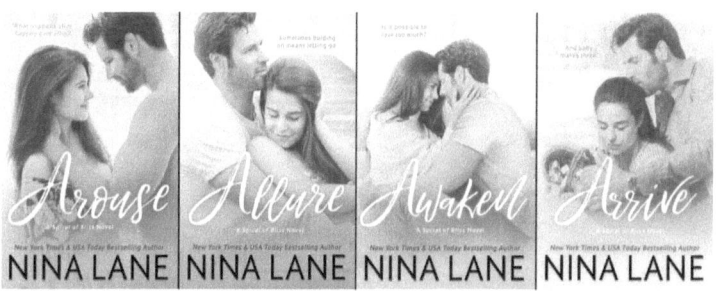

"Give me a kiss, beauty."

From an exhilarating crush to the intensities of marriage, Liv and Dean West embark on a passionate lifelong journey together. As the medieval history professor and his beloved wife face both personal challenges and painful battles, they never lose sight of the hope, humor, and devotion that belong only to them.

Liv and Dean's everlasting romance will melt your heart, turn you on, and enchant you with the power of a love to end all loves.

First we fell in love. Then we fell apart.

Shattered by tragedy a decade ago, two lovers fight the secrets that could destroy them.

"This book is a work of art."

A woman fleeing scandal. A town's mysterious recluse.

Lust and secrets collide in this provocative romance.